New Additions

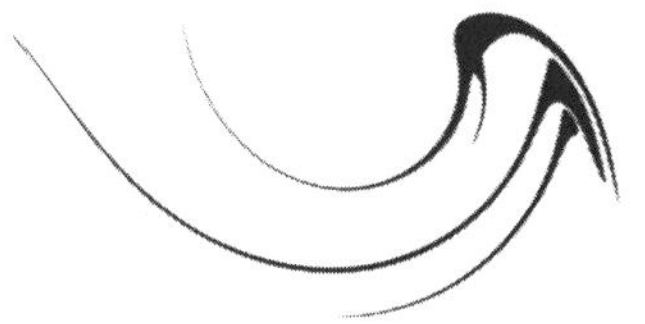

BECKY HARMON

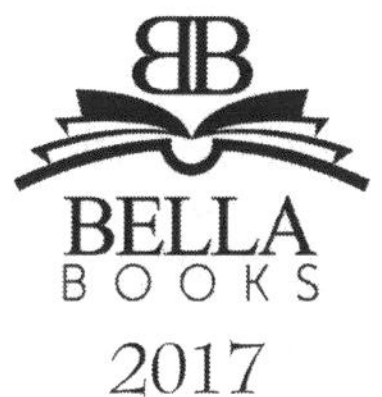
BELLA BOOKS
2017

Bella Books, Inc.
P.O. Box 10543
Tallahassee, FL 32302

Printed in the United States of America on acid-free paper.

First Bella Books Edition 2017

Editor: Medora MacDougall
Cover Designer: Sandy Knowles

ISBN: 978-1-59493-527-5

Other Bella Books by Becky Harmon

Tangled Mark

Acknowledgments

Thanks to Ruth and Laura for your valuable input and endless encouragement. Your humor always makes everything better.

To Linda and Jessica Hill, thank you for choosing me to be a part of Bella. Thanks to the many Bella authors for making me feel welcome and for the wonderful advice so freely offered.

Once again, Medora MacDougall, you have managed to turn my story into something I can be proud of. Thank you for all the corrections and the nudges that sent me in the right direction.

Thank you, Sandy, for creating a cover that speaks for the book and to Judy for all the behind the scenes fine tuning.

Thanks to all the readers who continue to crave new books. I hope you find this one enjoyable. Unfortunately, Lake View Resort and the town of Riverview do not exist except in my mind.

About the Author

Becky Harmon was born and raised just south of the Mason-Dixon Line. Though she considers herself to be a Northerner, she moved south in search of warmth. Romance has always been her first love and when she's not writing it, she's reading it. Her first book, *Tangled Mark*, was released by Bella Books in 2016. You can reach Becky at beckyharmon2015@yahoo.com.

Dedication

For Ruth and Laura

CHAPTER ONE

"I really don't understand why I'm here." Cassie Thomas swallowed hard as she stared at the woman sitting across from her. The intense blue eyes looking back were making it hard for Cassie to concentrate, but they didn't stop irritation from surfacing in her words. "Is there a problem with using my farm in the summer youth program?"

"No, there's no problem, and I'm really sorry we scheduled your appointment on such a busy day. I'm sure you noticed all the people downstairs."

"And the lack of parking."

"Yeah, that too." Kathleen gave her an apologetic smile. "This is our final spring registration week for potential adoption families. We hold one the last week in March, April and May. Each group home in the Fosters' system will have an open house next weekend, and anyone interested can visit as many homes as they like. They have to appear in person and be fingerprinted during one of the registration weeks though."

After many years in law enforcement, Cassie was good at reading people. Kathleen Masters did not strike her as the rambling type, and yet she was struggling to stop speaking. Kathleen was professional in her appearance and mannerisms, but she was obviously nervous about the reason that had prompted her to summon Cassie to her office.

"That makes sense." Cassie forced a smile, trying to ease the edge in her voice. Kathleen had been nothing but pleasant, though slightly evasive. The entire interaction was leaving her with an uneasy feeling in the pit of her stomach. What was she missing?

Cassie appraised Kathleen across the small oak desk. Her light brown hair hung barely past her shoulders and was pulled back from her face, revealing strikingly attractive features. Her white button-down shirt was open at the collar, hinting at what lay beneath. Cassie found it very professional and at the same time unusually seductive. Normally not so easily distracted, Cassie was ashamed to admit it had taken her several minutes after she entered Kathleen's office to remember where she was. Even now her thoughts were jumbled. She needed to move this conversation to whatever the issue was, and clearly Kathleen needed some prompting. "So…I'm here because…?"

"I know you're a returning client," Kathleen hesitated, "but we wanted to touch base with you in person before assigning your kids for this year."

Cassie frowned. Last year, she had participated in the "city to country" program sponsored by Fosters Incorporated, a privately owned Florida foster care system. The program allowed children in and around Pensacola who were already in the foster care system to spend their summer in the country.

Cassie pulled the binder she had brought from her lap and opened it. "I brought additional information about the farm and the resort."

"No, no," Kathleen said immediately. "Your application was fine. There's something else we wanted to talk with you about."

Cassie opened the water bottle she had been offered when she arrived and took a drink. She could see Kathleen was gathering her courage so she let the silence stretch between them. Kathleen pushed her laptop to the side of the desk and leaned forward. Her open appraisal caused goosebumps on Cassie's arms and she resisted the urge to shiver. She leaned forward herself, meeting Kathleen's gaze, and raised one eyebrow.

A smile spread across Kathleen's face, and Cassie felt her irritation begin to dissolve.

"What possessed you to volunteer to take on two teenagers again?" Kathleen asked.

Cassie laughed, shaking her head. This was not the question she had expected, but it was easy to answer. "It sounded like fun?"

Kathleen laughed with her and Cassie felt the tension between them begin to fade. She no longer cared why she had been called here. She was enjoying this meeting more than she would admit.

"I enjoyed having Greg and Mandi with me last summer. I would have taken them again." Cassie smiled as she remembered the teenagers. "Greg was sixteen when they arrived and Mandi was fourteen. My only request when I signed up was that the kids be the same gender. The whole raging hormones issue wasn't something I wanted to deal with all summer. When they arrived, I was a little disappointed, but then Mandi emerged from the van and informed everyone that she was a lesbian."

Cassie felt her face begin to flush as if she was disclosing her own orientation. She looked away for a second before meeting Kathleen's eyes again. Seeing nothing but the open, welcoming look Kathleen had displayed from the moment they met, she continued. "Greg took to Mandi immediately, and they became inseparable. Greg turns eighteen in the fall so he's working now and trying to save enough money to get out of the foster system as soon as possible." Cassie's smile widened. "Mandi has a new home, and there's a good chance they'll adopt her."

* * *

Cassie's earlier frown had completely disappeared from her face, and Kathleen was pleased to hear the happiness in her voice. She had a pleasant smile. Kathleen hoped what she had to say wouldn't make it disappear again. It was obvious Cassie had truly cared about Greg and Mandi.

Kathleen knew now she had made the right decision. She had spent hours reviewing applications before coming up with this idea, and she was confident Cassie's resort would be a perfect location. Now she needed to convince Cassie of that. Taking a deep breath, she blurted the question she had been avoiding. "Would you consider taking four kids instead of two?"

Cassie tilted her head, but her smile remained in place. "Jumping in with both feet now?"

Kathleen's shoulders gave a slight shrug, but she remained silent, giving Cassie a chance to process the question. On paper the jump from two kids to four didn't seem like much, but she knew how much attention each child would require. Housing the kids was not enough for Kathleen. She needed to know that Cassie cared, and the only way to do that had been to see her face to face before making the request.

She had reviewed Cassie's background and was impressed with her career. As an army brat, Cassie had been homeschooled and graduated from high school two years early. She had earned her law enforcement degree and joined the West Virginia State Police immediately upon graduation. Moving quickly up through the ranks and halfway to retirement, she had been recruited and then elected to the chief's position in a small West Virginia town where she stayed until taking early retirement several years ago. Kathleen had no doubt that Cassie could handle the four girls she needed to place. The girls weren't trouble as long as rules were clear and enforced.

"Seriously," Cassie finally spoke, shaking her head. "I don't think I could manage the resort and the farm and give the kids enough supervision if I had four."

"Space is not an issue then?" Kathleen tried to keep the excitement from her voice. Cassie had not said no.

"Including my own, there are four bedrooms upstairs and another one downstairs that I use as an office, so no, space is not the issue. Beds might be."

"I think you sound perfect." Kathleen sat back in her chair as she realized what she had said. She felt her face burn with embarrassment. "I mean, your place sounds perfect. How do I convince you this would work?"

Cassie shook her head. "I really am sorry, but I don't think I can."

Kathleen could hear the hesitation in her voice so she pushed forward. "Can we talk about your concerns before we rule it out completely?"

"I guess so." Cassie sat back in her chair, taking a deep breath. Her eyes focused on the wall behind Kathleen.

The concentration displayed on her face was intriguing, and Kathleen was surprised at the swirl of attraction she felt. Quickly pushing the feelings aside, she studied the woman across from her. Cassie's short dark hair still swayed from her movement, barely brushing the tops of her shoulders. It wasn't a masculine or feminine cut but clearly one of efficiency. Cassie owned and operated a four-cabin resort as well as a small farm, and her tanned arms showed the hours she spent outside. The top two buttons of her beige blouse were unfastened, revealing more brown skin. Kathleen wondered where the tan lines stopped, or if they did. She quickly moved her eyes back to Cassie's face and met the soft brown eyes studying her.

"I worry the most about being able to provide proper supervision. With four teenagers, the farm and the resort, I can't be everywhere." Her eyes narrowed. "This isn't the real issue is it? What are you still not telling me?"

"I understand your concern." Kathleen continued, ignoring Cassie's question. She needed to get Cassie to agree before she told the rest of the story. "What if Fosters was willing to provide additional supervision?"

Cassie raised an eyebrow. A look Kathleen was quickly beginning to find irresistible. "Okay," Cassie said slowly, dragging out each syllable.

Cassie might not be convinced, but Kathleen had heard the agreement. She quickly delved into a possible solution for Cassie's concerns.

"During the summer months, we have an influx of college students looking for full-time work. Normally they drive around and check on the kids that have been placed but what if we could place one of those students full time at your farm? Their priority would be monitoring and supervising the kids. Would that take away your concern and help this work for you?"

"You make a good case." Cassie leaned forward again, and Kathleen knew she was seeing the stare that had probably made many criminals confess. She knew she had stalled as long as she could.

"I have to ask again. Why are you pushing this with me?"

Kathleen sighed. "I have four girls that really need a place for the summer. They've had a rough year, and I would like to keep them together. Not many of our applicants could handle four teenagers." She took a deep breath. "And they are all lesbians."

Cassie's face was blank, and Kathleen tried to read her expression. Sexual orientation was not something that was asked about on the Fosters' application, but with a quick Internet search she had been able to locate the website for Cassie's Farm, Lake View Resort. It provided the basic information needed to pique someone's interest if they were already looking for a getaway, but she didn't feel it had the draw to convince those who weren't. Kathleen was disappointed that it didn't give as much information as she would have preferred, but it did clearly state the resort was gay- and lesbian-friendly. It didn't matter to Kathleen if Cassie was a lesbian. Well, it didn't matter as far as the kids were concerned, but Kathleen found herself hoping there might be some truth there.

Cassie frowned. "That brings the raging teenage hormones question back into the picture."

"Currently the girls all room together at one of our homes without any issues. Our biggest problem is their presentation. I have one with a shaved head, one with body piercings and one who can only find clothes two sizes too big."

"I'm afraid to ask about the fourth one."

"That would be Dani, and she is a twelve-year-old sweetheart."

"Twelve? And a lesbian?"

"Well…self-proclaimed lesbian."

Cassie laughed. "Is there any other?"

Kathleen grinned. This was going better than she had hoped. "So what do you think?"

"I think if you can provide me with another…" Cassie paused and used her fingers as quotation marks. "'Adult,' then I would say yes."

Kathleen jumped up and strode to the door. "Tiffany, call Joyce. It's a go!"

Cassie stood as Kathleen turned back toward her. Kathleen couldn't stop her fingers from grazing Cassie's arm as she approached. "I'm sorry if we seem crazy. We've had a hard time finding a good location for the brat pack and, well, when I read about your farm, it really seemed perfect."

Cassie returned her smile, but Kathleen could read something else in her eyes. *Confusion?* She realized she was still touching Cassie's arm and quickly dropped her hand, trying to appear casual. "I hope you don't feel like we pressured you."

Cassie shook her head and the clearness returned to her eyes. "Brat pack? Really? Should I be worried?"

"Absolutely not," Kathleen said. "Don't get me wrong. They're still teenagers and I can't say you won't have a few more gray hairs by the end of the summer, but they're hard workers and enjoyable to be around."

"A 'few more,'" Cassie said with a groan.

Kathleen grimaced as her words echoed. Cassie's round youthful face didn't reflect her forty-two years even with the speckling of gray in the dark strands. She didn't want to appear flirtatious with her new client, but the gray only made her look more attractive. "If you had any to speak of then, I would say they only made you look more distinguished."

"Oh, man," Cassie groaned again. "Are you trying to make it better? 'Distinguished' is the same as 'old.'"

"I agree with Kathleen." Tiffany, the young receptionist, stepped into the doorway and brazenly entered their conversation. "Distinguished…and fine."

"Better than fine." Kathleen mumbled without thinking as she turned back to her desk. *Seriously, what is wrong with me today?*

Safely behind her desk, Kathleen met Cassie's eyes. She knew Cassie had heard her comment, and she resisted the urge to act like she hadn't just told a client she looked fine. The faint flutter in her stomach told her she didn't want to ignore the spark she had felt between them. She wanted to fan the flame. She openly appraised Cassie, allowing her eyes to penetrate deeper into her as she dared her to disagree with the assessment she had made.

Looking from Kathleen to Tiffany, Cassie almost looked a little panicked. "Do you need anything else from me?" she asked, moving toward the door.

"We're all set from here," Kathleen said. "The girls and a supervisor will arrive June twelfth. It will probably be late afternoon before we can get out to your place. One of us will give you a quick call when we leave the city."

"A call would be great." Cassie looked straight at Kathleen.

The heat flooded her entire body as Kathleen fought to break their contact. Her eyes rested on the resort brochure in Cassie's hands. "Can I keep that?" she asked.

"Sure. I have plenty. Maybe you could pass it around. I could use the business."

As everyone laughed, Cassie made her way quickly to the door. Kathleen watched her, longing for something more. She knew there was nothing she could say that wouldn't come across as unprofessional. She could only hope she would have an opportunity to talk with Cassie again. Cassie hesitated in the doorway, but then she started walking again without looking back. Kathleen sighed and leaned against her desk as Tiffany followed Cassie out.

She knew her desire to see this woman in person went beyond testing the waters for the brat pack. Cassie was intriguing, and Kathleen had wanted to see if she could still hold her interest after they met in person. Now she knew the answer to that question…but she wasn't sure what it meant.

Pulling a photograph from her top drawer, she leaned back in her chair. It had been several months since she had taken the brat pack to animal rescue but it had been their first outing as a group. Kathleen smiled as she studied her own face centered between the girls. The picture captured the joy they each had felt at the end of a very long day. Their arms wrapped tightly around each other displayed the bond that had been formed between them.

Dani, the youngest, had cried for the newly arrived homeless and abused dogs, but the other girls had helped her put action to that pain. Together, they coaxed and cuddled four dogs through baths and checkups with the technicians. When everyone, including the two-legged creatures, was covered in enough water to fill the bathtub, they took their charges outside for playtime.

It was a day Kathleen would never forget. She had learned the secret to reaching the forgotten kids she wanted to help. Sharing more than just her time, but a part of herself. These girls and most of the kids she dealt with only needed to feel valued. Exactly what she had desired as a foster kid and was finally able to find as an adult.

She had applied to be event coordinator at Fosters because of Joyce Clark's diligence. Joyce owned and operated Fosters and had a reputation for taking in the kids the state couldn't place in homes—the kids that were passed from group home to foster family and back again. Joyce took the time to find the right fit for each child before placing them and then made sure they were nurtured to grow. Kathleen longed to be a part of something so emotionally profitable.

The brat pack had touched her in ways she could never have imagined. She saw a little of herself in each of them. Although Morgan and Shauna, the two oldest girls, had been passed through the most homes, Dani had been in foster care for the longest. With the death of her parents and no family members to take her in, Dani had been fed straight into the system. Kathleen could find no reasons for two-year-old Dani to never have found a permanent home. She was a happy kid with a positive attitude but thankfully a power larger than Kathleen had brought the four girls together.

Dani's outlook on life had changed the others' perspective so much that in the last three months there had been no runaway attempts or acts of violence. The group home they were in now, though crowded, offered them support to explore their own individuality. The four girls had become a family within the system and were learning to trust again.

"Way to go!" Tiffany exclaimed, interrupting Kathleen's thoughts as she stepped back into the doorway. "Ms. Thomas is safely out of the building."

Clearly she wasn't the only one infatuated with Cassie. Showing people out went above and beyond Tiffany's usual duties.

"The brat pack is going to be so excited."

"It didn't take much persuading. She was open to the idea." Kathleen knew that was only a small lie. She was pleased her initial judgment of Cassie hadn't been wrong.

She seldom dated outside her comfort zone, and Cassie was way outside of that. Kathleen liked being in control; she gravitated toward women who never stood up to her. They weren't challenging or potential mates, but then Kathleen wasn't interested in having anyone share anything in her life.

"I thought she was cool as soon as she walked in," Tiffany said, pulling Kathleen back into the conversation.

"Yes, I thought so too." Kathleen couldn't stop the smile from spreading across her face.

"Uh…what's that smile for?" Tiffany raised her eyebrows.

Kathleen stepped past her, ignoring Tiffany's question. She knew Tiffany wouldn't let it go without an adequate amount of harassment, but right now she only wanted to find Joyce so they could celebrate. The brat pack would get to leave the city for the summer and be somewhere safe and accepting. She couldn't help feeling a little jealous that they would be spending the summer with Cassie.

CHAPTER TWO

Cassie finished off the bottled water before pulling into traffic. She felt jittery and unsettled at the feelings Kathleen had stirred in her. It had been an agonizing five years since Nett had passed away, and she was finally content with her life. She had the farm she had always dreamed of with a small income from the resort and two fur-covered partners to share her house. Unfortunately logical thoughts weren't pushing the feelings inside her away. She hadn't felt anything like this since she met Nett twenty-five years ago, but she could still remember the thrill of wanting something she couldn't have. Kathleen made her feel things she didn't want to feel.

Thoughts of Kathleen blurred into panic about what she had agreed to do for the summer. When she had been sitting with Kathleen, it had seemed like an acceptable plan but what was she going to do with four kids? And a supervisor, who was not much more than a kid too? She should call Fosters and tell them she had changed her mind. Kathleen's smiling face appeared in her mind and she couldn't stop the rush of heat that quickly spread throughout her body. No, she couldn't disappoint Kathleen. Tomorrow she would order more beds and break the news to Dillon. Helping her take care of the farm would no longer be his only responsibility for the summer. Giving the girls a place to stay was really the only option. She found herself looking forward to the challenge.

The entire situation was Nett's fault anyway. Buying the farm and resort might have been Cassie's dream but taking in the kids from the city was all Nett. It had been a constant discussion between them on when to have children. Never if, only when. Nett was ready when they moved in together, but Cassie's goal was to retire early and then begin their life. Nett's cancer had ruined those plans. After her death, Cassie had finished out the remaining two years on her term as chief of police and then she had fled.

The sadness she had felt when she moved to the farm almost consumed her but then she heard about the "city to country" program. It wouldn't bring Nett back but it felt like a way to redeem herself. Her first year as chief, she had spent ninety percent of her time behind a desk and was miserable. In her search to find a way to change that situation, she had started a D.A.R.E. program. She studied the Drug Abuse Resistance Education program and learned how to teach kids ways to avoid drugs, membership in gangs and violence. Her interaction with kids became preventative instead of reactionary.

She knew how to develop a rapport with kids in a short amount of time and how to make them feel comfortable about speaking out. Though neither Greg nor Mandi came from violent backgrounds, they had helped Cassie realize quickly that her skills reached into other areas too. She wondered what she would face with Kathleen's brat pack. She had no doubt that Kathleen would provide details about each girl if she asked, but she was a firm believer in a clean slate. She wouldn't let past mistakes or actions form her opinions.

Turning her thoughts again on home, Cassie was surprised to see she was already entering Riverview and only a couple of miles from the farm. It was close to six p.m. and Dillon would have everything closed down for the night. At twenty-five, Dillon was more than an employee. Having grown up on a nearby farm, he had taught her about the animals and even remodeled two of the cabins. Now she was able to rent all four and pay Dillon a salary.

Cassie's gaze drifted across the rolling hills and focused on the giant black iron arch crossing above her driveway and the words "Lake View," written in block letters that welcomed guests. She felt a sense of peace as she drove under it. Her two-story wooden cabin with the old-fashioned wraparound porch always made her smile. From the first time she had pulled into the driveway, she felt like she was coming home.

The big red barn and house blocked her view of the office that adjoined it and of the first cabin beyond. She could see Cabin Two ahead and to the left across the lake were Cabins Three and Four. The farm was enclosed on three sides by fifty wooded acres, which provided a barrier from the world around them.

Cassie parked and sprinted up the steps into the office. Dillon's wife, Shelley, stood behind the counter bouncing between three open college textbooks. Her face was tense, and she looked relieved at the interruption. She worked three days a week at the farm while taking a full schedule of online college classes.

"How was your afternoon?" Cassie asked, joining her behind the counter. Shelley matched Cassie's five-foot-nine height, but she was leaner in all the places Cassie was muscular. Though she preferred to work in the office and had a very feminine appearance, she could still throw a bale of hay if they needed her help.

"Not bad. Things have been quiet. Mr. Jackson in Cabin Four and one of his sons would like to ride horses in the morning at ten. I put it on the schedule and told Dillon."

"Easy enough."

"Dillon already fed the fur babies," Shelley said, referring to Cassie's two dogs.

"Wow, that's great. I didn't expect that, but I'm sure they appreciated it."

"They hung outside with him all day, and when he came in earlier, he swung through the house and fed them. They're in the backyard now."

Cassie logged onto the computer and took a quick look at the business email account.

"I checked a little while ago. There haven't been any new ones since you left this morning."

"Okay. Thanks for staying late. Drag Dillon with you on your way out. He can call me if there's anything that can't wait until tomorrow."

"Sounds great," Shelley said, throwing her books and laptop into her backpack. "See ya."

"See you on Friday," Cassie called.

She clipped the farm radio to her belt and went through the side door into her house. The radio was the only means of communication she needed after five p.m. when the resort office closed. All of the guests had radio base units in their cabins and her cell number for emergencies. They also had mobile units with about a two-mile range. She kept a handful of long-range units in the office for anyone headed into the surrounding woods.

She detoured past the doggie door in the dining room and called for Zoey and Pandy. Within seconds, they flew through the door and amid lots of squealing, whimpering and petting, she was able to make it as far as the kitchen to preheat the oven for her dinner. Before she could relax for the evening, she needed to check on the rest of her animals.

As soon as she stepped outside, she could see six of the horses in the big pasture eating hay from the round bale. She walked through the open doors of the barn and saw the other four horses, grazing nearby. She inhaled the aroma of horses and hay; it felt good to be home. A buckskin horse with black feet approached the fence as soon as she stepped out of the barn. She loved all the horses, but Cheyenne was her favorite.

She took a few minutes and stroked Cheyenne's soft black nose. Patting her neck, she continued along the fence line for a closer view of the pygmy goats. She leaned on the fence and watched two of them fight to stand on one of the platforms in the pasture. Each goat was only about two feet high, but they liked to jump and climb. She had worried about them getting out of the pasture, but after Dillon had built several climbing apparatuses, they seemed content to stay. Dillon had only selected females without horns from animal rescue. They were gentle and liked to be petted, if you could catch them.

As she returned to the house, Pete and Rory from Cabin Two were grilling by the lake. She waved but didn't head their way. The thought of small talk made her feel even more tired though she knew either man could carry the conversation without her participation. They were retired and arrived every May, staying for the entire month. Neither one was shy and would let her know if they needed something whether she stopped to talk or not.

Cabins One and Three were empty this week. The Jacksons were in Cabin Four. It was her largest one and the last one built. With three bedrooms and two baths, it could hold Ryan, Judy, three boys and one girl comfortably. Ryan and the youngest boy, Darby, had ridden horses earlier in the week and were probably the ones scheduled for tomorrow as well. The other boys preferred to ride bicycles on the trails, and she hadn't seen much of the girl. They would be leaving on Saturday, and a week later a new family would come into Cabin Four. She couldn't remember their names, but she would know them by the time they checked in.

She locked the office doors and headed back into the house. Sliding a frozen pizza into the oven, she climbed the stairs two at a time, glancing into the small bedrooms as she passed. It would be a tight fit to add an additional bed to each room, but she could make it work. Four teenagers would bring a lot of activity and probably some drama into her life. Surprisingly, she was looking forward to sharing her living space with them.

The house often felt too big and empty, even with the dogs around. By the end of the summer, though, she would be happy to have her space back. She was sure of that. At the end of the hall she entered the master bedroom, where she changed into gym shorts and a T-shirt. With ten minutes left on her pizza, she collapsed into the recliner and flipped on the DVD player. Her favorite television show, *NCIS*, resumed in mid-episode.

* * *

Kathleen pulled into her driveway and switched off the car engine. Leaning her head against the back of the seat, she stared at her two-story townhouse. She didn't see the red brick siding or the flowers that she had planted in front of the porch last weekend. What she saw was the hope of seeing Cassie Thomas again. She hadn't been able to get her out of her mind since their meeting earlier. There was something about the soft-spoken "country girl" that Kathleen couldn't let go.

She was attractive, of course, but there was something else that pulled at Kathleen, keeping her off-balance. Cassie had moved and spoke with a confidence that displayed her years as a law enforcement officer. The few times she had given in to a blush, she still managed to maintain an edge of control. Kathleen still couldn't believe how Cassie's smile had made her heart race. She had to admit the soft brown eyes had rocked her a bit, causing her body to respond like that of a kid with her first crush. She liked the way Cassie's dark hair fell around her face softening her features. Oh, and then there was the single raised eyebrow.

Kathleen sighed. Maybe she could convince Travis to trade duties with her in June. Chauffeuring the kids to their locations for the summer was a good excuse to see Cassie, but could she wait that long? Maybe there was another reason she could come up with. Of course, it had to be one that didn't make her sound like she was losing her mind.

Kathleen jumped as a hand rapped lightly on the window inches from her face.

"Are you all right in there, Kathleen?" Mrs. George called, pressing her face in close to the window.

Kathleen sucked in a deep breath, barely muting the startled scream that was hanging on the end of her tongue. She unlocked her door and pushed it open as her elderly neighbor stepped around the open door, leaning in for a closer view of Kathleen's face.

"Yes, Mrs. George. I'm fine." Kathleen stepped out of her car, gently forcing Mrs. George to take a step back.

"Well, I wasn't sure. I saw you pull in and then when I carried my dinner plate to the kitchen you were still sitting there. Are you sure everything is okay?"

Kathleen smiled, hoping to ease her worry. "I was lost in thought about my day."

"One of those kids got you all stirred up again. I don't know how you do that job."

"No, everything is going well, in fact. Very well." Kathleen smiled at her again.

Mrs. George studied her.

Kathleen touched her softly on the arm. "I really am fine. Thank you for your concern."

"Well, okay, if you're sure everything is all right."

Kathleen could hear Mrs. George mumbling as she turned toward her own yard, and she couldn't help but smile. Mrs. George was always there when you needed her and, yes, even when you didn't. She'd probably been standing at the window watching her from the time Kathleen had pulled into the driveway. Mrs. George kept a close eye on the neighborhood. Kathleen appreciated that, especially when she was away, so times like these were easily forgiven.

She tossed her car keys on the hall table and went straight for the kitchen. After opening a bottle of wine and throwing together a salad, she headed upstairs to change her clothes. She returned to the kitchen in comfortable pajama pants and a T-shirt and took her meal to the living room. She turned on the television, flipping randomly through news channels and sitcoms as she ate her dinner from the coffee table. While her eyes watched the television, her mind returned to the day's events. Normally she hated having anyone else in her house, but she couldn't stop herself from trying to see how Cassie would fit. With a sigh, she ate the last cherry tomato and sat back with her glass of merlot. Tomorrow, after a good night's sleep, she would be rested and able to analyze this attraction logically and things might look different.

CHAPTER THREE

As usual, Cassie was awake by six thirty a.m. without setting an alarm. Dillon would arrive by eight a.m. He would take care of any chores she hadn't completed, so she never felt any pressure to rush. She took a shower to wash the sleep from her face and pulled on jeans and a T-shirt. Grabbing a flannel shirt for the cool morning, she clipped her radio to her belt and headed downstairs with the dogs on her heels.

She put kibble in the dog dishes and made herself a slice of peanut butter toast, placing a thawed chicken breast into a bowl of marinade for dinner. She forced herself to make dinner preparations early in the day to keep from eating pizza every night. Taking her breakfast out on the back porch, she relaxed in one of the chairs. She loved her solitary hours, but for a second she found herself mentally picturing Kathleen sitting beside her.

Would she like the quiet of the farm after living in the city? Would she feel at peace here too? Cassie shook her head. Thoughts about a woman she would never see again were not what she needed to start her day. She dropped her breakfast dish in the sink and crossed to the office. Setting the Keurig to brew a cup of hazelnut coffee, she checked for any work emails or voice mails.

After bringing the horses in from the pasture and feeding them and the goats, she used the golf cart to swing by Cabins Two and Four to check for housekeeping tags. There were no requests for anything, so she returned to the office and sent out welcome emails to the guests coming in on Saturday. The Jacksons in Cabin Four would be leaving and two new couples would be coming in. The lesbian couple had a ten-year-old daughter, so she would place them in Cabin Three. She was enjoying her second cup of coffee when she saw Dillon's truck pull up outside.

"Good morning," Dillon said as he strode through the door.

"Good morning," Cassie returned as she sat back to watch his morning ritual. He was a man of few words in the morning, and she knew better than to attempt to engage him in conversation before he had his coffee.

He headed straight for the Keurig and inserted his favorite breakfast blend, deep roast coffee cylinder into the machine. He stared at the machine as his cup filled and then joined her behind the counter. Pulling one of the barstools over beside her, he slid onto it, stretching his long legs out in front of him. Taking a deep breath of the rich aroma and then a small sip, he sighed contentedly.

The sun had turned his light brown hair almost blond and his muscular arms a deep brown. She could see the tanned skin beneath his light-colored T-shirt. They both tried to prevent farmer tan lines from taking over their bodies in the summer, but she could see Dillon was more successful than she was. Unfortunately, she always had the markings of a sports bra and shorts branded on her body.

"Best part of the day." Dillon inhaled deeply again. "Shelley makes coffee every morning, and she can't see the difference between hers and this."

"Well, you better let her keep thinking hers is the best or she might not make anything for you."

Taking another long sip, he put the cup down on the counter. "What's on today's schedule?"

"Ordering beds."

"Hmm, beds?"

"We have agreed to take four kids this summer instead of two."

Dillon leaned back on his stool. "*We*? What in the world would make *you* do something so crazy?"

Cassie focused on her email, avoiding Dillon's stare.

"Oh, I see." Dillon lowered his voice conspiratorially. "Must have been a girl."

Cassie looked at him and raised one eyebrow.

"Okay, a really hot woman then," he said with a smile.

"Well, that wasn't the reason I agreed, but, yes, she was really hot." Cassie couldn't stop herself from grinning.

Kathleen really was hot and her only regret was not asking her out. She thought about the quick easy smile and the beautiful blue eyes and then the swell of Kathleen's breasts beneath the white shirt. Cassie felt her face grow warm, and she shifted away from Dillon's gaze while she reined in her emotions.

Surprised at Dillon's silence, she finally looked up to see his entire body shaking with laughter. Cassie returned her gaze to the computer screen and tried to ignore him. She knew she wouldn't be seeing Kathleen again so it didn't matter what she thought of her anyway. Besides, they didn't have anything in common. Kathleen was a city girl, and Cassie had no plans to leave her farm.

"Well, alrighty then!" Dillon said energetically, granting her a reprieve from the harassment she was expecting. "What do we know about these four kids?"

"Not much except they're all girls."

"Well, that's cool. Girls have a way with the animals and are usually less trouble."

"These are foster kids so I'm afraid trouble might be their middle name." Cassie thought for a minute. "We have one with a shaved head and at least one with body piercings." Cassie looked at him to see how he would process this information.

Dillon wrinkled his face. "That's not trouble. That's just how they show their individuality. Trouble would be running away or destroying property."

"Aren't you Mr. Diversity?" Cassie shoved him off his stool.

Positioning his stool out of Cassie's reach, he sat down again. "I love kids and this is going to be fun. I'm sure these girls will have a good time here."

"I can't wait until Shelley is ready to start your family. You desperately need some kids of your own if you think having four teenagers is going to be fun."

Dillon's face turned serious as looked down at her. "Yeah, that ain't gonna happen for a while. She's talking about taking classes in Pensacola this fall."

"Really? Would she want to move or commute?" Cassie hoped she didn't sound selfish. She knew there was always a chance Dillon would leave one day, but she couldn't help hoping it would never happen.

"I don't know. I guess I haven't been very understanding when she wanted to talk about it. I just don't want to have to leave here."

"Ignoring her wants won't make them go away."

"I hear you, but I really don't want to think about it right this moment." He stood and started toward the door. "Are we picking up the beds or are they being delivered?"

"We have two weeks so delivery should be fine. Then they can carry them upstairs and set them up. We'll need to move some furniture to make room though."

"Works for me. I'll let the horses out and clean the stalls, then I'm all yours."

"I'll sit here at the computer and make online purchases while you're out working up a sweat."

Dillon tipped his hat at her and strode out the door. She knew how lucky she was to have him around. He was always agreeable and in a good mood. She had seen him angry but never with an uncontrolled temper. To her he was more of a friend than an employee, and she hoped he felt the same way. They didn't have deep emotional discussions, but their actions showed their feelings more anyway.

She pulled up the closest mattress store that had an online site and started making selections. She needed two twin beds for upstairs and a queen for her downstairs office, which she would convert to the guest bedroom for the supervisor. She doubted the college student, male or female, would want to share a bathroom with the girls upstairs. Last summer, without any prompting, Greg had voluntarily made the trek to the bathroom downstairs, allowing Mandi to have her own space. The brat pack would have to make things work upstairs, but Cassie had to imagine they were used to sharing space with others.

* * *

Kathleen pushed back from her desk and stood. Mistakenly, she had thought an early morning trip to the gym would help her focus on her real job. She spent more hours at her part-time job at Fosters Incorporated, but doing website design was what paid the rent and allowed her to work from home. This morning she needed to complete a few minor corrections on a website she had just launched for a new client, but after staring at the screen for over an hour, she wasn't any farther along than when she started.

Picking up her laptop, she moved from her home office to the kitchen table. Normally, she preferred the limited window view in her upstairs office, but today she gave in to her wandering mind. Setting the teakettle on the burner, she opened the sliding glass door that led into her small privacy-fenced backyard. She stood in the doorway and enjoyed the cool breeze blowing through, allowing the images that had been playing at the back of her mind to take over. Cassie leaning across the desk as they talked. Cassie smiling when they reached an agreement. With the sound of Cassie's laughter ringing in her ears, she went into the hall and grabbed the travel brochure from her briefcase.

Leaning against the counter, she savored the feel of the glossy, tri-folded pages. Across the top of the front page in large letters were the words "Lake View Resort." The brochure, the same as the website, listed four cabins in varying sizes with a picture of each and a small description. Another picture showed the pasture with a horse grazing beside several little goats and another shot of a small child in a riding cap sitting astride a dark-colored horse. The last picture on the back showed a crystal-blue lake the size of a football field circled by a walking path with old-fashioned streetlights and park benches. Kathleen folded her fingers into a fist as she imagined the feel of Cassie's hand in hers as they enjoyed an evening stroll.

The teakettle started to whistle, drawing her out of her fantasy and she grabbed it, pouring water into her cup. Before she could analyze what she was about to do, she pulled her cell phone from her pocket.

"Fosters Incorporated, Tiffany speaking, can I help you?"

"Hey, Tiff, it's Kathleen. Is Joyce around?"

"Yep, but she's on the phone. Is there something I can help you with?"

"I was thinking about the woman I met with yesterday." Kathleen paused to pick her words before she blurted too much.

"Oh yeah…The big, tough cutie…And what exactly were you thinking?" Tiffany teased.

"Uh, yes, that would be…uh…her. Has she had a home visit this year?"

"Gee, I wonder why you would be asking about that."

"Well," Kathleen ignored Tiffany's continued teasing, taking a professional tone, "we want to make sure we follow all the laws. With us being a private facility, it would really be easy for the state to pull our license, especially if we don't follow all the guidelines. Everyone in the 'city to country' program is supposed to have a home visit at least once a year."

"Well, I have to say that was a real load of crap that you just spewed, but Joyce is off the phone now so let me check with her." Kathleen could hear Tiffany's laughter before the elevator music told her she was on hold. She picked up her cup of tea and took a sip. Pushing the cup away from her, she glared at the tea bag still lying on the counter.

"So, Joyce agrees with me," Tiffany said as the music stopped.

"About what?" Kathleen asked in confusion.

"That you are spewing a load of crap," Tiffany cackled, and Kathleen could hear Joyce laughing in the background.

"Thanks a lot." Kathleen called loud enough for them both to hear through the speaker.

"But seriously," Joyce said. "I guess it would be a good idea for a home visit, but, I don't know...who could we convince to drive all the way out there?"

Kathleen laughed with them. "Don't you worry, boss. I'll find someone to take care of it."

"Okay, but don't get so excited about driving out there tomorrow that you forget the weekly Friday morning meeting at nine. You can't go until after that."

"I'll see you in the morning." Kathleen hung up before either of them could say anything else.

Now maybe she could get some work done. Knowing she was going to see Cassie tomorrow made her heart race, and she felt giddy with excitement. She wondered if Joyce was reading her interest in Cassie or if she should have brought it up. Honesty had always been important to her, which was why she had disclosed her sexual orientation in her initial job interview. Joyce wasn't judgmental or condescending. She also was never shy about confronting someone if there was an issue. Kathleen was confident that if Joyce had a concern she would voice it.

Pushing aside the thoughts of an awkward conversation with Joyce, she let the thrill of seeing Cassie again wash over her. She couldn't believe how she was letting her imagination run away with her. She and Joyce had never discussed anything personal in the past and technically there wasn't anything to tell now anyway. So she thought Cassie was attractive. She wasn't her co-worker and neither held any influence over the other's job. If something developed, she'd bring it to Joyce's attention; otherwise there was nothing to tell.

Feeling the queasy stomach roll of anticipation, she considered giving Cassie a call to let her know she was coming, then decided against it. Home visits were supposed to be a surprise for the client. She was only following protocol and doing her job after all.

CHAPTER FOUR

Cassie was still sitting behind the computer when she saw Ryan and Darby crossing to the barn. She knew Dillon would be tied up now for a couple of hours, so moving furniture would have to wait. Cassie joined them, knowing Cheyenne would follow the other horses into the little pasture in hopes of getting some attention. She brushed Cheyenne and then jumped on her bareback, taking her for a short ride around the lake before turning her loose in the pasture again.

She returned to the office as Dillon, Ryan and Darby set off on their ride. An hour later, Cassie was surprised to find herself still staring out the window at the fountain in the middle of the lake and drinking cold coffee. She dumped the remaining coffee and pulled sandwich ingredients from the refrigerator in the small kitchen behind her office. Dillon arrived a short time later, and they moved silently around each other as they made sandwiches, carrying their plates outside to a picnic table.

"Did you get the beds ordered?" Dillon asked.

"Yep, two twin beds to add to the rooms upstairs and a double for the office downstairs."

"You're giving up your office?"

"Not giving it up exactly. I just thought it should have a bed in it, so I'd still have at least one guest room in the house."

"What's wrong with the guest room upstairs?" Dillon frowned, looking confused.

"Oh right. I forgot to tell you," Cassie shook her head. "Fosters is going to give us a college student for the summer to help with supervision."

"That's cool. What did you have to promise in return?"

Cassie rolled her eyes and took another bite of her sandwich as she watched Darby and his brother, Derek, running toward their table.

"Can we take a canoe out on the lake?" Darby gushed.

"Of course, Darby," Dillon said. "You guys need any help? Canoes can be tricky."

"Nope, we got this." Derek strolled toward the lake with Darby on his heels.

"Okay, have fun then," Cassie called, glancing at Dillon. "Do you think they have any idea how easy a canoe is to roll over?"

Dillon laughed. "No, I don't." He slid around the end of the picnic table joining Cassie so he could watch the boys.

"I think we're about to get a show with our lunch."

"At least they're both wearing swim trunks."

Cassie noticed Ryan and Judy watching from their cabin porch and waved. The boys reached the lake and pushed one of the canoes into the water. Darby climbed into the boat while Derek held it, but when Derek tried to climb in the boat it tipped, dumping Darby into the lake. Both boys were squealing with joy as they righted the boat and attempted to get in again. After two more attempts that ended with the boys in the lake, Cassie got up from the table and slipped off her boots and socks. When she got down to the lake, she rolled her jeans up to her knees and waded in. She held the boat steady while the boys climbed in.

"Hold on a second, boys." Cassie walked over to the storage shed and grabbed two of the child-sized life jackets hanging on the side. When she returned, she waded in far enough to hang a life preserver over each boy's head, reaching in to help Darby secure the buckles.

"We can swim, you know," Derek said, wrapping the safety strap around his waist.

"Life preservers are for more than just helping someone who can't swim. If you capsize, they will help you surface more quickly."

"Well, I don't know about Darby, but I don't plan on capsizing," Derek stated.

Cassie laughed. "I don't think anyone ever plans on it."

"What's 'capsize'?" Darby looked back and forth between Derek and Cassie.

"Capsize means tipping over and ending up in the lake," Cassie explained.

Darby giggled.

"Are you ready to go, boys?" Cassie asked.

They both screamed, "Yeah!"

Cassie pushed the little canoe away from the shoreline. Both boys dipped their paddles into the water and began to row. Cassie tried to shout directions to them to help with their paddling, but eventually she gave up and went back to Dillon. Rory and Pete sat on bicycles beside the picnic table.

"That was an adventure." Rory nodded toward the boys.

"Good kids, but I don't think they know anything about paddling a canoe." She laughed.

"Well, you tried." Pete shrugged. "We could hear you up here."

She watched the boys as she only half listened to the guy's conversation. They were good kids. Darby especially was very polite and courteous. Derek and the oldest brother, she still couldn't remember his name but she was sure it was another D name, were typical teenagers. On Monday she had tried to tell them about the bike trails and show them a map, but they weren't interested in listening to her. She was glad to see that their dad had gone with them the first day, and she hoped that on succeeding days he made them at least take a radio. The woods around the lake were made for exploring and were fairly safe, but you could never anticipate an accident.

"…And it's all because of some hottie…" Dillon's words registered as he drove an elbow into her side. "She's probably dreaming about her now."

"What?" Cassie elbowed him back.

"I was just telling the guys about your new kids."

"Sounds like you guys will have a very eventful summer," Pete said.

Cassie sighed. "Eventful is fine. It's traumatic that I want to avoid."

The guys laughed.

"Are you worried?" Pete asked.

"Well, yeah." Cassie frowned. "Worried and scared."

"We're going to have a blast," Dillon insisted.

His confidence pushed the anxiety that was starting to build in her aside. Two weeks to prepare seemed like forever and no time at all.

"So tell us about the woman. What's her name?" Rory leaned toward her over his bicycle handlebars.

"Her name is Kathleen, and she works at the agency that takes care of the kids. She was very nice and not at all what I like in a woman, so you guys can stop the third degree."

Rory held up his hands. "A bit defensive, aren't we?"

"I think there's too much protesting," Pete joined in.

"What's not to like?" Dillon chimed in. "You said she was hot."

"Really, guys. She would not survive a day on the farm. She's a city girl. Nice to look at. Okay, well, very nice to look at, but probably not a keeper. Plus," she held up a hand to keep them from interrupting her, "she lives in the city and I don't have any plans on driving there again in the near future."

Clearly she wasn't the only one not convinced by her statement; the guys were laughing when she walked away from the picnic table. Zoey and Pandy, dripping wet, joined her when she crossed the driveway. Happily, they both laid down in the sun when she went inside so she brought them a bone to chew on.

Wandering through the upstairs bedrooms, Cassie began thinking about how to move the furniture to accommodate the new beds being delivered next week. Arranging the different ideas in her mind, she quickly realized she needed to order smaller dressers for each room. She returned to her office and pulled up the furniture store on her computer again. She quickly selected four small dressers and added them to her already scheduled delivery date. The large dressers already in the kids' rooms would need to be moved; one could go into the guest room upstairs and one downstairs. That was definitely a job she needed Dillon's help with.

The afternoon passed quickly, and Cassie was glad to shut the office down at five and retreat to her house. The grill heated quickly and she placed vegetables in an aluminum foil pack beside the chicken. She fed the dogs and then sat outside watching them chase each other around the yard. After moving into Lake View, she quickly decided she needed the company of a dog. Dillon had insisted she needed two. When she went to pick out her puppies, the woman only had one left. She bonded with Pandora immediately and then spent a miserable night listening to Pandy cry for her missing family. The next morning she sent Dillon on a mission to find another two-month-old labradoodle and he had come back with Zoey.

Both dogs were primarily black, but the white mark on Pandy's chest was larger than the one on Zoey's. Though they got along well, they had stopped being inseparable after the first couple of months. Now each one was independent. Pandy preferred to be outside with people, and Zoey preferred the peace and quiet of being alone. Both were friendly with guests, but they didn't roam the resort without Dillon or Cassie.

Cassie ate her dinner in the dim light coming from inside the house. She watched the lightning bugs blink across the yard until she couldn't hold her eyes open. Dropping her plate into the dishwasher, she climbed the stairs. She had spent much of the day trying to push thoughts of Kathleen out of her mind. What she had told the guys earlier was true. Kathleen was a city girl and wouldn't fit into Cassie's lifestyle. Though her farm wasn't rustic, you couldn't walk down the street for coffee or anything else for that matter. The town of Riverview was at least a fifteen-minute drive away and on a road that was narrow and not made for pedestrians. Unfortunately, all the logic in the world didn't stop her from dreaming about Kathleen even before she fell asleep.

CHAPTER FIVE

Kathleen's thoughts wandered in and out, torn between the excitement of her planned day and the important agenda Joyce was covering. When the meeting finally ended, Kathleen bolted back to her office before anyone could stop her to chat. Noticing Tiffany getting coffee in the breakroom when she passed, she grabbed her briefcase and hurried past the empty reception desk. Tiffany would make her pay for sneaking out without telling anyone, but right now she just wanted to get on the road.

The two-hour drive to Riverview, unfortunately, would give her plenty of time to run scenarios in her mind. A home visit was an opportunity to get to know the host family a little better and that's what she intended to do. She would be utterly professional. She couldn't help that the visit was bringing her a large amount of pleasure. If she was lucky maybe Cassie wouldn't see through the explanation for her visit.

* * *

Cassie and Shelley went through each room rearranging and mentally placing the new furniture. Cassie repeated everything she knew about the girls' arrival while they worked, but Shelley asked more questions than Cassie could answer.

She shrugged for what felt like the hundredth time. "I don't know."

"You didn't ask specifically for a female supervisor?"

"I want them to choose the best candidate, male or female."

"Did you at least ask if the girls had any violence in their past?"

"No. It doesn't matter to me. I want to take them at face value and deal with what they give me." Cassie's excitement was increasing as her anxiety faded. As a police officer, she had dealt with a lot of juveniles from broken or no homes; few of them had had any love for law enforcement. Playing a different role was a challenge. She looked forward to making an impact in each girl's life.

Shelley wrinkled her face. "I guess I understand and I don't mean to sound callous but what if you're bringing a thief into your house?"

"I trust Kathleen's judgment."

Shelley rolled her eyes. "You don't even know her."

"I know enough." The words made Cassie's stomach lurch. She didn't know Kathleen actually, and yet she felt like she did. She hadn't been far from Cassie's thoughts in the last forty-eight hours. She'd almost decided, in fact, to call her. Why not? It had been so long since she'd asked someone out that she couldn't remember what it felt like to be rejected. Besides if she rejected her, wouldn't that be easier to take over the phone?

Cassie smiled to herself as she pushed the heavy dresser toward the hallway. The thought of hearing Kathleen's voice again made her want to stop what she was doing and call her right now. She looked up to find Shelley standing in her path. Her eyes squinted as she studied Cassie's face.

"It's almost eleven thirty. Call Dillon and tell him to get his ass in here and help us."

Wiping the smile from her face before Shelley could ask any questions, Cassie pulled the radio from her belt and keyed the microphone. “Hey D, time to lift some weights.”

“Busy.”

“Doing what?” Cassie frowned. Her mind filled with Kathleen and the girls, she wondered what she had forgotten.

“Jason is here.”

“Well, crap,” Cassie groaned as she climbed around the dresser and headed for the stairs. “I don’t remember the farrier being on today’s schedule.”

“I don’t remember seeing that either,” Shelley called after her.

Cassie left the house at a trot with both dogs on her heels. Trimming the hooves on eight horses was a job that took most of the day, and normally she and Dillon both helped out.

As she approached, Dillon was holding the bay mare and Jason was filing the hoof on her right front foot.

“What’s up, guys?” Cassie asked, joining them in the small pasture.

“Juliet was limping a little when they came in to eat this morning and I could see something stuck in the tip of her hoof. Since it was more in her hoof than in her foot, I gave Jason a call. He was down at the Myers Farm so he came straight over.”

“That’s cool. Thanks for coming so quick, Jason.”

Jason gave a little nod without taking his attention from Juliet’s foot. “Glad I was close by.”

Dillon pulled a small metal object from his pocket and tossed it to her. “Looks like a fence staple. Guess we better ride the fence line today and make sure we don’t have any holes.”

Cassie groaned. “Better to ride the fence line than to chase goats once they escape.”

Dillon nodded. “I was coming in to move furniture. I swear I was.”

“Sure you were, but don’t think you got out of it because I have Shelley on the job.”

Dillon groaned, causing Jason to laugh.

“I’ll be in as soon as we finish here. No need to put it off ’cause *she* will find me.”

"Yep, even if she has to ride a horse to do it," Cassie teased.

Glancing up from his work, Jason smiled. "That must be a story I need to hear."

Cassie looked at Dillon.

"Go ahead. Jason will hound me until I tell him anyway. You can have the pleasure of telling him."

Cassie leaned against the side of the barn. "Apparently Dillon had forgotten his radio and Shelley panicked when she couldn't reach him. She chased him across the pasture and must have really let him have it because I don't think he's forgotten his radio since that day."

"I wasn't gone that long and no one would have ever known about it if you wouldn't have seen Shelley coming back on the horse."

Even in the bright sun, Cassie could see the faint blush on his neck. "Shelley would have told me eventually. She was really pissed at you."

Jason laughed. "Married life. And people ask me why I haven't taken the leap yet." He placed Juliet's foot on the ground and looked at Cassie. "She looks good."

"Any follow up?" Dillon asked.

"Check it for the next day or so, but I don't think you'll need the vet. I was able to clip and file where the staple went in."

"Want to grab a cup of coffee while I write you a check?" Cassie asked as she turned toward the office.

"Be right there," Jason said, holding the gate closed without latching it, waiting for Dillon to catch up.

"So we have two guys to help now," Shelley said as the guys walked into the office.

"Oh no, Jason, you've been roped into moving furniture." Dillon gave him a push back toward the door. "Get out while you still can."

Jason blushed and scuffed his boots on the floor. "I'm on my lunch break anyway, so I can help for a while."

"Geez, man, you didn't even put up a fight." Dillon shook his head.

Cassie handed Jason a check and nodded to the Keurig. "Grab a cup and then we'll put you to work."

* * *

Jason and Shelley grabbed the first dresser and headed down the hall to the guest bedroom. Dillon and Cassie took the other one and headed down the stairs.

"How did we end up with the stairs?" Dillon whined.

"Didn't you see how fast they jumped on moving the other one down the hall? They knew what they were doing all the time."

Before they had made it halfway down the stairs, Shelley came running down the hall and squeezed around them. "I hear a car."

"No, don't let us get in your way," Dillon yelled at her back as she bolted through the door connecting to the office.

They maneuvered the dresser around the corner at the bottom of the stairs and headed down the hall toward the downstairs guest bedroom.

Dillon shifted his grip, almost dropping his end. "Where the hell is Jason?" he whined again.

Cassie laughed. "When did you become such a whiner? You used to be such a big tough guy."

Dillon picked up his pace, forcing Cassie to stumble backward. "Having trouble with your end there, Cass?"

"No trouble, if you'd stop pushing me." She gave a little shove on the dresser, pushing it into Dillon's stomach.

"You aren't whining, are you?"

"I am not whin…oomph." Cassie exhaled as Dillon and the dresser slammed her back against the wall at the end of the hall.

"I think we missed our turn," Dillon crooned sweetly.

They both collapsed across the top of the dresser laughing. The door from the office slammed.

"About damn time we get some assistance," Dillon yelled to Shelley with laughter in his voice.

"How about some manners, mister? We have company," Shelley chastised him, her professional tone causing Cassie to stop laughing and lean around Dillon to look at her.

With a sharp intake of breath, Cassie caught a glimpse of the woman standing behind Shelley.

"What are…I mean, how or…uh…why…?" Cassie stuttered.

"Well, I guess I don't have to ask who this is." Dillon stepped around Shelley and reached out his hand to Kathleen. "I'm Dillon."

"Kathleen Masters."

Cassie struggled to catch her breath while she watched Kathleen chat comfortably with Dillon and Shelley. Shiny clips held her hair away from her face, displaying the openness Cassie had experienced the first time she met her. She was dressed in soft tan chinos and a dark blue button-down dress shirt. Her delicate low-heeled shoes definitely were not made for a farm. Kathleen was there on business.

Crap. A home visit. This was not a good start. Cassie started to walk toward her and realized that she was still pinned between the dresser and the wall. She tried to catch Dillon's eye to get his assistance, but his attention was on Kathleen and Shelley was watching him with an approving look as she listened to the conversation.

"Uh, Dill…" Cassie started to say as a loud crash came from upstairs.

"Jason," Shelley and Dillon said together as they raced up the stairs.

Kathleen looked toward the stairs and then back at Cassie. As their eyes made contact, Kathleen grinned, realizing Cassie was trapped.

"Do you need a hand?" Kathleen stepped forward and pulled the end of the dresser back far enough to allow Cassie to slide out.

Cassie stuck out her hand. "It's good to see you again." Kathleen's hand was soft. She wondered if hers felt rough to Kathleen. Feeling self-conscious, she attempted to withdraw her hand, but when Kathleen didn't let go, Cassie's eyes searched her face.

"I'm sorry to drop in on you like this," Kathleen said as she dropped Cassie's hand and casually leaned against the wall.

"Are you?"

"Okay, no, I'm not. I volunteered."

Cassie raised one eyebrow but made no comment.

Kathleen nodded toward the dresser. "Were you headed somewhere with this? Or did you plan to leave it in the hallway?"

"Actually, we're clearing space for new furniture in the kids' rooms upstairs." Cassie nodded toward the doorway on the right. "The bedroom down here has more room for this big dresser."

"Well, let's move it." Kathleen squeezed down the hall, positioning herself at the other end of the dresser.

The dresser was more bulky than heavy, but Cassie wasn't sure Kathleen would be able to carry it as far as she needed. She looked very stylish in her professional attire. Cassie bit her tongue to keep from commenting on her genteel appearance. She moved to the other end of the dresser. "Ready, on three."

"Is that lift on three or one, two, three and then lift?" Kathleen gave her a wink.

Cassie's stomach dropped, and she struggled to recover quickly from her surprise at Kathleen's flirting. "Really? Just lift the dang thing."

"Wow, here for more than five minutes and all pleasantries go out the window." Kathleen held her end off the floor, waiting for Cassie to lift hers.

"Now you're family." Cassie lifted her end and together they walked into the bedroom, placing the dresser under the window.

Cassie glanced around the room as Kathleen studied it. This was the one room in the house she hadn't really decorated. There was a wooden desk with a chair on one side and a filing cabinet on the other. A small bookshelf sat near the door.

"This was your office?" Kathleen asked.

"Yes, but I didn't use it much."

"Are you going to put a bed in here?"

"I thought the supervisor would prefer the privacy and their own bathroom." Cassie took a step toward the door and then turned to find Kathleen only inches from her. She was captivated by the fleeting look of desire that crossed Kathleen's face. Quickly taking a step back and stuffing her hands in her pockets, she was surprised to hear the gravelly tone in her own voice. "Do you have anywhere else you need to be?"

"There's nowhere else I would rather be." Kathleen's voice was soft and Cassie's heart skipped a beat.

"Well…um…do you want to get lunch?"

Kathleen blushed. "Well, I didn't think through my plan very well since I arrived right at noon, but I'm not on a schedule. Is there somewhere we can go? My treat."

"That's a nice offer that I'll hold you to one day, but how about a sandwich for today? We keep a variety of stuff in the kitchen behind the office and we can take care of business while we eat."

"That sounds great. I love 'stuff.'"

CHAPTER SIX

Shelley and the guys quickly made their plates and disappeared outside.

"Is it okay if we eat with everyone?" Cassie held out a bag of chips.

"Of course, we can still talk about the farm, right?"

"Yes, and you'll get input from everyone. Neither Dillon nor Shelley is shy, if you haven't noticed already."

"I like them."

Cassie smiled. "We'll see what you think after lunch."

Zoey and Pandy met them on the porch and followed them to the picnic table.

"Sit here, Kathleen." Shelley slid toward Dillon on the bench, giving Kathleen the end spot. Cassie took a seat beside Jason and across from Kathleen.

"Those are beautiful dogs." Kathleen watched Zoey and Pandy stretch out in a shady spot nearby.

"Thank you," Cassie said, sticking a chip in her mouth.

"They're spoiled rotten." Shelley grinned, keeping her attention on her sandwich and avoiding Cassie's hard stare.

"They might be, but neither one is at the table begging for food," Kathleen countered.

"Cassie wouldn't allow that," Dillon chimed in.

Kathleen looked at Cassie, laying her sandwich on the plate. "Are you strict?"

Cassie narrowed her eyes at Kathleen's scrutiny. "Maybe, but I couldn't allow them to run around loose without manners. As long as no one feeds them from the table they listen pretty well." She turned her glare back to Shelley.

"I would never feed them from the table." Shelley laughed. "I only give them their treats in the appropriate locations."

"They hang close to the house and the stalls." Dillon shoved the last of his sandwich in his mouth and picked up his bag of chips. "They never go far or visit the guests without either Cassie or me. None of the guests have ever complained about them."

Kathleen gazed over Cassie's shoulder toward the lake. "This place is really peaceful."

Cassie didn't have to turn around to see what Kathleen was seeing. She knew the fountain centered in the large lake would be making ripples across the crisp blue water, pushing continuous waves toward the shore. She also knew that when the cabins were occupied peacefulness could be sparse.

"For the moment, yes, but in five minutes the Jackson boys from Cabin Four will return from lunch and the world will erupt in screaming and kid play."

Cassie ate another chip, ignoring her sandwich. She wasn't sorry to be sitting across from Kathleen. She had the best view of everyone. No matter how she tried to resist, her eyes gravitated to Kathleen's face, pulled by the movement of her lips when she talked. She was surprised her mind was able to stay in the conversation.

"Yeah, we think it's peaceful too." Dillon shot Cassie a rebuking look.

Kathleen winked at Cassie. "So, convince me to spend my money here."

Cassie coughed, quickly taking a sip of water to cover her surprise. Kathleen's easy flirting was certainly welcome and enjoyable, but it was not something Cassie was used to. Nor were the feelings it invoked deep inside her. She was used to being in control of her emotions, and she couldn't help feeling a little out of sorts.

"Oh, that's easy," Dillon jumped in before Cassie could regain her speech.

"Really." Kathleen leaned around Shelley so she could see Dillon. "Let's hear it."

"We offer trail riding on horses or bikes and a beautiful lake for swimming or boating. We have twenty acres with paths for watching the wildlife. The property backs up to the Conecuh National Forest with connecting trails. Or you can just hang on the beach and do nothing. On Friday nights we have a big cookout and roast marshmallows." Dillon took a breath.

"The girls are going to love it here," Kathleen said softly.

Dillon smiled. "We'll make sure of it. They'll have responsibilities, but we'll let them decide how involved they want to be."

Cassie took a few minutes to put some distance between her emotions and the woman across from her. Finally finding her voice, she continued Dillon's sales pitch. "We have four alike but different cabins. One cabin has three bedrooms, one has two and one has one. The last cabin is a large open room. All are fully stocked with general appliances and cooking supplies. Each one has a gas grill on the back deck, and we provide charcoal for the grill pits by the lake."

"Housekeeping is provided upon request. Fresh towels and linens are always available in the office, or they can fill out their housekeeping tag and we'll do it for them," Shelley added.

"Housekeeping tag?" Kathleen asked.

"It's a tag that they hang on their cabin door each morning. They can mark whatever housekeeping items they would like to have done that day," Shelley explained.

"That's a great idea," Kathleen agreed. "You don't bother them unless they need something."

"And the staff is pretty friendly too." Jason put in as he stood and tossed his plate into a nearby trash can. "This has been fun, but I gotta get back to work."

"Cookout tonight, if you're free," Cassie invited.

"Sounds great," Jason said with a wave as he started toward his truck. Looking back over his shoulder, he reminded them. "Don't forget to check your fence line."

"Oh yeah," Dillon groaned. "I guess we better go do that." He glanced at Kathleen and then at Cassie. "Maybe I should go alone?"

"No. Well, maybe, I am not sure," Cassie frowned. She wasn't ready for Kathleen to leave, but it would take Dillon late into the evening to make the check on his own.

Kathleen stood quickly. "I can go. I don't want to keep you from your work."

"You could stay with me," Shelley suggested.

"Or…" Cassie scanned Kathleen's clothing down to her shoes. "You could go with us?"

"Okay," Kathleen eagerly responded.

Shelley laughed. "Not dressed like that, you can't, but I think we can hook you up. Come with me." Shelley cleared the table of trash and grabbed Kathleen's hand, tugging her toward the house.

"Well, all right then." Cassie stood, taking a deep breath. "Let's saddle some horses."

Dillon frowned. "Did we mention we'd be riding horses?"

"I don't think so, but she's going to find out soon enough."

* * *

Kathleen quickened her steps to keep up with Shelley. *What have I agreed to?* She didn't really know, but she did know she wasn't ready to leave. She also wasn't ready to think about how unprofessional her feelings were becoming. Cassie was a host for Fosters, a company she was employed by. Was she crossing a line? Maybe. She only knew she couldn't remember the last time she felt this good. She felt more comfortable with these strangers than people she had known for years. Flirting with Cassie and watching her blush was certainly worth hanging around a little longer for.

CHAPTER SEVEN

Cassie stepped into the small paddock and whistled for Cheyenne and Dakota, while Dillon gathered the materials they might need for fencing repairs. After she saddled both horses, she selected a mahogany bay mare for Kathleen. She and Dillon were attaching supplies to their saddles when they heard the sound of Kathleen's laughter. They turned to see Shelley and Kathleen walking toward the stables arm in arm, their heads bent close together.

Dillon chuckled. "I think she might be a farm girl after all."

No kidding. Cassie's eyes widened at the sight of Kathleen. Obviously, she had made a rash decision when evaluating Kathleen's ability to fit into life on the farm; the transformation in front of her made her light-headed. Kathleen had untied her hair, letting it fall in disheveled waves around her face. A light, long-sleeved T-shirt hugged every curve of her breasts and grazed the top of her borrowed blue jeans. Cassie's eyes had barely made it to the cowboy boots covering her feet when the two women stepped into the barn.

"Close your mouth, Cass." Dillon bumped Cassie with his shoulder, knocking her off balance as he pushed past her and approached the women.

Cassie fell against the wall of the stable, and she casually leaned there as if that was her intent all along. Her face heated when she met Kathleen's eyes, taking in the smile that covered her face. Kathleen had clearly heard Dillon's comment. Cassie was going to have to kill him.

"My lady, your horse awaits." Dillon gave a mock bow, holding out his hand to Kathleen.

She looked at Cassie and then Shelley before allowing her hand to be swallowed up by Dillon's larger one.

"Have fun." Shelley kissed Dillon and turned, placing a wide-brimmed hat on Kathleen's head.

Dillon headed for the paddock with Kathleen, swinging their hands between them like small children on the playground. Cassie swallowed the lump starting to form in her throat. Her friends had pulled Kathleen into their inner circle, and she looked quite comfortable there. The sweet sound of her laughter touched Cassie. Grabbing her Stetson from the tack room, she hurried to catch up to them and join the conversation.

"So, are you seeing anyone?" Dillon's voice reached Cassie as she approached.

Cassie slammed to a stop, instantly regretting her precipitous arrival, but she couldn't help leaning forward in hopes of catching Kathleen's answer. Her words were only a low murmur, but Cassie didn't miss Dillon's evil grin as he looked back at her. She groaned. Dillon was having way too much fun at her expense. He had never had the opportunity to meet anyone Cassie was interested in and he was completely aware of her discomfort. To distract him, she took Angel by the reins and led her beside the mounting platform.

Dillon raised his arm, assisting Kathleen as she climbed the three concrete steps beside the mare. Taking the reins from Cassie, he smiled at Kathleen. "Have you ridden before?"

"Yes, but only on guided tours." She grinned. "And it's been a few years."

Dillon laughed. "No worries. Cassie picked a great horse for you. This is Angel." He gently guided Kathleen's hand to the bay's neck. "She is very gentle and great at following."

He folded the reins into Kathleen's hands as she settled in the saddle. "Hold right here in a relaxed grip, using both hands. Pull back if you need to stop, but you probably won't have to. She will follow us and stop when we do."

Cassie climbed on Cheyenne's back and guided her beside Kathleen. "All ready?"

"As ready as I'll ever be," Kathleen said hesitantly.

"Hold on tight." Cassie winked. "Injuries make my insurance go up."

Kathleen choked out a laugh. "That's nice. Your concern for my welfare is touching."

Cassie and Dillon maneuvered their horses out of the paddock with Kathleen in the middle. The goats scurried away from the horses' feet but followed close behind them.

"We're being followed." Kathleen turned back and forth in her saddle to watch them.

"They'll lose interest shortly. Once we get to the platform out there." Cassie pointed at a wooden four-by-four platform about three feet off the ground.

"What's that?" Kathleen asked.

"Playground equipment."

"What?"

"Just watch." Cassie pointed again as three of the goats ran up the ramp and began pushing each other off the platform. "See, they've already forgotten about us."

"They're very cute." Kathleen laughed when a fourth goat squeezed herself onto the platform, shoving another one off.

"It was easy for Dillon to convince me to rescue them."

"Very easy," Dillon added. "I think we should head straight for the stream since that's our weakest point."

"Sounds like a plan." Cassie pulled her gaze from Kathleen and glanced at Dillon. "If we don't find anything there, we can separate and follow the fence line back in both directions."

"Is the fence broken?" Kathleen asked.

"Possibly. Dillon found a fence nail in one of the horse's hooves this morning so we need to check. The goats can wiggle out of really small holes and predators can get in so it's not worth the risk. Although with so much sandy dirt around here, things get dropped and then churn up years later."

* * *

As they entered the tree line, Dillon took the lead and Cassie dropped to the rear. It was difficult to talk in single file so they rode in silence. Cassie was happy to follow and keep an eye on Kathleen. The long sleeves on Kathleen's T-shirt made her shoulders look even narrower and the material molded to her back, moving as she moved. Cassie was sure she had already memorized every inch of Kathleen's body and could trace the curves in her mind.

Dillon nudged Dakota into a trot when they cleared the trees and headed across the open pasture to the fence line. He dismounted, jumping back and forth across the little stream. He looked up at Cassie as they approached.

"I don't see anything," he said, shaking his head.

Cassie dismounted and looked up at Kathleen. "Would you like a chance to stretch?"

"Yes, but I might need help getting down and back up again."

"That's no problem. One of us will help you." Cassie dropped Cheyenne's reins, leaving her to graze beside the stream. She stepped to the side of Angel, putting one hand on the saddle horn to balance Kathleen as she dismounted. "Just swing your leg over and drop."

"Have you seen the length of my legs?"

"Yes, as a matter of fact, I *have* seen your legs." Cassie's face flushed, but she didn't look away. Kathleen had started the flirting, and Cassie couldn't let the opportunity pass.

"Then I don't have to tell you they won't reach the ground." A slight smile played on Kathleen's lips, but she didn't acknowledge Cassie's comment.

"Put your hand on my shoulder, and I'll support you until your stubby little limbs reach the ground."

Kathleen laughed. "I would say something smart but then you might not help me down."

"True, but there's always Dillon."

Kathleen swung her leg over the back of Angel and slid down into Cassie's arms. Their faces inches apart, Kathleen leaned forward and whispered in her ear. "I prefer you."

Cassie's breath caught and her fingers tightened on Kathleen's waist. The soft material covering Kathleen's skin didn't protect Cassie's fingers from the heat, and she quickly stepped away. *Crap!* Cassie avoided Kathleen's gaze and walked toward the fence line. "See anything, Dillon?"

"Nothing so far."

"Bummer," Cassie mumbled. The sparks Kathleen had caused moments ago still raced through her body, and she had hoped they could return to the stables quickly. "I guess we better walk the rest of the fence line."

"Works for me. Meet you back at the house." Dillon called as he turned and began a slow pace along the fence away from Cassie and Kathleen.

Cassie picked up Cheyenne's reins and began walking in the opposite direction. "I guess you're stuck with me unless you hurry and catch up to Dillon."

"Tempting." Kathleen took Angel's reins and followed her.

Cassie couldn't help feeling that she should apologize for what almost happened, but she wasn't ready to put her attraction into words. She didn't think she would ever experience this feeling of enchantment with another person again and she would feel like an idiot if it was one-sided. She didn't think it was, though. The look of desire she had seen in Kathleen's eyes had mirrored her own. It had been a while since she had seen it, but she was pretty sure about what she was seeing.

Cassie stopped and waited for Kathleen to catch up. She turned to face her before speaking. "I'm sorry—"

Kathleen's fingers touched her lips. "There's nothing to be sorry for."

Static crackled from the radio on Cassie's belt, and they both jumped.

"Hey, Cassie," Dillon's voice boomed.

Cassie turned the volume down and keyed the microphone. "Yes." Her voice was hoarse and scratchy.

"I found the spot. Looks like something heavy climbed the fence and tore it down."

"We're headed back your way."

Cassie dropped Cheyenne's reins and stepped beside Kathleen. "It will be faster if we ride." Taking Angel's reins from Kathleen, she interlocked her hands, placing them below the stirrup. "Use my hands as your step and I'll help you swing your leg over."

Kathleen placed her left hand on the horn and her right on the rear of the saddle. Placing her left foot into Cassie's hands, she allowed herself to be pushed up onto Angel's back. Cassie handed the reins up to her. "All good?"

"We're all good." Kathleen stated with a smile, making Cassie's chest flutter. She could get used to this feeling. It had been a long time since she had felt any stirrings of interest for anyone, and she was starting to enjoy it.

"Okay. Yeah." Cassie flashed Kathleen a big grin. Putting her left foot in the stirrup, she swung her leg over Cheyenne's back.

Angel fell in behind Cheyenne as they trudged down the fence line. It wasn't long until they spotted Dillon. He had already cut a piece of fence to strengthen the damaged section. Cassie jumped down and grabbed the bag with the supplies in it. While Dillon held the fence in place, Cassie tapped a couple of new fence nails into the posts. When she finished, Dillon pulled out the wire cutters and wrapped all of the open ends around the standing fence.

The two of them worked together in silence and after a few minutes they had patched the damaged portion. Cassie checked in with Shelley on the radio and let her know they were on their way back. With Kathleen positioned between them, they cleared the trees and headed back across the pasture.

Kathleen shrugged. "I guess I should take this opportunity to ask my questions, and then I can get out of your way."

"What?" Dillon asked. "You can't leave before the cookout."

"You guys don't need an extra body in the way all afternoon and I should head back home."

"You won't be an extra body if we put you to work," Dillon said, trying to persuade her.

"Don't worry, Dillon," Cassie said, cutting off Kathleen's response. "She's going to stay."

"I am?" Kathleen asked.

"You are." Cassie gave her a wink. "We have your clothes."

Kathleen laughed.

"So, no work for now. You can enjoy the ride." Cassie smiled. "I'll give you a tour and answer all your questions when we get back."

"I like that plan." Kathleen returned her smile.

CHAPTER EIGHT

Cassie listened distractedly as Shelley relayed a phone message she had taken from a returning guest. Acknowledging the information, Cassie quickly stepped around her. She was disappointed to see Dillon had already helped Kathleen down from Angel, and she gave him a glare. His response was a big smile over Kathleen's head as he helped her remove the bay's saddle.

Together the four worked quickly to remove saddles and brush the horses before releasing them into the pasture.

"I am going to head over to Mac's," Dillon announced.

"I made you a list." Shelley pulled a piece of paper from her pocket and handed it to him.

"Why don't you go with him?" Cassie suggested. "We're just going to be hanging around and he could use the help."

"You only want her to watch me," Dillon said, pretending to be upset and stomping off. "Everywhere I go, everything I do, she's always watching me," he mumbled to himself. When he reached his truck, he held the door open and turned to Shelley. "Coming, sweetheart?"

Shelley rolled her eyes at Cassie and Kathleen. "You gotta love him." She handed Cassie the phone. She gave Dillon a peck on the cheek before sliding behind the wheel and across the seat.

Dillon gave them an evil grin, climbing in behind Shelley. When the truck had pulled away, Cassie clipped the phone to her jeans and looked at Kathleen.

"Shall we?" She motioned toward the first cabin before stuffing her hands in her pockets.

Kathleen fell into step beside her. "So, who or what is Mac's?"

"Oh right, you're not from around here. It's a local meat market where we get everything for our Friday night dinners."

"What's on the menu? Since I've been so kindly invited to stay."

"Steaks and burgers, but we always have hot dogs or chicken if you prefer. We can even do a portabella mushroom, if you're against meat."

"A steak sounds great."

"They'll be back in an hour to start prepping everything. Is there anything specific you want to see around here before then?"

"No, I'm perfectly content." Kathleen slid her hand into the loop of Cassie's arm.

Goose bumps erupted up and down Cassie's arms, and her body felt like it was on fire. The flirting earlier had caused Cassie's stomach to flutter, but Kathleen's touch was sending electric pulses throughout her body. Talking was the last thing on Cassie's mind, but she felt like she should be open before things went too far.

"You know…I mean…I'm sure it's obvious." Cassie struggled to find the right words and looked up to see Pete and Rory waving from their porch at Cabin Two.

Kathleen dropped her hand from Cassie's arm, and Cassie glanced at her, surprised. She knew she definitely had to say the words now. She didn't want a misunderstanding between them.

"Hey," Pete yelled, waving them over.

"One second," Cassie called back, turning her back to the guys. She searched Kathleen's face with her eyes. "You know I'm a lesbian, right?" Cassie asked, her brow furrowed.

"Well, yes. I mean. I assumed."

"I wasn't sure if you were shying away from me or them." She nodded toward Pete and Rory.

"I didn't want to put you in an awkward situation in front of your guests."

Cassie gave the guys a wave and took Kathleen's hand, leading her up the steps to Cabin One. She unlocked the door and pulled Kathleen inside. Closing the door behind them, she turned to face her.

Kathleen's eyes were filled with curiosity and a hint of desire. The speech that had been on Cassie's tongue seconds before was history, replaced by a desire to kiss the soft lips in front of her. Still holding Kathleen's hand, Cassie kept space between their bodies as she gently touched Kathleen's cheek. Before she could think of a reason not to, she slid her hand to the back of Kathleen's neck, pulling them closer. Kathleen's eyes were closed, and Cassie gently brought their lips together.

She was about to take a step backward to break the kiss when Kathleen's tongue met hers. Instantly aroused, she stepped forward and pushed Kathleen back against the door. Deepening the kiss, she slid both hands into her hair. Her stomach muscles twitched under Kathleen's hands as they moved lightly up and down her sides. Her touch felt hot through Cassie's T-shirt.

Kathleen dropped her head to Cassie's shoulder. "I need to breathe for a second."

"You can't kiss and breathe?" Cassie asked, struggling to catch her own breath.

"It seems I can't with you."

"Well, while you are breathing maybe I should take a step back."

Kathleen slid her hands across Cassie's stomach, giving her a little push. "I guess that would be a good idea unless you're thinking about finishing what you started?"

"I'm willing." Cassie gave her an evil grin as she stepped into the living room, placing the kitchen bar between them.

Cassie watched Kathleen take a deep breath and let it out slowly as she looked around the one-room cabin. It was sparsely furnished with two barstools against the counter, a love seat and a recliner facing the rear deck. A double bed covered with a patchwork comforter was against the far wall. The wooden floors were covered with rugs of mauve and dark blue that matched the comforter on the bed and the pillows on the love seat.

"This is really cute." Kathleen walked past Cassie to look out the rear window. "And a hot tub. Nice."

"Each cabin has one, and we keep them open year round. The bathroom is in that corner, by the way. Dillon did all the renovating."

Kathleen walked into the bathroom. Cassie heard her praising the detail but didn't follow her in. Knowing she wasn't ready to be in a small space with Kathleen, she leaned against the breakfast bar and waited for her to return.

Kathleen stepped out of the bathroom. "I love the space around the sink and the walk-in shower."

"Those are my favorite parts too. My bathroom and the other cabins are designed the same way." Cassie spoke without thinking, "If you want, you could stay here tonight."

Kathleen stopped and looked at her. "Really? That would be great."

"We do have guests checking in tomorrow, but that's not until three."

"I'll clean up after myself in the morning so you don't have to clean it again."

"That's okay. You can call me when you get up, and I'll take care of it."

Kathleen shrugged as she took Cassie's hand in hers. "Thank you so much. I'm really looking forward to this evening now. Without the drive hanging over my head, I can relax."

"And have some wine with dinner?"

"Yes, I think I will." She gave Cassie's arm a pull as she walked toward the door. "We should leave now."

"But we're just starting to have fun," Cassie joked.

Kathleen stopped and pulled Cassie hard against her. She ran her fingers through Cassie's hair, pulling her head down into a kiss, a deep one that seemed to caress Cassie's lips. Before Cassie could tighten her grip, Kathleen had pulled away and was leading her toward the door again.

Cassie groaned.

"You have guests waiting to talk with you," Kathleen reminded her.

"Oh, wow. I totally forgot about them." Cassie shook her head. "You really mess me up."

Kathleen stopped on the porch and waited for Cassie to lock the cabin door. "That's the nicest thing anyone has said to me in a while."

Cassie took her hand and led her down the steps toward Cabin Two. "Get used to it. I have more to say."

Kathleen smiled.

* * *

"Hey," Dillon called when Kathleen entered the house, pulling the office door closed behind her.

"Those steaks look awesome." Kathleen stared down at the slabs of red meat marinating in several baking dishes on the counter. "Cassie's on the phone. Can I help?"

"Dillon will make the burgers with his special recipe, but you can help me cut the vegetables for a salad," Shelley suggested as she piled slices of tomato in the plastic container with other hamburger toppings.

Kathleen washed her hands in the kitchen sink and then glanced around the room as she dried them. She had noticed when she arrived how warm and comfortable the house felt. There were a few pictures on the wall and some knickknacks in a corner curio cabinet in the dining room, but mostly the room was free of clutter. Dark blue was the dominant color in both rooms, but the kitchen was brighter with some yellow mixed in. The window behind the kitchen sink and the sliding glass door opposite it in the dining room allowed both rooms to be bathed in natural light.

Kathleen took a seat at the bar separating the kitchen and dining room, and Shelley pushed a cutting board toward her along with a head of lettuce.

"Go ahead and use the entire head. Cassie will eat on it all weekend if it doesn't get eaten tonight."

Kathleen cut the lettuce head in half and began slicing it. "So you guys live nearby?"

"About five miles down the road." Shelley's voice was muffled as she pulled additional vegetables from the refrigerator.

"Cassie offered to let us build here." Dillon paused and glanced at Shelley. "We're thinking about it."

"That would be convenient." Kathleen sensed an edge of tension between them. "Is there a drawback?"

"Not really." Dillon shrugged. "Shelley would like to live in the city though."

"I certainly understand that. I do like where I live and being in the city has some advantages, but it's nothing like being out here." Kathleen couldn't explain the instant feeling of calm she had felt when she crossed under the Lake View sign. She didn't understand it herself. "It's like entering a different world."

"We're still trying to figure out how we can do it all." Dillon again glanced at Shelley.

Shelley gave him a small smile. "I've been taking online college classes through City College and I'd like to enroll on campus this fall."

"I have a two-bedroom townhouse if you would like to split your time between here and there," Kathleen offered.

"Really? Are you sure?" Shelley's voice filled with excitement. "I might take you up on that."

"I'd love the company."

"We'd really appreciate that." Dillon grinned, the tension gone from his voice. "I love my job here, but I want Shelley to have what she wants too. I can't imagine living in the city, and Shelley couldn't wait to graduate high school and move away."

"Sounds like a match made in heaven," Kathleen joked.

Shelley slid the containers holding salad and hamburger toppings into the refrigerator.

"Why don't you show Kathleen the kids' rooms while I mix my secret recipe," Dillon suggested.

"Dillon swears he's a closet chef." Shelley bumped her hip into his.

"I'd love to see the rooms upstairs, but I promise not to peek if I'm forced to stay in the room with you." Kathleen gave him a wink.

"I'm not sure you can be trusted and I know Shelley can't be." Dillon bumped his wife back, pushing her toward the stairs. "Get out."

"We'll leave the room, but you need to wrap the potatoes in foil after you do the burgers," Shelley instructed him.

Dillon waved them away with both hands.

"Right this way." Shelley disappeared into the living room and headed toward the stairs. "You got to see the downstairs bedroom earlier, didn't you?"

"Yes, but it's not going to be used for the girls, right?"

"Right."

At the top of the stairs, Kathleen paused, looking out the window at the scene in front of her. She could see all of the cabins, the lake and the trails where they disappeared into the tree line. The girls would be overwhelmed with the openness and their newfound sense of freedom. It was heavenly. *Was it possible to be more in love with the property than with the woman? Love? Where did that word come from?* She thought about the gentle way Cassie had helped her off the horse. Tender and caring. Her face flamed when she remembered the possessive way Cassie had pushed her against the cabin door when she kissed her. She preferred one-night stands with no complications, and yet this woman already had her wishing there might be more.

"It's beautiful, isn't it?" Shelley's voice stopped Kathleen's analysis and she turned to follow her.

Shelley stopped at the first door on the left. "This room connects to the bathroom, but the other bedroom for the girls is across the hall. We have two more single beds and four small dressers coming next week."

Kathleen looked around the large bedroom with one single bed, then stepped into the connecting bathroom. "This is certainly nicer than the group home they're in now. They might not want to leave."

Shelley laughed. "Careful, Cassie might let them stay."

"She's pretty sweet, huh?" Kathleen looked down the hall toward the two other open doors. One of them had to be Cassie's bedroom and the curiosity to see it tugged at her. Instead she followed Shelley across the hall into the second girls' room.

"She pretends to be tough, but she's pretty good with the kids. We all enjoyed having Greg and Mandi around last summer, but Cassie was really bummed when they left. Do you know who'll be coming with them to supervise?"

"Not yet. I am trying to get a female, but believe it or not most of our applications come from young men."

"A female would probably work better with the house arrangements, but I know Dillon would be happy to have another guy around."

"He shouldn't feel too left out. I think he'll find the girls very interested in the animals and in him. None of them have had a male in their lives, at least not one as easygoing as Dillon. I bet they fall in love him."

"He's very easy to be around and this place is more than a job to him."

"That's very clear with both of you, actually. You've all given me a wonderful break from work."

"How long will your drive back be?" Shelley asked.

"I came from the office. It only took about two hours to get here, but I live closer to the beach so it might take a little longer to get home." She hesitated, unsure of what Shelley's reaction might be to Cassie's offer to use the cabin. "But Cassie offered to let me stay tonight."

"Really?" Shelley raised her eyebrows.

Kathleen grinned. "Not here, but in one of the cabins."

"Oh, that's great. We'll have a fun evening. Nothing better than s'mores and wine."

"So," Kathleen whispered, "are you going to tell on me if I sneak a peek at Cassie's room?"

CHAPTER NINE

"Hey, what's going on?" Cassie glanced around the room, not seeing Shelley or Kathleen. She moved closer to Dillon and whispered. "Where are they?"

"Shelley is showing her the kids' rooms."

Cassie took a step back and released the breath she had been holding. She had thought for a moment that maybe she had scared Kathleen away. "That's cool." She busied herself with opening the bottle of wine sitting on the counter.

"Quit worrying." Dillon laughed. "They haven't been up there very long, and Shelley doesn't know all of your secrets."

Cassie frowned. "I'm not worrying."

"What happened while we were at the store?"

"Why? What did Kathleen say?" Cassie tried to control the blush that was starting at the base of her neck. She turned her back to Dillon and began wrapping the potatoes in foil. "I showed her the inside of the cabins."

"The empty ones?"

Cassie knew his question wasn't really a question. The heat spread, covering her face. "Well, I couldn't very well show her the ones that were occupied." She tried for nonchalance but knew she was failing.

Dillon laughed again. "No, you're right. You had no choice but to take the beautiful woman into an empty cabin."

"Geez, man. Give me a break."

"Give you a break? Why do you need a break?"

Cassie could feel his gaze penetrating her back.

"Cassie?"

She knew he wouldn't give up so she turned to face him.

Dillon took one look and collapsed with laughter. "You should never in your life play poker."

"Why?" Cassie raised her eyebrow.

"Confess already."

Cassie shook her head.

"What did you do? And how good was it?" Dillon asked.

Cassie shook her head again and turned away from him.

"Come on, Cass. I've never had the opportunity to give you the third degree."

Cassie took a deep breath. Dillon was her best friend. It wasn't like she was betraying confidences in the high school locker room. "We kissed and it was awesome."

Dillon whooped.

"Hush." Cassie looked up at the ceiling, hoping their voices wouldn't carry that far.

Dillon began dancing around the kitchen, and the dogs barked, joining in the excitement.

"Dillon!" Cassie frantically shoved him. "Stop it." She squeezed a piece of aluminum foil into a ball and whipped it at him. Both dogs dove to retrieve the ball when it bounced off his shoulder. When the second ball connected with Dillon's head, he finally stopped dancing and took cover behind the kitchen's center island. Cassie launched several more balls over the counter and she could hear the dogs' nails on the floor as they raced to retrieve them. Dillon slid around the counter and launched a barrage back at her. Several of the balls hit her in the chest, leaving wet spots from the dog drool.

"Honestly! A drool ball?" Cassie yelled at him. "I'm going to kick your ass."

Cassie and Dillon froze as Kathleen and Shelley came around the corner. Shelley stared at both of them.

"What's going on down here?" Shelley asked with a stern face, biting back her laughter.

Cassie stood and pointed at the wet spots on her chest. "Dillon drooled on my shirt."

"Dillon?" Shelley looked inquiringly at him.

Dillon stood to face her. "You know she lies, Shell. It's not my drool and I didn't technically put it on her shirt."

Cassie laughed. "Well, he's right. It's dog drool and it got on my shirt from an aluminum foil ball." Cassie pointed at Dillon. "That he threw."

"I think I've heard enough," Shelley said. "It's time to carry the food outside."

Dillon stepped around Shelley and whipped another ball at Cassie, hitting her between the shoulder blades. Kathleen, who had moved into the kitchen to help Shelley pull containers from the refrigerator, took a couple steps away from Cassie.

"I was talking to you, Dillon!" Shelley shoved several stacked food trays into his arms.

"Yes ma'am." He hung his head and followed Shelley, throwing an evil smile over his shoulder at Cassie.

Cassie grinned at Kathleen. "You can come back over now."

Kathleen stepped beside her, running her hand over Cassie's back. "You have a little bit of drool on your back too."

Cassie watched Kathleen's bottom lip start to quiver as she tried to hold back her laughter. Cassie gave her a gentle push. "I thought you were on my side."

"Oh, I am, but I can still appreciate the drool spots on your shirt."

Cassie stepped into the pantry and filled two dog bowls with kibble, setting them in the elevated feeder. "That should stop them from eating aluminum foil." Cassie took a step toward her. "Did you have a nice tour?"

"I did." Kathleen backed into the counter. "Did you have a nice drool ball battle?"

"I did." Cassie placed her hands on the counter on either side of Kathleen and stared into her eyes. She wasn't sure what she was searching for, but the smoldering look of desire she found in Kathleen's face pulled her forward. Gently their lips met and their tongues entwined. Unlike the earlier kiss, this one deepened immediately. The soft lips were familiar to Cassie now and she longed for more. Kathleen's fingers slid up her neck and into her hair, sending bolts of lightning through Cassie's body. She slid her leg between Kathleen's and felt the vibration of Kathleen's moan. The front door slammed, and Cassie spun, concealing Kathleen with her body.

Shelley glanced at them and quickly pulled the last container from the counter. "I'll just grab the potatoes and go." She stopped in the doorway her back to them. "Dillon started the grill so no need to hurry."

Cassie didn't move until she heard the door close behind Shelley.

"Sorry about that." Cassie turned and pulled Kathleen against her.

"Nothing for you to be sorry for. I don't think Shelley was upset and I'm certainly not."

"I guess we should head outside." Cassie reluctantly picked up the bottle of wine and started toward the front door.

"Or upstairs?" Kathleen's voice was soft but teasing.

Cassie stopped, taking a deep breath and Kathleen walked past her onto the porch, bumping Cassie's shoulder as she passed. "Maybe I can get the full tour later?"

CHAPTER TEN

Cassie glanced around at the crowd as they approached the large brick grill surrounded by picnic tables. Dillon turned the grilling duties over to Cassie with a wink, but to her relief he didn't offer any additional harassment. Unfortunately, she knew he would save it for later but she didn't care—the kiss had been worth it.

Shelley took Kathleen by the arm and began introducing her to everyone. Unable to keep her eyes off her, Cassie watched as she chatted comfortably with the guests, occasionally looking back to meet Cassie's eyes. She was still dressed in the borrowed jeans from the earlier horseback ride. She had joked about their length earlier, but in the dark jeans, Kathleen's legs looked long and lean.

"What are you smiling about?"

Cassie was surprised to find Kathleen next to her. She struggled to think of something cool to say, but when smoother words wouldn't come she blurted the truth. "I was admiring your legs in those jeans."

Kathleen smiled, offering her wineglass to her.

"Thank you." Cassie took a sip and passed the glass back.

"Thank you." Kathleen dipped her glass at Cassie before putting it to her lips.

Cassie stepped away from the grill and put her arm casually around Kathleen, speaking softly. "No, thank you."

"I get the feeling we're talking about a lot of different things here."

"Well, I appreciate you sharing your wine and for you being here with me."

"Not so different then. I can't think of anywhere else I'd rather be."

Cassie couldn't remember feeling so happy. She looked around at the group of people, talking and laughing, her gaze taking in Ryan and Judy's oldest son, David, sitting at the farthest picnic table with his sister. Cassie frowned when their eyes met and he continued to stare in their direction. She leaned in close to Kathleen's ear. "I think we're being watched."

"I noticed some interest."

"Do you think it's us together or one of us individually?"

"I'm not sure."

Cassie took the wineglass from Kathleen and drained the remaining liquid in it. "How about a refill?"

Kathleen took the empty glass. "Clever."

She watched Kathleen walk toward the picnic table covered with drinks and food. When she glanced over at David, she saw that he too was focused on Kathleen. Watching his eyes follow Kathleen on her path back, Cassie dropped her gaze from him and relaxed.

She greeted Kathleen with a smile. "Oh, it's you, baby."

Kathleen laughed. "Baby…really?"

Cassie couldn't stop the blush from covering her face so she turned to flip the meat on the grill. She hadn't meant to say that. "Sorry, that just slipped out," she said softly as Kathleen stepped close.

"I like that you say what comes to mind. Honesty is not overrated."

"Except at poker. Which is why Dillon says I'm never allowed to play."

"I can see how that could be bad for you."

Cassie called to the group. "I have rare ready to go. Any takers?"

Pete and Ryan jumped up from the table and grabbed plates.

"I was starting to worry you were making rubber out of that luscious looking piece of meat," Pete berated Cassie.

"Some folks don't like to chase their meat on their plate," Cassie joked back at him.

Turning the remaining steaks, she allowed them to cook a little longer before calling the next group. Kathleen appeared with two plates, and Cassie gave her a huge smile. "You read my mind."

Kathleen gave her a wink as she walked away with their plates balanced in her hands.

Cassie spread a small amount of sauce on the remaining steaks and looked around to see where Kathleen had settled. She stood beside the farthest picnic table with the two oldest Jackson kids. Cassie smiled when Kathleen took each of them by the hand and led them over to join the rest of the group.

"Looks like you lost your assistant," Shelley said as she handed Cassie the remaining plates. She nodded toward Kathleen. "I'm really starting to like her."

"What's not to like?"

Shelley distributed the remaining plates as Cassie filled them. Kathleen passed on her way to the cooler and slid her hand across Cassie's lower back. Goose bumps erupted on her arms and Cassie couldn't fight the shiver that ran down her body.

To distract herself from the erotic thoughts the touch had sparked, Cassie began stabbing potatoes from the depths of the charcoal and passing them around. She found an empty spot between Kathleen and Shelley and happily took it. Kathleen was attempting to engage David in conversation.

"You guys are from Louisiana?" Kathleen asked, glancing at Judy for assistance when David only nodded.

"Yes, just outside Shreveport," Judy answered.

"School must release early for the summer there?"

"We start early in the fall to allow days for hurricanes, but this year we didn't have any."

"Our kids don't get out until the first week of June." Kathleen took a bite of her steak. "Oh, this is good." She moaned, nudging Cassie with her elbow. "And she can cook."

"I'm not sure grilling qualifies as cooking." Dillon jumped in before Cassie could answer.

"I made the burgers too," Cassie added, making the group around her laugh.

"I was tempted to try both, but I couldn't resist this steak."

Dillon leaned around Shelley and Cassie. "There are plenty so you can have one of them too."

"Oh, I don't think I could, but thank you."

Cassie bumped her shoulder. "Then it will be lunch tomorrow."

"I may never go home."

Kathleen's voice was soft, and Cassie wasn't sure anyone else had heard her comment. She pressed her thigh a little harder against Kathleen's and felt her return the pressure. Giving up on paying attention to the conversations around them, Cassie reveled in the closeness of the woman beside her. She was definitely getting used to having Kathleen around and there wasn't anything she could do about the smile she could feel stretching from ear to ear.

* * *

Cassie lit citronella candles and placed them on the tables as the evening light began to fade. The old-fashioned streetlights around the lake came on automatically, bringing muted light to the picnic area and drawing moths. Cassie saw Darby and Derek follow Dillon to gather firewood, and she knew the evening would be ending shortly. She looked around the group, searching for Kathleen. She hoped to have a moment alone with her and see what her plans were for the next day. Did she need to rush back to Pensacola or could she talk her into hanging around for a while? Cassie wanted to convince her to stay as long as she could.

When she finally spotted Kathleen, she was pleased to find her looking in her direction. Cassie forgot everything around her as her body responded to the intensity of her gaze. When Kathleen turned to acknowledge a comment from Judy the connection was broken. Cassie felt the loss; she needed to be near her. She crossed to the food table and began helping seal plastic containers as she listened to their conversation.

"David seems to prefer watching from the outside rather than participating." Kathleen glanced in David's direction as he watched Derek and Darby, returning with their arms full of firewood.

Judy nodded. "Derek and Darby have their father's natural athleticism, but unfortunately David is exactly like me. We're still hoping he'll have a growth spurt before school starts."

Kathleen's hands rocked the half-full wine bottle back and forth. "That doesn't have to be a bad thing as long as he understands everyone is different."

Cassie took the wine bottle from Kathleen's hands, substituting a water bottle. Even in the dim light, she could see the strained look on Kathleen's face and she wanted to ease it. "You're on vacation. Relax."

Kathleen smiled at her.

"Contrary to what Shelley believes, I don't think wine goes well with s'mores." Cassie passed a bottle of water to Judy.

Judy laughed, taking the bottle and turning to watch her squealing boys as the flames from the fire stretched toward the sky.

"I'm not sure I can eat any s'mores after that steak," Kathleen moaned, laying her head against Cassie's shoulder.

"What?" Cassie stepped back, pretending to be offended. "You have to eat a s'more."

"I'll give it some thought, but first, I think I'll take a walk."

"I need to supervise the marshmallow distribution, but I'll save you a seat. Pandy will go with you though."

Cassie smiled as if on cue Pandy appeared at their feet. Kathleen stroked her head as they walked toward the path.

Judy had silently watched the interaction between them. "She's a very intuitive woman. I enjoyed talking with her."

"She works with foster kids." Cassie watched Kathleen stop beside David. "She's one that really cares."

"It seems like she might care about you too."

Cassie's heart gave a flutter. She tried to keep her face neutral, but a little smile slipped out.

"I asked Kathleen if my son was making her uncomfortable, but maybe I should ask you the same question."

"Not at all."

"He seems to be quite taken with Kathleen. She has a very gentle approach, and he is clearly drawn to it."

"His infatuation will pass and Kathleen doesn't seem uncomfortable." Cassie watched as Kathleen, David and Pandy began walking around the lake.

"We've had a wonderful vacation and I certainly wouldn't want it to end on a bad note."

"There's nothing to worry about. You guys are welcome back anytime."

"Ryan and I have already talked about booking for next summer. Since you only have one cabin that will hold us all, I'd like to book it before we leave tomorrow."

"Next summer is still pretty open, so if you know what dates you want we can do it when you check out."

"The boys would like to visit the zip line place in Milton next summer."

"Remind me and I'll pick up some coupons before you arrive."

"Thanks, again, for everything."

"My pleasure." Cassie put her arm around Judy's shoulders. "Shall we join the fire bugs?"

Cassie picked up several bags of marshmallows, chocolate bars and a box of graham crackers as they moved closer to the fire. After distributing the marshmallows and sticks, she took a seat in one of the chairs Dillon had pulled from the storage shed. As she placed her marshmallow on the end of a stick, she tried to locate Kathleen around the lake, but the glow from the fire reduced everything outside its range to a blur. Trying to scan the dim light around the lake, she stood, sticking her marshmallow into the fire in the process.

She felt Kathleen's breath on the back of her neck before she spoke and the goose bumps emerged on her arms again.

"You're on fire," Kathleen whispered softly into Cassie's ear.

"Yes." Cassie turned to face her. "And you're to blame." She pulled the burning marshmallow up to her face and blew out the flame. Pulling the black glob from the stick she held it up, offering Kathleen the first bite.

"It's burnt." Kathleen took a step back and Cassie followed her. "No, it's not just burnt, it's charcoal." She glanced over her shoulder as she took another step back.

"It's supposed to be burnt. It's the best way to eat them. Otherwise they're just a sugary glob." Cassie narrowed her eyes as they passed under the light and she caught a glimpse of the desire on Kathleen's face. "This way," she continued breathlessly, "they melt in your mouth." She took another step, pushing Kathleen into the shadows behind the shed. Sandwiching Kathleen's body between her and it, Cassie held the marshmallow up between them.

Kathleen raised her eyebrows. "Why do I get the feeling I'm going to eat it or wear it?"

"Oh, you're going to eat it all right." Cassie shoved the marshmallow into her own mouth and licked her fingers clean. She almost choked with laughter at the surprised look on Kathleen's face.

She braced her hands on the shed with Kathleen centered between them and brought their lips together. Opening her mouth, she felt Kathleen slide her tongue inside. The sweetness of the marshmallow mixed with the succulent taste of Kathleen's mouth, and Cassie lost all sense of control. Kathleen's hands slid inside her shirt, and she felt a jolt of arousal pulse through her as her thumbs stroked across the thin layer of cloth covering her hard nipples. Distantly she heard Dillon call to her and she broke the kiss, remembering they were barely concealed behind the shed. She collapsed against Kathleen, stilling her hands between them.

"Seriously." Cassie exhaled roughly.

"Seriously, I'll never eat another marshmallow the same again."

"Cool." Cassie mumbled, her face buried in Kathleen's neck.

"Not cool. Very hot, in fact, and you need to stop breathing on my neck or we're headed back to your house right now."

Dillon yelled again, and they laughed when Shelley told him to shut up.

"I think our absence has been noticed." Cassie pulled her head from Kathleen's neck.

"I was thinking about calling it a night anyway, but I guess I should say goodbye to everyone first."

"I'll grab you some clothes to sleep in and meet you by the office with the key to the cabin."

"Leaving me to face the firing squad alone?" Kathleen groaned.

"Believe me, they'll go a lot easier on you without me there." Cassie squeezed her hand and turned before Kathleen could convince her to change her mind.

Cassie walked toward the house, resisting the urge to shake her head. The number of times she had lost control today was growing fast and she wasn't sure she recognized her own behavior. Normally quiet and reserved, she was not the kind of person who pushed a woman against a wall and devoured her mouth. Yet that's what she had done more than once today and, honestly, it was what she wanted to do right now.

From the first moment she had met Kathleen, she felt an attraction. But what was even more shocking was that everything she felt, she saw mirrored in Kathleen's face. They seemed to be sharing a connection that pulled them together and set their bodies on fire. Every time they kissed, Cassie felt the passion overwhelm them. It made her heart race to even think about it. She couldn't remember ever having this constant feeling of giddiness. If she did really like this woman, and she did, she needed to get her hormones under control. Taking advantage of her at the first opportunity would not convince Kathleen that she was looking for a serious relationship.

Cassie took the stairs to her bedroom at a jog. *A serious relationship?* A week ago she would have said, "Hell no." Yesterday she would have said, "Probably not." Today? Well, today she was thinking about what it might be like to wake up every day next to Kathleen.

Cassie pulled one of her softest T-shirts from a drawer along with blue cotton boxers. Her chest was heaving from the sprint, and she leaned against the wall, pulling the clothes against her body. She closed her eyes and thought about Kathleen wearing this T-shirt over her bare breasts and she imagined running her hands across the soft material. Pushing off the wall, she grabbed a long-sleeved T-shirt and a pair of thin sweatpants from her closet. She added her newest pair of running shoes and socks to the growing bundle and then crammed it all into a duffel bag.

Kathleen was waiting on the porch swing outside the office. David sat beside her, and Pandy and Zoey lay at her feet.

"David's going to escort us to the cabin." Kathleen stood, giving Cassie a wink over his head.

Cassie smiled at him. "That's very gentlemanly of you, David."

They strolled together followed by Zoey and Pandy.

Kathleen looked at the bag in Cassie's hand. "Did you pack me a bag?"

"I want you to be comfortable. It's just clothes and a pair of running shoes. You'll find a spare toothbrush and stuff like that in the cabin. Look around until you find what you need. Or call me."

Kathleen pulled her cell phone from her pocket and began typing. "What's your number?"

Cassie gave her cell number. "You can also use the radio on the counter."

"And no one else can hear the conversation?"

"Well," Cassie hesitated. "Yes and no. I have each cabin set on a different channel so when they call me I know which cabin I'm talking to, but anyone could change the channel, I guess."

"That's good to know then. I think I'll stick to my cell phone if I need to call you."

Cassie stepped onto the porch of Cabin One and unlocked the door. Reaching inside, she turned on the entryway light and then handed the key along with the duffel bag to Kathleen.

"Call me if you need anything, okay?" Cassie gave her a quick kiss on the cheek.

"Don't worry. I will." She looped her arm through Cassie's as she turned to David.

Reaching out her empty hand, she gave his hand a shake. "It was very nice to meet you, David."

"You too, Ms. Kathleen." He shyly dropped his head before walking away.

"You can contact me anytime," Kathleen called after him.

He gave her a little wave and continued toward Cabin Four.

"I gave him my business card in case he wants to talk. I doubt he'll call though."

"He's very shy." Cassie gave her hand a squeeze. "Good night, Ms. Kathleen."

"Do you want to come in for a drink? Oh wait…do I have any drinks to offer?"

"There are a few small bottles in the cabinet, but I think I should say no. I haven't shown very much restraint where you're concerned, and I should help Dillon and Shelley clean up."

"Oh, I should help too. I didn't even think about that." Kathleen started down the steps after her.

"No. We got this. Go settle in for the night. Call me in the morning when you get up and I'll come visit."

Kathleen pulled her close, giving her a gentle kiss on the lips. Cassie held on to her a moment longer, wishing she could take the kiss deeper but knowing she couldn't. When she released Kathleen, her body felt cold and empty.

"Good night."

"Good night, Cassie."

CHAPTER ELEVEN

The picnic tables were clean and almost empty, so she grabbed the last of the containers and carried it up the steps to her house.

"Cassie-nova returns," Dillon announced.

"I told you we're not torturing her tonight." Shelley glared at Dillon as she placed the containers from Cassie's arms in the refrigerator. "Let her bask in the glow until Monday and then you can dog her." She shot Cassie an evil grin and pushed Dillon toward the door. "Leftovers are in the fridge. Enjoy your weekend."

"Monday!" Dillon yelled as the door shut behind them.

Cassie leaned against the counter and sighed. Opening a bottle of beer from the refrigerator, she tossed the cap in the trash can before walking onto the rear deck. She settled into an Adirondack chair and let her head fall back. She needed some time to unwind before she would be able to sleep.

* * *

Kathleen paused in the doorway and watched Cassie stride into the darkness. Today she had developed a new love for a well-worn pair of Levi's. The way they hung from Cassie's hips, pulling tight below her butt with each step. Kathleen quickly closed the door to keep herself from calling after her. If Cassie came back now, Kathleen knew she wouldn't be able to let her leave. She had known that when she invited Cassie inside for a drink but had ignored the warning bells. Thankfully, at least one of them had been thinking.

She opened the cabinet and searched through the small bottles of alcohol, selecting a merlot. Pouring herself a glass, she crossed to the sliding glass doors and stared at her own reflection. The dim light from inside the cabin slowly revealed the deck outside and her eyes widened. She had forgotten about the hot tub. Setting her wineglass on the counter, she carried the bag Cassie had given her to the bed and pulled everything out. She stripped off her clothes and pulled on the thick terry cloth robe hanging on the bathroom door. Grabbing a towel and her glass of wine, she slid open the door and stepped out onto the deck. The night was quiet except for the chirps of a few frogs and crickets. Flipping on the heater and massage jets, she slipped out of the robe and quickly slid naked into the water.

Though the water wasn't heated yet, it was still warm and relaxing. She shifted around the jets to a more comfortable spot. Today had been an amazing day. Better than she could have imagined. The connection she had felt with Cassie was real, and she missed being with her. She considered calling to tell her good night again or maybe to invite her over. Her body seconded the motion, throbbing with anticipation. Okay, maybe that wasn't such a good idea. She slid her shoulders down into the warm water and leaned her head back, closing her eyes.

It had been at least twelve months since her last date and her body was quick to remind her it had been even longer since she had sex. Women were never what they appeared to be on the surface; many, it seemed, were ready to move in before their bodies had even dried from the first morning-after shower. She had always lived alone, and the thought of having another woman in her space made her palms sweat. She had even stopped inviting dates to her house. She couldn't stand it when they took liberties with her personal space like borrowing her clothes.

She thought about the bag Cassie had packed for her tonight. *Did it feel invasive to Cassie for her to give up her clothes?* She had offered willingly and Kathleen was surprised to find she was looking forward to pulling on the soft T-shirt, knowing it would have Cassie's fresh, wild scent. She thought about Cassie's naked body inside the shirt where hers would soon be and she flashed to earlier when her hands had grazed soft skin and hard nipples. She wasn't sure she could make it through the weekend without feeling Cassie's warm skin against hers. She wasn't sure she wanted to even try.

* * *

Cassie couldn't believe that she hadn't asked for Kathleen's phone number. Almost two hours had passed since they parted at the cabin; she must be asleep by now. She had tried to reach her on the cabin radio, but apparently it was turned off or Kathleen wasn't within hearing distance.

Cassie rummaged through her dresser for an acceptable T-shirt to sleep in and wondered why she had given Kathleen her favorite one. Would Kathleen know it was her favorite? Was she wearing it right now? Or maybe she slept naked. Cassie groaned. Thoughts like that would quickly undo the relaxing effects of the beer and the shower she had just taken. She glanced jealously at Pandy and Zoey stretched out on their dog beds sleeping peacefully. She had barely pulled the covers back on her bed when the music from her cell phone broke the silence and startled her. Smiling, she grabbed the phone and looked at the screen to identify the caller. Pensacola.

"Hello."

"Whacha doin'?" Kathleen's voice purred through the line.

Cassie sat back up as she tried to read Kathleen's tone. "Do you need something? I can come over."

"No, everything is fine. Perfect in fact."

"Well, I could still come over." Cassie lay back down.

Kathleen laughed.

"Perfect, huh?"

"I had a glass of wine and soaked in the hot tub. Both were wonderful."

"I could come over," Cassie suggested again.

"Well, that would certainly make things more perfect."

Cassie hesitated. Was that an invitation or only an observation? Before she could inquire, Kathleen took a deep breath and let it out slowly.

"That would probably be a bad idea, wouldn't it?"

"I'm not sure I want to answer that." Cassie gave a little laugh.

"Yes, it would be a bad idea and we both know it."

"Am I supposed to agree with you?"

"I wish you wouldn't."

The silence grew between them as Cassie struggled to rein in her desire and resist the urge to run to Kathleen.

"I do. Agree with you, I mean." Cassie gave a little sigh. "But I don't want to. I can't seem to stop thinking about you."

"I'm having the same problem here."

"I certainly haven't shown much control around you today. It doesn't appear I can be trusted."

"And that would be a bad thing?"

"Oh, hell no!" Cassie exclaimed and then laughed, enjoying the smooth sound of Kathleen's laughter in her ear.

"Maybe we should say good night before I change my mind."

"I just have one question."

"Okay," Kathleen said slowly.

"What are you wearing?"

"And on that note…I'm hanging up."

"You can't blame a girl for trying."

"Let's leave it to your imagination?"

"You *are* very dangerous." Cassie's voice strained with desire.

"Good night."

"Night."

CHAPTER TWELVE

Cassie opened her eyes and stared at the cold, wet nose inches from her face. Zoey stood beside the bed with her head resting on Cassie's pillow and her tail wagging enthusiastically. Pandy watched from the comfort of her nearby dog bed. Cassie gave Zoey a scratch behind her ears as she glanced at the clock. It was still early, but she needed to get her work finished so she could spend time with Kathleen.

She was glad she had returned home last night instead of doing something either of them might have regretted. Putting some distance between them had cooled the intense fire, though Cassie's stomach still quivered at the memories of yesterday. She showered quickly and actually thought about what she was going to wear. She could hear Shelley's voice in her head telling her to pick something nice, but she ignored it and chose her usual attire. Jeans and a T-shirt were appropriate for a farm, so why would she wear anything else?

She was surprised to find two mini-quiches thawing in the refrigerator and sent a silent thank-you to Shelley for her thoughtfulness. Placing the quiches in the toaster oven on low, she mixed a pan of blueberry muffins and slid it into the oven before feeding the animals inside and out. She filled the horses' water buckets while she waited for them to finish eating so she could release them back into the pasture. Her phone rang as she was finishing, and the readout brought a smile to her face. *Kathleen.* She had saved her number last night after Kathleen's late-night call.

"Good morning, sleeping beauty."

"Don't even tell me. You've been up for hours, right?" Kathleen yawned loudly.

"Barely an hour. Can I come over?"

"Absolutely."

"Be right there."

* * *

Cassie returned to the house to take the muffins out of the oven, checking the quiches before sprinting to Kathleen's door. She knocked softly and Kathleen whipped open the door, pulling her into a tight hug.

"Good morning to you too," Cassie said hoarsely as Kathleen's touch ignited a new fire in her.

"I just wanted to thank you for a wonderful getaway. I didn't realize I'd been working so much lately."

Cassie nodded, slipping from her arms and moving into the room. Distance. She needed space and distance. She gathered the bedding Kathleen had already stripped off the bed along with the other items to be washed and dropped them all into the washer. Pulling clean sheets from the closet, they made the bed together, their movements fluid and comfortable as they worked.

"I can't even tell you were here," Cassie teased as she tossed the disposable cleaning towels into the trash. "Are you hungry or do you need coffee first?"

Kathleen came out of the bathroom where she had been cleaning. "Coffee would be great."

"I need to let the horses out, but you can go on over to the office and make a cup."

"That'd be great and then I'll catch up with you."

"Okay, but it won't take me long. There are blueberry muffins cooling in the house if you want to wait there."

They left the cabin together and parted at the stairs to the office. Within a few minutes, Kathleen joined her in the barn with a cup of coffee in one hand and a muffin in the other. She sat down on a bale of hay and watched as Cassie circled one of the horses.

"What are you doing?" Kathleen asked, sipping her coffee.

"Checking for injuries and such." Cassie ran her hand down the horse's leg and caught his hoof when he lifted it, removing dirt and debris from the bottom.

"How many horses do you have?"

"Eight horses and six goats."

"Are they a lot of work?" Kathleen took a bite of the muffin. "These are still warm."

Cassie released the horse into the pasture and turned to watch Kathleen as she licked the crumbs from the edge of her mouth.

"Would you like a bite?" Kathleen asked, holding the muffin out to Cassie.

Without a word or even a thought, Cassie crossed the distance between them in two strides and took a bite of the muffin Kathleen held. Her lips unintentionally brushed Kathleen's fingers, sending a pulse of desire through her body. Kathleen's eyes widened and Cassie froze as their eyes locked. Moving away quickly, Cassie let the next horse out of her stall. Out of the corner of her eye, she watched as a slow smile spread across Kathleen's face.

"So, are the animals a lot of work?" Kathleen asked again.

Cassie liked the deep huskiness of Kathleen's voice as she tried to return to their conversation. She couldn't help but be pleased with the effect she was having on her. Especially since her own body was still reeling from the unexpected touch.

"Not to me. Dillon and I share the workload during the week. Weekends are pretty quiet with guests checking in and out."

"I really enjoyed riding yesterday. I was a little nervous at first, but I'd like to do it again."

"You did great. A real natural." Cassie gave her a wink.

"Would you like a drink?" Kathleen held up her coffee cup as Cassie closed the gate behind the last horse.

"I should probably get my own cup," Cassie suggested with a devious grin.

Kathleen nodded and slid her hand into Cassie's as they returned to the office. Cassie liked the easy comfort between them. Though the touch earlier had been unintentional and very arousing, Kathleen's grasp of her hand now was neither of those things, and she basked in the warmth of the friction between their fingers.

* * *

While they waited for Cassie's cup to brew, Kathleen moved around the office, taking in the things she had missed when she arrived yesterday. Several paintings hung on the wall and clearly had been selected by Cassie. Kathleen smiled as she studied a remake of the Norman Rockwell painting of a Massachusetts State Trooper and small boy sitting in a diner. Cassie's painting showed a female officer with a young girl sitting in front of an old-fashioned ice cream soda fountain.

She thought about the ease with which Cassie handled the animals and her responsibilities. Her confidence, and Dillon's too, soothed others around them, allowing them to relax. It was easy to imagine Dani and even Kaitlyn having the self-assurance to interact with the horses. They would love the animals. Morgan and Shauna would use the freedom to find peace and quiet away from everyone else. She had been trying to get both of them to open up about their appearances. Morgan's piercings and Shauna's shaved head drew unwanted attention when she took them out in public, yet each had chosen to be noticeable.

Interrupting Kathleen's wandering thoughts, coffee cups in hand, Cassie led them back into the house. The smell of something yummy cooking greeted them. Kathleen peered over Cassie's shoulder as she placed the dishes on the top of the stove to cool.

"Is that a quiche?"

"It is and they taste as good as they smell. I'd like to take credit for them, but Shelley is actually the cook."

"Impressive."

Cassie grabbed two muffins, handing one to Kathleen as they headed out to the deck with Zoey and Pandy on their heels. They each took a seat in an Adirondack chair and stared out at the horses and goats in the pasture. The silence was comforting, and Kathleen didn't want to break it. She felt Cassie's glance several times before she finally spoke.

"I was thinking..." Cassie let the sentence hang.

Kathleen met her eyes. "Yeah?"

"You should stay another night."

Kathleen glanced away, focusing on her empty coffee cup. She wanted to stay and that's why she knew she shouldn't. "I'm not sure."

"I'm sorry," Cassie said quickly. "I didn't mean to push, and I wasn't implying anything. You can sleep in the spare bedroom or move to a different cabin."

Kathleen couldn't help but smile. Cassie's rare display of insecurity was very endearing, but she didn't like that her hesitancy was the cause of it. She didn't have any doubts about her feelings toward Cassie. "I don't want to overstay my welcome."

"Well, it's not an overstay if I offer." Cassie held up her hands. "Let's hang out on the beach for the afternoon and make the big decisions later."

"That sounds great." Kathleen sighed internally. The big decision wouldn't be any easier later, she was afraid. Cassie would still be attractive and desirable, especially in a swimsuit. She swallowed hard to cover her growing arousal. "Is it time for quiche yet?"

"Go ahead and sample. I'll run over and switch the laundry to the dryer."

"Okay. I'll try to save some for you."

* * *

Kathleen stole another bite from the plate beside her before leaning over to stroke Pandy's belly. She was surprised when both dogs had remained with her instead of following Cassie. Zoey lay in the sun with her head tilted toward the house. She opened her eyes at the sound of Cassie's return but made no effort to move.

Cassie dropped into the chair beside her. "You waited. How sweet."

"I might have stolen a couple bites."

"Hard to believe it was frozen, right?"

"There's no way this was frozen. It tastes fresh and the crust is flaky."

"The toaster oven works magic on leftovers. Shelley likes to bake, so I encourage her and then I find all kinds of surprises in my freezer." Cassie took a bite. "So, how did you end up working at Fosters?"

"I grew up in the system…" Kathleen twitched, shocked by her admission. She bit her cheek to keep from saying more. She lifted her water glass and sipped slowly, giving herself time to gauge Cassie's reaction. She *had* grown up in the system and she hadn't been a good kid waiting for a home. She had been a rebellious teenager with a huge chip on her shoulder. Being deserted by one parent would have been hard, but when her father left too, Kathleen had become angry at the world.

She didn't talk about her childhood with anyone, especially about the fact that she had been a foster kid. She watched Cassie stare into the pasture, clearly giving her room to talk, but she didn't have anything more to say concerning those years. She had put that experience behind her years ago and now she helped to make sure other kids didn't have to go through the rejection that she went through. There wasn't any judgment or sympathy showing on Cassie's face, so Kathleen filled the growing silence. "I wanted to make a difference," she said softly.

Cassie glanced across the table and reached out, gently touching Kathleen's hand. "I didn't mean to pry."

"You didn't." Kathleen laced their fingers together, gripping Cassie's hand tightly. "Sharing is not one of my qualities. I was astounded at how easily I responded to your question. I was waiting to see what else I might reveal."

"Your secrets are safe with me, but I really didn't mean to delve into your personal life. I thought I was asking a work-related question."

"Okay, then," Kathleen said, taking a deep breath. "Let's pretend that's what we're talking about."

She squeezed Cassie's hand when she started to withdraw it.

"I was going to use that hand."

"You can use the other one. I want to keep this one for now."

Cassie laughed and, laying her muffin down, picked up her coffee.

Kathleen studied Cassie's profile as she again stared into the pasture. There wasn't only one single thing she found herself liking about Cassie. She was the complete package. Personality, warmth and sex appeal. Kathleen loved the full cheeks that gave her a youthful appearance. Her body was curvy, leaving no doubt she was all woman though she hid it behind her flannel shirts. Kathleen met Cassie's eyes and watched a teasing grin cover her face.

"What's that grin for?"

"Do you want me to tell the truth or say that I was watching the goats play?"

Kathleen followed her gaze into the pasture and laughed. "Since there aren't any goats in sight, let's start with the truth."

"I was enjoying the feel of your skin beneath my fingertips."

"Oh." Kathleen hadn't expected Cassie's response to be so bold. She had been enjoying the feel of Cassie's touch as well, but she knew talking about what she felt would move them past the flirting stage. She wasn't sure if she could resist the next stage as she had the last.

"Oh?" Cassie prompted.

"I was waiting for the warning bells in my head to stop going off."

"'Danger, danger!'"

"You said it best last night. You *are* so dangerous."

"No, I said *you* were so dangerous."

"Let's agree to disagree." Kathleen looked at her watch. "What time is checkout?"

"Eleven." Cassie glanced at her own watch. "I should probably go hang out in the office. They'll show up soon."

"Okay, let's get to work then." Kathleen stood. Pandy immediately jumped to her feet as well, but when Kathleen reached down to pet her head, Pandy collapsed onto her back. Kathleen ran her hands back and forth across Pandy's stomach. "I'm starting to get attached to this dog."

"I think the feeling is mutual."

Zoey joined Pandy on the deck and quickly rolled belly up as well.

"See what you started now." Cassie pulled Kathleen away from them. "They'll never get enough, so you have to spread it out throughout the day."

Both dogs jumped to their feet and followed Cassie and Kathleen into the house.

* * *

Cassie stopped at the door to the office. "You don't have to go with me, you know? You can stay here or roam around."

"I'll look over your shoulder for a while if that's okay."

"Absolutely."

Cassie went straight to her desk and checked emails. Pressing the voice mail button, she jotted down the dates a former guest wanted to return. She tore off the page and taped it to the monitor screen.

"We'll call them back on Monday. I don't return any calls or emails on the weekend unless it's time sensitive."

"Is there anything I can do to help out?"

"Not really. Make yourself at home. Look around, snoop or whatever."

"Would you like another cup of coffee?" Kathleen moved around the desk to the Keurig.

"I think I'd like tea instead."

"Any specific kind?"

"I like the vanilla green tea. If you don't see any on the carousel, I have more in the back."

"There's one," Kathleen said, placing the small canister in the pot to brew. "Where are the refills? I'll restock."

"In the kitchen cabinet to the left of the sink."

Kathleen disappeared into the small kitchen behind the office. Cassie returned to checking email, leaving the majority of messages marked as unread to be answered on Monday. Noticing Zoey and Pandy with their noses pressed to the door, she walked over to let them out. When she opened the door, she found Pete standing on the porch.

"Good morning."

"Morning." He glanced back over his shoulder. "Rory's on his way over too. Do you have any bread we could use to make sandwiches? We bought some homemade rolls but realized this morning that they're moldy."

"Sure. Come on in."

Cassie led the way through the office and into the small kitchen. Kathleen was browsing the video shelf between the office and the kitchen.

"Morning, Kathleen," Pete said as they passed.

"Good morning. I thought you guys were off on a bike ride this morning."

"We aren't early risers when we're here, and even when we do wake up before eight we don't start moving until at least ten."

"There's nothing wrong with relaxing, as Cassie is teaching me this weekend."

"She should try it herself too," Rory said, appearing in the doorway.

"No kidding," Pete agreed.

"If you guys are finished, I'll give you your lunch choices." Cassie gave them each a silencing glare.

"We're listening," Rory said, giving her a little bow and motioning for her to proceed.

"I have sliced bread or hamburger and hotdog buns. The bread and hamburger buns are both from the bakery."

"I think the hamburger buns would be best," Rory said.

"I concur," Pete agreed.

"The Jacksons are coming in," Kathleen said to Cassie as she handed her the hamburger buns. "I'll stay back here out of sight. I said my goodbyes last night. No need to do it again. If that's okay?"

"Of course. I'll take care of them."

Cassie quickly checked the Jacksons out and recorded their reservation for next summer before returning to the kitchen. "All right, boys, time to clear out of here. We're going to spend the afternoon at the beach." She shoved the container of hamburger buns into Rory's arms. "Now go."

Laughing, the guys disappeared out the door. Finally alone, Cassie turned to Kathleen. "Are you hungry? Do you need anything before we head to the beach?"

"No, I'm good on food for a couple more hours."

"Great. Let's go find you something to wear."

CHAPTER THIRTEEN

Kathleen followed Cassie up the stairs to find a swimsuit, but in the back of her mind she couldn't help wishing it was for another reason. She faltered on the top step and Cassie turned to look at her. One glance at Cassie's face and Kathleen knew they were having the same thoughts. Kathleen felt a flicker of fear pulse inside her and she glanced away. If they kissed now, there would be nothing to interrupt or stop them from going farther. What if too much too soon would ruin everything?

Cassie quickly closed the distance between them and pulled Kathleen against her. "This doesn't have to be a decision-making moment. We're only picking clothes to swim in."

Kathleen exhaled the breath she had been holding. The comfort of Cassie's arms settled around her and she gave a soft laugh. Panic wasn't normally her first emotion when faced with the possibility of having sex and certainly not with a woman she found more attractive than any she had slept with in the past.

Cassie stepped behind her, placing her chin on Kathleen's shoulder as she wrapped her arms around Kathleen's waist.

Bound together, they took the last couple steps into Cassie's room.

Kathleen paused in the doorway, taking her time to appreciate the spacious room with more than the passing glance she had during Shelley's tour the previous day. The queen-sized bed centered between two identical nightstands was covered with a quilted light brown comforter. The color of the stitched blue swirls matched the curtains and the subtle blue tint in the tan carpeting. A matching chestnut dresser opposite the bed was long, holding nine drawers and a mirror above it. There were small pictures and what looked like event tickets held in place by the frame down both sides of the mirror. The top of the dresser was clear of any clutter or personal belongings. On the right nightstand, there was a stack of books and a digital clock, but the left was empty. There was a long, squishy dog bed against both walls on either side of the bed.

"Does it pass inspection?" Cassie asked, giving her a squeeze.

"It certainly fits you."

"Unfortunately, I have to give Shelley most of the credit. She narrowed my selections and made sure all the colors matched. I just wanted blue, but she forced me to pick other colors too."

"So blue is the color of choice?"

"Oh, yes. Everything should be blue."

"Let me guess, you had a crush on Smurfette?"

Cassie spun Kathleen in her arms and sat her on the edge of the bed before pulling open a drawer on the dresser. "I thought about it, but she and Jessica Rabbit were both a bit too feminine for my taste."

Kathleen laughed.

Cassie held out two sports bras, one black and one purple. "I should have warned you. I don't do bathing suits. Just sports bras and running shorts. I have plenty of tank tops too, if you want to cover your stomach from the sun."

Kathleen pulled the purple bra from Cassie's hand and took it into the bathroom. She paused as the feel and smell of Cassie surrounded her. There was one sink and the remaining counter space was covered with bottles, sprays, brushes and two hair dryers. All a contradiction to the casual appearance of the woman on the other side of the door. The floor was blue and white ceramic tile with deep blue rugs in front of the sink and shower. The L-shaped shower was larger but identical to the one in the cabin and ran along the back to a small dividing wall that separated it from the toilet.

Kathleen removed her shirt and bra, laying both on top of a three-shelf unit at the entrance to the shower. The sports bra was a bit tight, but after some stretching it fit well enough to wear for a few hours. She would definitely need a tank top to cover it though.

"Will that work?" Cassie called from outside the door.

"It'll be fine. Can I get a tank top too, please?"

A few seconds later the door opened a crack and a pair of green shorts with purple trim and a purple tank top came flying through.

"Thanks," she called as the door quickly shut again.

Kathleen pulled on the remaining clothes. When she opened the door, she found Cassie lying on the bed with her feet on the floor. She was wearing the black sports bra and black running shorts. Kathleen sucked in a deep breath as her eyes roamed Cassie's lean stomach and the curve of her breasts. All exposed skin was a light bronze, and she wanted to run her fingers across Cassie's stomach and feel the swell of her breasts. She imagined her pale skin contrasting with Cassie's tan as she straddled her body, the hard tips of Cassie's nipples under her thumbs.

Cassie's eyes flew open and she jumped to her feet, pulling on her tank top. "Ready?"

Her face was flushed and Kathleen wondered if they each had been thinking the same things. Not willing to risk another moment alone with Cassie in her bedroom, Kathleen led the way back downstairs.

She watched as Cassie added a couple bottles of water and clean towels to an already packed beach bag. Zoey and Pandy eagerly led the way and took the first swim before finding a shady spot nearby. Cassie pulled two long towels out of the bag and handed one to Kathleen.

"Do you have sunscreen in there too?" Kathleen asked.

"I do." Cassie grabbed the bottle and held it up. "Shall I?" She stood up and approached Kathleen.

Turning her back to Cassie, she pulled her hair off her shoulders. She had wanted to say no as soon as she saw the bottle was a lotion instead of a spray, but she knew the word wouldn't come out. She wanted Cassie to touch her. To feel Cassie's hands on her body. She heard Cassie rub her hands together, warming the lotion before she felt the gentle touch. Cassie massaged her shoulders around the straps of clothing before sliding her hands down Kathleen's arms. Closing her eyes, Kathleen basked in the warmth of the sun and the heat radiating from Cassie.

When she could take it no longer, she spun, sliding her arms around Cassie's neck and running her fingers through her shoulder-length hair. She leaned forward, pressing her lips to Cassie's. The kiss was soft and gentle but quickly deepened as their tongues met. Cassie slid her hands under Kathleen's shirt and across her bare back. All thoughts were gone except the feel of Cassie's touch. For the first time she wasn't analyzing her feelings or what was happening between them; she was simply letting it happen.

A shrill catcall from the tree line made Kathleen jump and she stepped away from Cassie.

"Geez," Cassie exhaled. "I may kill them."

Kathleen caught a glimpse of Pete and Rory as their bicycles disappeared into the trees.

She collapsed onto her towel. "And I may help you."

"I'm going to take a dip and cool off. Want to join me?" Cassie asked as she stripped off her tank top.

"I better let the sunscreen soak in a little, but I'll stick my feet in." As she followed Cassie toward the water, she rubbed lotion onto the spots that had been missed. Her body was hot from the sun and even her own touch felt sensual.

She watched Cassie enter the water quickly, diving under and then swimming toward the floating dock. The muscles on her shoulders rippled as her arms stroked through the water. Looks weren't everything to Kathleen, but what she knew about

Cassie, inside and out, was better than she could have imagined. Cassie's relaxed personality didn't show any signs of knowing how attractive she was; she only seemed confident in who she was. All of this only made her more desirable.

When Cassie reached the dock, she turned back toward the shore. The rays of sunlight danced off her body and a huge grin covered her face. She'd barely been there twenty-four hours, but Kathleen felt lost. She quickly dipped her hands into the water and ran them across her face. She wasn't ready to admit there was only one thing that might curb the heat coursing through her body, but from the moment she had shaken Cassie's hand in the hallway yesterday she had either had her hands on her or had been dreaming of it.

She picked up a towel and met Cassie when she emerged from the lake, water dripping from her body. Kathleen quickly handed her the towel before turning away, the desire to lick every drop of water off Cassie's body hitting her hard. She was in for a long afternoon. She turned and walked back to her towel, dropping down on it. Like a ton of bricks one thought hit her. *Why am I fighting this attraction?*

Her life was organized and planned. She didn't have feelings this strong toward the women she knew. She had to have everything defined perfectly before she agreed to spend the night with someone. One-night stands didn't involve any of the passion she was feeling now. This was uncharted territory and she wasn't sure how to handle it. She watched as Cassie lay down on the towel beside her, closing her eyes. She couldn't think of a single reason not to embrace the moment and give into her desire to ravish this beautiful woman.

Cassie opened her eyes and gazed at Kathleen, lifting an eyebrow.

"I'd like to stay tonight, if the offer still stands."

"Absolutely." Cassie closed her eyes again, but a smile played at the corners of her lips.

Kathleen lay back on her towel. She felt Cassie's fingers entwine with hers where they lay on the sand between them.

* * *

Cassie opened her eyes and sat up, grabbing her cell phone from the bag to check the time. It felt like she had been asleep for hours, but barely twenty minutes had passed. She tossed her phone back in the bag and pulled out a bottle of water. Turning it up, she drank half of it before taking a breath. She turned her head to look at Kathleen and found her watching her.

"Did you have a nice nap?" Kathleen sat up and took the water bottle Cassie offered.

"I think I did, but my head is fuzzy now. I hope I wasn't snoring or drooling."

Kathleen laughed. "No, you were very dignified. I wouldn't even have known you were asleep except that each time I moved my hand in and out of yours to change positions, you never moved."

"Are you bored?"

"Not at all. I just want to avoid a sunburn because that will put a damper on my plans for tonight."

Cassie could feel Kathleen watching her as she stared at the lake. She replayed Kathleen's words over in her head. Surprise quickly gave way to a feverish need as she realized what Kathleen was implying. They had at least three hours before new guests began arriving and there was no way she could wait until tonight. Standing, she offered her hand to Kathleen and pulled her to her feet. She shoved everything but a towel for each of them into the bag.

Holding Kathleen's hand, she pulled her toward the water. Now that she had been given the green light, her desire was overwhelming. Her first thought had been to head straight for the bedroom, but she knew that she wouldn't be able to take things slowly. She had fought these feelings for the last twenty-four hours and now they were about to be released.

"Are we swimming?" Kathleen asked. Her eyes filled with questions as she followed Cassie.

Cassie didn't answer but stopped at the edge of the water, pulling Kathleen into a tight embrace. Her body was warm from the sun and she knew the water would be mind-numbingly cold against their skin. She tilted her head, capturing Kathleen's mouth with her own. Slowly she deepened the kiss until their tongues danced and then she began walking backward into the water. Kathleen froze when the water reached the top of her legs.

"Oh," she gasped, breaking their kiss. "That's cold."

"I was trying to distract you," Cassie whispered into Kathleen's ear.

"Don't stop. It might be working."

Cassie began to gently nibble her neck and across her jawline. When their lips met again, she took two more steps deeper into the water. Kathleen pulled her legs up and wrapped them around Cassie's waist to avoid the water. Cassie turned to step deeper but lost her footing, dropping them both into the water.

Cassie found her feet first and grabbed Kathleen's arm, pulling her into a standing position.

"I cannot believe you just did that." Kathleen wrapped her arms across her stomach, teeth chattering violently.

"I am so sorry. I swear that was not the plan." Cassie put her arms around Kathleen to help warm her.

"You're lucky I believe you, but we need to work on your moves."

"I'm not very smooth, am I?" Cassie nuzzled her neck. "Are you too angry to swim out to the dock now?" she teased, glad to see the smile on Kathleen's face return.

Kathleen laughed, pushing her away. "I think I can make it." She dove into the water and started swimming toward the floating dock.

Cassie followed, catching her as she grabbed the ladder and started to climb onto the dock. She wanted the feel of the water surrounding them as well as the cover it provided. She gave a gentle tug on Kathleen's hips and caught her as she slid back into the water. Kathleen didn't let go of the ladder, but she leaned back into Cassie's embrace.

Cassie slid her arm around Kathleen and grasped the ladder to hold herself afloat. With one hand and some help from Kathleen, she pulled Kathleen's tank top over her head and tossed it up on the dock. For a few seconds, Cassie stared down into the water at the creamy white of Kathleen's skin. She no longer felt the cold from the water as desire surged through her.

She slid the purple bra strap off Kathleen's shoulder and down her arm as far as it would go. Her tongue danced along the top of Kathleen's shoulder and up her neck. She slid her left hand across Kathleen's chest, pushing the bra away from her body until she could dip her fingers inside. Kathleen shivered as Cassie firmly cupped her breast, sliding her thumb over the protruding nipple.

Cassie's heart raced and she struggled to breathe. She wanted more. Needed more. The cold water had done nothing to cool the heat between their bodies or to slow her pace. She needed to feel Kathleen's body beneath her hands. She let go of the ladder rung and sputtered as the water covered her mouth and nose.

"Was that part of your plan?" Kathleen asked when Cassie surfaced beside her. She turned slightly and grasped Cassie's waist, pulling her to the ladder.

Cassie ran her hand through Kathleen's wet hair. "I wanted to touch you so bad I forgot why I was holding on to the ladder."

Her eyes followed her hand as it traveled down Kathleen's neck to the top of a breast barely visible through the water. Her fingertips touched the hard nipple through the fabric and she inhaled deeply. "I want you so bad."

"I think we need to put this off until later," Kathleen suggested.

Did she hear regret in Kathleen's words or was that only her own feelings? Cassie wasn't sure. "I don't think I can wait and we still have a couple hours."

"Let's go then." Kathleen grabbed her tank top from the top of the floating dock. "It won't be enough time, but it's a start."

CHAPTER FOURTEEN

Cassie wrapped a towel around Kathleen and grabbed the rest of their stuff. She glanced at Kathleen several times as they walked, dreading that she might see a shadow of doubt but each time the smile that met hers was a match of her own. In the office, Cassie pulled her cell and radio from the beach bag before tossing it toward the back of the office to be unpacked later.

She turned as Kathleen locked the exterior door, leaning casually against it. The tension she had felt from trying to resist the pull between them was gone and she let out a breath. Kathleen's gaze held her own as she savored the look of desire on her face. She took Kathleen's hand and they followed the dogs into the house.

Her heart skipped a beat as they climbed the stairs without hesitation this time. Her body was consumed with arousal; she couldn't wait to touch and be touched. She closed the bedroom door behind them and tossed the radio and cell phone on the top of her dresser.

Cassie knelt, kissing slowly across Kathleen's stomach before pulling her shorts to the floor. Her skin was still cool from the water, and Cassie warmed her with her mouth. Standing, she lifted Kathleen's bra over her breasts and removed it in one fluid motion. She tossed it onto the bathroom floor and added her own bra and shorts to the wet pile. Finally naked, Cassie hesitated. Her pulse raced, but her mind taunted her with how long it had been since she had shared more than a bed.

Kathleen's touch was gentle as she pushed Cassie back onto the bed. Straddling Cassie's stomach, she looked into her eyes. Cassie met her gaze, knowing Kathleen had felt her hesitation. She studied the emotions she saw on Kathleen's face and was quickly reminded of the surge of desire passing between them. She grasped Kathleen's hips and guided her on top of her. Kathleen lowered herself over Cassie's center, stroking her with her body.

With an arm on either side of Cassie's head, Kathleen bent and kissed her, running her tongue across Cassie's lips before sweeping inside her mouth. The kiss fueled Cassie's desire, and she pushed Kathleen's body upright, breaking the kiss. Sucking first one and then the other breast into her mouth, Cassie held them firmly as her tongue stroked each hardened nipple. Kathleen opened her legs wider, pushing harder into Cassie as her pace increased. Their bodies were slick with wetness and the feeling pushed Cassie to the edge.

She opened her eyes as she felt Kathleen shudder. Her hair fell around her face and Cassie's breath caught at her beauty. Her stomach clenched at the unexpected emotions. How had she captured this woman? And could she hold on to her? She pulled herself into a sitting position, wrapping both arms around Kathleen. Their chests pressed hard together, but she wanted to be closer.

She kissed the racing pulse in Kathleen's neck, quickly finding her mouth. Pulling Kathleen's body hard into her own, she allowed Kathleen to push her back on the bed. She braced both hands just below Kathleen's breasts and brushed her thumbs across her nipples. Cassie felt her own desire surge and pushed up, meeting Kathleen's stroke. Grasping for release, she let herself go as her body exploded. She felt Kathleen give a few more hard strokes before she collapsed on top of Cassie.

Cassie's hands were trapped between their bodies, still encasing Kathleen's breasts. Several minutes passed before Cassie attempted to move them, and when she did Kathleen moaned as her hands brushed across her nipples. Cassie slid her hand down Kathleen's back, gently rolling her until they lay side by side, gazing into each other's eyes. Kathleen's contented smile filled her with eagerness to start everything over again. Cassie pulled their lower bodies together, sliding her leg between Kathleen's, wanting to feel the exhilarating pressure again and eliciting another moan from Kathleen.

Cassie caressed her face, tracing her cheekbones before leaning in for what she intended to be a gentle kiss. She had always enjoyed kissing, but Kathleen's lips were intoxicating. They were soft but demanding, and Cassie was consumed by them. Her desire bubbled to the surface again as her hips began a slow stroke. She wasn't finished yet, and it appeared neither was Kathleen.

* * *

When Cassie lifted her head to check the clock, Kathleen attempted to still her movement. "You have to stop," she moaned.

Cassie crawled up beside her and pulled her into her arms, covering them both with the sheet. "You win but only because it's two thirty."

Kathleen's eyes grew wide and then she smiled. "You need a shower. And don't forget to wash your face."

"I need a shower? And you?"

"I'll take a shower too, but first I am going to change these sheets."

Cassie raised an eyebrow.

"I can't sleep in all this sand tonight."

Cassie laughed, squeezing her tight. "I agree."

Climbing from the bed, she strolled naked into the closet and pulled out a set of sheets, laying them on the dresser.

Kathleen's appreciative stare brought Cassie to a stop, and she barely resisted the urge to climb back into the bed. "Join me and I'll help you change the sheets when we get out."

"Tempting, but…" Kathleen shook her head. "I can't do it. My body needs a respite from you."

"Okay, but get plenty of rest and drink lots of fluids because I still have plans for you tonight."

Kathleen covered her face with the sheet. "Get out of my sight before I drag you back into this bed."

Cassie laughed and walked into the bathroom. She turned on the shower and set the temperature before leaning over the sink to stare into the mirror. She was starting to get faint wrinkles at the edge of each eye which got larger the bigger her smile, and right now, her smile was big. Kathleen was more beautiful and more intelligent than any woman Cassie might have imagined. She closed her eyes, recalling every inch of the beautiful body that was laying in her bed. Opening her eyes, she realized Kathleen was leaning against the doorframe watching her.

Cassie felt her face flush as she looked into Kathleen's eyes.

Kathleen laughed. "I won't ask. Just get in the shower. You barely have twenty minutes."

"I'll be quick." Cassie stepped into the shower.

"Not too quick. You have a very distinctive odor that needs to be gone before you greet your new guests."

"The sad part is they might not show up for another hour or two."

"Or they could arrive in ten minutes." Kathleen leaned against the doorframe, watching her through the glass window.

Cassie showered quickly and was surprised to find Kathleen still standing in the same spot when she exited the shower. Her eyes were closed and her head rested against the frame behind her. Cassie watched her for a few seconds before she spoke. "When you're finished, the shower is all yours."

Kathleen's eyes flew open and her face quickly turned pink.

Cassie laughed. "Whatever you're thinking will happen tonight."

"You are so right," Kathleen said as she disappeared into the shower.

Cassie's breath caught at Kathleen's words, and her entire body pulsed with anticipation.

She quickly dressed in jeans and a T-shirt, tossing a few items on the dresser for Kathleen. She stepped into the bathroom and called loudly. "I laid some clothes on the dresser, but help yourself to anything you can find. We'll put the sheets on the bed later."

Kathleen stepped to the opening in the shower with her arm shyly covering her breasts. "Okay. Thanks."

Cassie crossed to the shower, sliding her hand around the base of Kathleen's neck. "You are so beautiful," Cassie said breathlessly.

Kathleen leaned in for a deep kiss but kept a few inches between them. Breaking the kiss, she pushed Cassie away. "Go before I make you wet."

"Too late," Cassie said, lifting one eyebrow. "I'll be in the office."

CHAPTER FIFTEEN

Cassie ran next door and took everything out of the dryer. Hanging the robe on the bathroom door, she folded the towels and sheets and put them away. Back in her office, she pulled the folder for her new guests and began brushing up on their names. John and Sara would be in Cabin One and had estimated they would arrive between three and four. The lesbian couple, Anita and Roz, and their ten-year-old daughter, Ana, would be in Cabin Three. She completed their check-in paperwork and made copies of the local information sheets to give each of them.

After checking to make sure she had a signed contract in each folder, she went in search of food. Her stomach was reminding her they hadn't eaten in hours. She made a platter with deli meats and cheese, adding several kinds of crackers and carried it into the house. Kathleen was descending the stairs, and Cassie recognized the khaki cargo shorts and blue shirt from her closet. Kathleen hadn't buttoned the shirt yet and the silky white bra it revealed immediately drew Cassie's attention. She was surprised at the surge of heat that raced through her body.

Kathleen glanced at Cassie and then pulled her shirt closed, quickly fastening the buttons.

"Please don't do that on my account," Casey said, raising one eyebrow.

Kathleen's eyes narrowed. "It's for your own good." Grinning, she quickly changed the subject. "Are you ready for your guests?"

"I am." Cassie watched longingly as the last bit of exposed flesh was covered. She sat the plate of snacks on the table. "Are you hungry?" she asked, pulling an apple from the basket on the counter.

"Very."

Cassie concentrated on slicing the apple and added it to the plate. She couldn't make eye contact with Kathleen, or she would lose the little bit of restraint she was trying to cling to. Although Kathleen had buttoned her shirt, Cassie was sure by the tone of her voice that she wouldn't resist removing it again.

Cassie quickly stepped into the pantry and took a deep breath. Regaining some of her composure, she returned with two bottles of water.

"Would it be okay if I washed some clothes? I should wear my own clothes home."

The thought of Kathleen leaving tomorrow hit Cassie hard, but she turned her back to cover her disappointment. Kathleen moved closer to her, rubbing a hand across her shoulder. "I've stayed longer than I should have."

The words stung as well as the flippant way Kathleen had thrown them out. Had she pressured Kathleen to stay longer than she wanted? Cassie searched Kathleen's face for regrets. Finding none, she continued to stare into Kathleen's blue eyes as her mind searched for words to express how much she enjoyed having Kathleen here. Afraid to push Kathleen farther away, she quickly chose simple rather than sappy, but the emotion in her voice betrayed her. "Please stay as long as you want."

Kathleen didn't answer, but she stroked Cassie's cheek before stepping away to grab a cracker from the plate. Cassie could see Kathleen wanted to say something more, but when she didn't Cassie pushed the worry of what her words might have been from her mind. For now she would focus on the remainder of their time together. There would be plenty of time later to agonize over the future.

"Is chicken stir-fry okay for dinner?" Cassie asked as she pulled two frozen chicken breasts from the freezer and put them in a bowl of cold water.

"That sounds great."

"Are there any vegetables that you don't like?"

"None that I can think of."

"We'll start dinner after everyone checks in so we won't be interrupted. If they were going to be later than six, they would have called by now."

"That's fine."

Cassie sat down at the table and layered a cracker with meat, cheese and an apple slice. "Do you want to watch a movie or something while we wait?"

Kathleen nodded her mouth filled with cracker.

"Why don't you pick something from the rentals in the office?"

As Kathleen disappeared into the office, Cassie carried the plate of snacks to the coffee table in front of the couch. In a few minutes, Kathleen returned, handing a copy of *Imagine Me and You* to Cassie.

Cassie loaded the DVD and grabbed the remote before taking a seat beside Kathleen on the couch. They quickly emptied the plate of snacks before the previews had finished. Cassie put her arm across the back of the couch and Kathleen snuggled into her. The opening scenes were barely beginning when the gate chime sounded on Cassie's phone.

She kissed Kathleen's head before jumping up and heading toward the office door. She pressed receive on her phone and said hello as she closed the door behind her.

* * *

Kathleen stretched her legs in front of her and took a deep breath of fresh air. She couldn't remember the last time she had done the same at her own house. The view there was nothing compared to the raucous play of the goats in the pasture or the horses grazing in the distance. She had tried to watch the movie when Cassie left, but it couldn't hold her attention. She had seen how easily her words had hurt Cassie when she talked of leaving, and she was struggling with how close they had become so fast.

This was just another one-night stand. *Right?* She knew it wasn't. She wanted it to be that simple, and when she had decided to give in to her desires she had told herself it was. Now, replaying the emotions that had been displayed on Cassie's face, she knew she was in deep and the giddy, happy part of her didn't care.

She heard the glass door slide open behind her and smiled when Cassie brushed her shoulder as she passed. Intimate gestures had always irritated and pushed her away from others in the past, and she was surprised at how different everything felt with Cassie. Kathleen couldn't take her eyes from Cassie as she watched her drop into the chair beside her. "Everyone all settled in?"

"John and Sara are happily tucked into Cabin One and were headed to the beach when I left them. You didn't have to stop the movie because I left."

"I wanted the fresh air."

"I understand. Would you like to go for a walk?"

"Sure. Can I borrow another pair of socks?"

"Of course." A flush covered Cassie's face. "I've enjoyed seeing you in my clothes. Well, except for the white bra, of course. I don't have anything like that, and it looks amazing on you."

Kathleen winked at her. "It was either that or go without."

"Go without. Always go without." Cassie smiled evilly.

Kathleen laughed as she climbed the stairs. She could still hear Cassie mumbling to herself about all the things she should go without. She pulled on a pair of Cassie's socks and the running shoes she had given her the night before. She couldn't resist grabbing the dark blue baseball cap she had noticed in the closet earlier. She pulled her hair through the opening in the back and glanced in the mirror.

Though she had made the decision to sleep with Cassie because she couldn't think of a reason not to, she could admit that maybe things weren't going to be as simple as she had hoped. What she couldn't think about, though, was where things would go after she left tomorrow. Maybe after tonight the initial lust that had consumed both of them would fade and she wouldn't feel the same as she did right now. She looked at herself in the mirror and smiled. There was something so intimate about wearing Cassie's clothes and the hat on her head with the simple West Virginia State Trooper label.

She glanced around Cassie's room. How had she not realized sooner that she felt at home here? With Cassie. She liked everything about her. The kindness and compassion that came naturally to Cassie was a constant surprise. Kathleen wasn't used to that. The women she dated were usually more concerned about themselves and what Kathleen could do for them. Cassie made her feel desirable. She didn't want to leave. How could she have this life and her own too? Didn't she have to return to Pensacola? This was a fantasy world that couldn't stand up to the test of time, but for now she would ignore the nagging thoughts in the back of her mind and enjoy another night of pleasure with a woman who was too good to be true.

"Nice." Cassie gave her an appraising look when she joined her again.

"I let my hair dry without doing anything with it, so now it needs to be covered to be presentable."

"I'll just say again that I love you in my clothes."

She slid her hand into Cassie's as they walked out the front door with the dogs following close behind. Pete and Rory were grilling on the beach and talking with the new arrivals so Cassie turned them toward the barn.

She laughed at Cassie's obvious detour. "Don't want to see the boys right now."

"Not hip on ever seeing them again after this morning."

"I remember there were some death threats being thrown around."

"I'll give them hell later, but I'm afraid they'll have some harassment for us too. Best to avoid that in front of the new guests."

They walked into the shade of the barn and leaned on the railing, watching the horses and goats that were within sight.

"I guess that could be embarrassing. Gay or straight. How do you handle that? Are you out with your guests?"

"It depends. I don't hide, but I also have never had a woman here to flaunt before."

"You want to flaunt me?" Kathleen grinned.

Cassie pulled her into her arms. "I want to do more than flaunt you." She bent to kiss her as the chime on her phone sounded again.

"I'll stay out here. Out of sight," Kathleen suggested.

"I don't think so." Cassie took her hand as they headed back toward the office.

She listened to Cassie's side of the conversation as she answered the phone. "Hello…Great. I'll open the gate in a second. Past the barn and the office is on your right…See you then."

* * *

Pandy and Zoey took up guard positions on the porch as Cassie and Kathleen entered the office. Cassie pressed the buzzer under her desk to open the gate remotely and in a few seconds a white SUV pulled in front of the office. Cassie watched as a small girl climbed out first, raced to the porch and wrapped her arms around both dogs.

"Ana, wait." A woman called climbing out of the passenger seat and quickly joining her daughter on the steps. "You should never charge a dog like that, honey. Wait for them to approach you so they don't feel threatened."

Cassie motioned to the two stools behind the counter, and Kathleen pulled one of them out of the way and took a seat. The voices on the porch drifted through the open window and Cassie watched as the other woman joined her partner and child on the porch.

"It's okay, Roz. It's clear these dogs are used to people."

"The next dog she meets may not be."

"She can't help she loves animals. Give her a break. We're on vacation." She held the door open for her to enter the office.

"Hello." Cassie stepped around the counter and offered her hand to both women. "I am Cassie. This is Kathleen."

The taller of the two women shook Cassie's hand and then stepped to do the same to Kathleen. "I am Anita and this is Roz. That's Ana on the porch mauling your dogs."

"They're loving it as much as she is." Cassie stepped behind the counter and opened the folder. "Sign here and we'll let you get settled." She marked the spot with her yellow highlighter. "Here's your information packet. It has most of the same information that was mailed to you except for the gate code. You'll find directions to the nearest grocery stores and lists of local attractions. You should find everything you need in your cabin, but if you can't just give us a call."

Cassie stepped to the window and pointed to the cabin directly across the lake. "That's Cabin Four. Cabin Three is the next one to the right."

"Great," Roz said, picking up the information packet while Anita signed her name to the paperwork.

"Is there anywhere close by to get dinner?" Anita asked.

"There is a small diner at the edge of Riverview. That's about eight miles west of here." Casey patted the information packet. "Directions are in here as well as to the grocery store in Riverview. Unfortunately the meat market closes at five on Saturday, but the bakery is open until six. They have wonderful muffins and rolls for breakfast. They even sell the mixes ready-made if you want to bake them yourself. If you can hold off on buying any burgers or steaks until you can make a trip back to the meat market, it's worth the drive."

"Thanks for the information," Anita said as they closed the door behind them.

Cassie waited until they had corralled their daughter into the vehicle before calling the dogs and locking the front door. Then she followed Kathleen and the dogs into the house.

CHAPTER SIXTEEN

"How can I help?" Kathleen asked, joining her at the counter.

"You could cut up the vegetables."

Cassie pulled an electric wok from under the counter and dropped a small amount of olive oil in it. She began pulling vegetables from the refrigerator. "If you see something you don't like, tell me."

"I'm pretty easy to please."

Cassie raised her eyebrow. "Good to know. Back to the vegetables, though, I will never learn your likes and dislikes if you eat whatever I make." She closed her mouth in surprise. Why was she talking like they were planning a future together? Tomorrow Kathleen would leave and she would return to cooking for one again.

"You'd have to serve something crazy like anchovies for me not to like it."

"You're safe with me. I won't eat anchovies."

Cassie cut the chicken into small chunks and added them to the olive oil. She added a few seasonings and then closed the lid. "Would you like some rice or pasta with it?"

"How about salad? Was there any left from last night?"

"Yep." Cassie pulled a plastic bowl from the refrigerator. "And I have some of Shelley's balsamic vinegar dressing too."

"That would be perfect."

Cassie stirred the chicken and tossed in several handfuls of vegetables before adding soy sauce and replacing the lid. She pulled a bottle of red wine from the rack under the island and held it out to Kathleen. "Yes?"

"Yes." Kathleen took the bottle and read the label.

"I'm not much of a wine connoisseur. I mostly buy what tastes good to me."

Cassie pulled the foil cutter and straddle-style wine bottle opener from the drawer and began opening the bottle.

"That's interesting." Kathleen watched Cassie slide the metal tongs on either side of the cork before twisting it out of the bottle.

"I learned to use this at San Sebastian Winery in St. Augustine. They claim a standard corkscrew can push pieces of the cork into the wine." She gave Kathleen a grin. "Besides I always found corkscrews difficult to use."

Cassie set plates and silverware on the table before placing the wineglasses on the counter in front of Kathleen. She poured a little in both glasses and held hers up to toast.

"To a relaxing weekend." She clinked her glass against Kathleen's.

"Is this what we were drinking last night?" Kathleen asked after taking a sip.

"Yes. Did you like it?" Cassie took a sip and then set her glass down to stir the chicken again. She turned up the heat and placed the lid in the sink. Picking up her wineglass and taking another sip, she continued to stir their dinner. When Kathleen didn't respond, she looked up to find her watching her. She smiled. "Did you like the wine last night? We can open something different if you want."

"I do like this wine. I was just admiring you at home in your kitchen. Trying to imprint the picture into my head." Kathleen slid off the barstool. "No wait." She patted her hips, searching through the pockets of her shorts. Holding her phone up, she looked at Cassie and quickly snapped several pictures.

"Oh, that's what we're doing, huh?" Cassie pulled her phone from her back pocket and held it up. "Me too." She reached across the counter and undid several buttons on Kathleen's shirt. Stepping back, she quickly snapped several shots of the bemused look on Kathleen's face before she could object.

"Enough indecent photos." Kathleen held her hands up in surrender. "Thanks for reminding me I need to put a load of clothes in the washer." She disappeared into the laundry room.

* * *

Cassie placed the salad bowl on the table and two plates filled with chicken and vegetables. When she turned to pick up Kathleen's wineglass, she noticed her phone still laying on the counter. She picked it up and snapped a shot of Pandy and Zoey, reminding herself she hadn't fed them yet. She placed Kathleen's phone back on the counter where she had found it and filled the dog dishes. She carried the bottle and wineglasses to the table and took a seat.

Kathleen joined her and they ate for a few minutes in silence.

"I almost starved you, right?" Cassie joked.

Kathleen smiled. "Actually you distracted me so well today I didn't really think about food. Who handles your website for the resort?"

"I do. Why?"

"I was just thinking about a few things that might draw more traffic."

"I had a woman design it for me, but I do the updates. What would you add?"

"Pictures of your guests. Ask them to email you pictures to add to it when they check out."

"I'm not sure I could set up a new page."

"I could do it for you."

Casey raised an eyebrow. "It's in DreamWeaver. Can you work in that?"

"I can. I could even design you a new site with a carousel of pictures on the home page."

Cassie pointed her fork at her. "You've been holding out on me. What other talents do you have that I might take advantage of?"

"Websites are what I do for a living."

"Wait! I thought you worked at Fosters?"

"I only work there part-time. I also own a website design company."

"I'm impressed. You are a fascinating woman." Cassie paused before laying her fork down. She stared into Kathleen's eyes. "Can I ask a personal question?"

"Of course." She narrowed her eyes. "How personal?"

"We haven't talked at all about our personal lives." She took a deep breath and continued. "Is there someone in your life?"

Kathleen smiled. "There isn't anyone. I haven't even been on a date in months."

Cassie loudly exhaled the breath she had been holding. "I should have asked that question before I ever kissed you. I'm sorry."

"What about you? Are you dating anyone?"

"I went out with a woman a couple times when I first moved here, but we decided to be friends instead."

"Can I ask why it didn't work out with her?"

"She was mean and kicked my dogs."

Kathleen laughed. "No, that wasn't subtle. You could have just said it's none of your business."

Cassie shrugged. "She was nice and not bad to look at."

Kathleen tossed her napkin at Cassie.

"Hey! You asked."

"I asked why it didn't work, not for details about how attractive she was." Kathleen pulled her foot up onto her chair and rested her chin on her knee, waiting patiently for Cassie to continue.

"She's a deputy sheriff and we got along well. She was looking for something permanent, but I wasn't ready for a relationship." Cassie frowned. She couldn't remember a day passing where she hadn't thought of Nett, let alone several.

"I was just out of a twenty-year relationship and not ready to move on yet." Cassie took a deep breath, laying down her fork. "Nett had cancer. It's been almost five years since she passed away." She couldn't remember when the empty feeling had left. Sometime in the last week she had started to feel whole again. She glanced at Kathleen, wondering if she had said too much. Finding Kathleen's blue eyes filled with sadness, Cassie knew she needed to give closure to the story of her life. "We had a lot of good years together, but the last couple weren't easy."

"I'm sorry for your loss," Kathleen said softly.

"Thank you. Today it feels like another lifetime ago. I'll never forget her, but I'm ready to move on now." Cassie picked up her fork and took a bite, chewing slowly. Kathleen followed her lead and for a few minutes they ate in silence. Cassie finally looked up and smiled. "Okay, your turn."

"The last woman I dated showed up for our second date with an overnight bag. I hadn't even decided if there would be a third date yet," Kathleen joked. "She was nice and not bad to look at though."

Kathleen ducked as Cassie threw her napkin at her.

"Seriously though, there wasn't any spark. I've always felt like I tolerated the women I dated. I couldn't wait to leave them and I never invited them to my house to avoid having to make them leave." Kathleen shook her head. "I hear myself and it sounds so horrible and very cold-hearted. I guess some of those women would tell you that I am, but it's not like that. I just wasn't willing to pretend. I wanted my heart to beat wildly and my pulse to race." She stretched her arm out and played with the tangled curl at the base of Cassie's neck. "Like it does with you." She pulled Cassie toward her and kissed her softly. "Is it time for bed yet?"

Cassie looked at the clock on the wall. "I should probably make another appearance. Do you feel like a walk around the lake?"

"One time and then I want to take you to bed."

"Works for me. How about a cup of decaf with some Baileys Irish Cream?"

"Yum."

Cassie carried the bottle of Baileys into the office, and they each brewed their selection of coffee, adding a shot of the liqueur. As they left the office, Kathleen slid her hand into Cassie's. "Is this okay?" she asked.

"Always. If anyone has a problem, they can leave. This is my home."

"I really like how you face life."

"I've spent a lot of years getting to this point, and I refuse to move backward. Some people might say that I live in a fantasy world because I surround myself with accepting people and avoid those who disagree with me, but why does our life have to have conflict? I want to live peacefully and happily each day."

"Can we pause this conversation?" Kathleen said as they approached the four guests sitting at the picnic table.

Cassie tightened her grip on Kathleen's hand and smiled at her.

Cassie had seen the boys as soon as they had stepped outside, and she was fairly confident they wouldn't say anything specific in front of John and Sara, but just in case she pulled Kathleen closer and it gave her comfort.

"Did you guys have a nice swim this afternoon?" Pete asked with a devilish grin.

Cassie saw Rory kick him under the table, shutting him up so she gave Rory an appreciative glance.

"It felt very cold after being in the sun, but it was refreshing." Cassie gave Kathleen a smile before looking back at Pete and Rory. "How was your ride?"

"Long and sweaty! The lake felt perfect to us," Rory said, laughing.

"Are you guys settled in?" Cassie asked, including John and Sara in the conversation.

"We're unpacked and stocked with groceries. Thanks to Sara. She did all the planning before we got here. We had lunch at the diner and still had time to hit the bakery and meat market before they closed."

"Most of my information came from the packet you mailed us," Sara added.

"I'm glad. That's why we send it."

"What of the newbies?" Pete nodded toward Cabin Three.

"I think they headed to the diner and then to grab some groceries."

"Did I see a little one?" Pete asked.

Rory kicked him again, and this time he didn't try to hide it. "Stop being nosy."

"Yes, a little girl," Cassie answered.

"It's a bummer there are no other kids for her to play with."

"I think the animals will interest her more based on how she attacked Zoey and Pandy when they arrived," Kathleen said, nodding at the dogs, who had found a shady spot nearby.

"They're very relaxed dogs," Sara said. "We have two at home and they'd be running around here crazy if we had brought them."

"Zoey and Pandy grew up here with people coming and going so they take it in stride," Cassie explained.

"Can I pet them?" Sara asked, getting up from the picnic table.

"Of course." Cassie turned and called them to her.

Both dogs came running and Cassie reached down to slow their approach. Pandy went straight to Kathleen's side, and Sara stooped down to pet her. Pandy immediately slid onto her side to expose her belly. Cassie shook her head and stroked Zoey's ears, encouraging her to wait her turn. Sara spoke softly to Pandy while she rubbed her belly. After a few minutes, Sara moved over to Zoey, who also went belly up as soon as the petting started. Pandy sat up and leaned against Kathleen's leg.

"I think they would lay forever if someone was petting them." Cassie looked at Kathleen. "I guess we better finish our walk."

Kathleen moved beside her as they stepped away from the group. Everyone said good night as the two started around the lake followed by both dogs.

"So back to this fantasy world that you live in." Kathleen smiled at her.

"Some people like conflict and it makes them feel alive. When necessary I will stand up for what I believe, but if given the option I prefer to not have the conflict. I spent too many years doing what was expected and hiding my own opinions. For the first time in my life, I have a say in who and what I surround myself with."

"Unfortunately when you live in the city you don't always get to pick the people around you."

"The majority of my days are spent here. If I don't like a guest's attitude, I can ask them to leave or tough it out for the week, but you can bet if they try to book again we won't have any availability."

"I wish my job was like that."

"The ladies I met at Fosters seemed nice."

"Oh, my office is fine. I'm talking about the close-minded people we have to deal with."

"Are you out at work?"

"Only with Joyce. I told her during my interview before she hired me. I didn't want it hanging over my head or for it to be something someone could use against me. She was cool about it and said she didn't see where it made a difference."

"I got a family vibe from Tiffany."

"Yes, I have as well, but I've never had a conversation with her. Nor do I plan to. I don't feel that it's important to how we do our jobs, and it wouldn't feel very professional."

Cassie squeezed Kathleen's hand, knowing her next question would tempt Kathleen to withdraw and she wasn't going to let her. "Do you have any siblings?"

"No."

"I have a sister. She visits occasionally. She likes to use the time to get away from her husband and kids."

"And your parents?"

"My dad was military and we moved around a lot. After he retired, they continued to move around. I think Jenny, that's my sister, said they were in Italy or maybe Ireland right now."

"You're not very close to them?"

Cassie could feel Kathleen starting to relax again so she continued to talk. "When I came out to them, they chose to not be part of my life. They've tried to make up for their initial withdrawal and now they visit about once a year. I try to be agreeable when their schedule brings them here, but honestly, their rejection did more damage than an occasional visit will repair."

"And your sister? How did she take your coming out?"

"Like my parents at first, but she quickly came around. She even stayed with me during Nett's final days. It wasn't easy for either of us but I was glad to have her there."

Cassie wasn't sure if the conversation was over or not so she walked along silently, listening to the croaking of the frogs around the edge of the lake. After a few minutes, Kathleen squeezed her hand and Cassie glanced at her. She wanted to ask questions and get to know Kathleen more but she wouldn't push any issue. Kathleen would talk when she was ready.

"My mom left when I was five. I don't remember much about her. Dad tried to tough it out alone, but he only lasted another two years. According to my case file, Mom returned to her career and didn't leave a forwarding address. Dad became a truck driver and it was easier to place me in foster care than to try to find someone to care for me while he was gone. Sometimes I think it all would be easier to take if they were addicted to drugs or alcohol, but they weren't. They each chose to abandon me."

"I'm sorry that happened to you." Cassie wanted to say more, but she knew Kathleen didn't need her sympathy or to be consoled. The edge in Kathleen's voice showed she would always be bothered by her parents' abandonment, but it no longer defined her.

"Did you ever try to find them?"

"No."

Kathleen's abrupt answer kept Cassie silent. She certainly understood why Kathleen wouldn't try to find them, but she was a little surprised. Curiosity usually got the best of most people.

"I survived the time in my life where I needed them. Why would I cause myself more pain? They could find me if they wanted to and I accepted a long time ago that they didn't want to."

There were no words that could fix what Kathleen went through and though Cassie's heart ached, she remained silent. Her grip on Kathleen's hand may have tightened because

Kathleen released it, flexing her fingers before sliding her arm through Cassie's. Meeting her eyes, Cassie tried to express her understanding. Though their backgrounds were different, Cassie still knew what it was like to feel a parent's rejection. Kathleen's smile reminded her that Kathleen didn't need her sympathy and she returned it.

Cassie hadn't wanted to interrupt their conversation so they had continued around the lake. As they passed Cabin Three for the second time, the white SUV returned and Cassie gave them a wave. Ana jumped out of the car and came running to pet the dogs. Cassie and Kathleen stopped walking to let her catch up to them.

"Hi, Ana," Cassie greeted the small girl now sitting at her feet. "I'm Cassie and this is Kathleen."

She smiled up at both of them.

"Do you have a dog at home?" Kathleen asked her.

"No. I've asked for one and Mom says maybe in another year or so. I have to be old enough to take care of it." She enthusiastically petted both dogs at the same time. "What are their names?"

"That's Zoey and that's Pandy." Cassie pointed to each dog as she said their name. "We need to go for now, Ana, but you'll have plenty of time to visit with the girls this week."

"Okay." Ana got to her feet and headed back to her parents.

Cassie gave them a wave as she and Kathleen continued their walk. Without discussing it, they both increased their pace to avoid additional delays. Cassie was glad to return her thoughts to the evening ahead of them. There would be plenty of time later for intense conversation.

CHAPTER SEVENTEEN

They returned to the house and without any effort settled into a comfortable routine. They cleared the dinner dishes and put the leftovers away. As Kathleen switched her clothes to the dryer, Cassie turned out the lights and locked the doors. She waited by the stairs for Kathleen to finish and they climbed to the bedroom together. While Kathleen was in the bathroom, Cassie placed a T-shirt and boxers on the bed for her, pulling on her own set. Then she lit a couple of candles and turned the music on low.

Kathleen paused as she came out of the bathroom, and Cassie watched a slow smile spread across her face. Cassie brushed her body against Kathleen's as she slid past her into the bathroom. When she returned moments later, the first thing she noticed was the sleep clothes she had laid out for Kathleen were now laying on the dresser. Cassie smiled and stripped her clothes off as she slid under the covers.

Her heart racing with desire, Cassie allowed Kathleen to roll her onto her back as soon as they touched. Clearly Kathleen had an agenda, and Cassie intended to let her accomplish it. Pleasure would come whether she challenged Kathleen's lead or not, so Cassie relaxed and allowed the passion to consume her.

The clock read four fifteen a.m. when Cassie managed to raise her head from the foot of the bed and focus on the digital numbers. Kathleen's body was sideways on the bed with her head on Cassie's stomach. Neither was covered fully by the sheet and the comforter had been thrown to the floor. Cassie slid from under Kathleen and stumbled her way to the bathroom. Her body was stiff and her thigh muscles screamed when she attempted to use them. She smiled. She hadn't felt this good in years. Maybe ever. After washing her hands, she filled a glass with water and drank it down without pausing. She refilled the glass and carried it with her to the bedroom, setting it on the nightstand. Pulling the comforter from the floor, she straightened the sheets on the bed. Kathleen stirred as Cassie straightened her body on the bed and placed a pillow under her head.

"Would you like a drink, baby?" Cassie whispered.

Without opening her eyes, Kathleen nodded, leaning up on her elbow and Cassie pressed the glass into her hand. She drank most of it and then reached the glass out blindly in front of her. Cassie took it and set it back on the nightstand. She crawled under the covers, spooning her body around Kathleen's and pulled the blankets over them. Kathleen's breathing had already returned to the steady sound of sleep. Cassie kissed her neck before falling back into a deep sleep.

* * *

The next time Cassie awoke, Kathleen was sitting on the side of the bed. Cassie threw her arm across her eyes and groaned at the light coming through the windows. Kathleen leaned down and kissed her softly on the lips.

"I don't know what time you normally feed the horses, but it's almost eight thirty."

Cassie groaned again and removed the arm from her eyes, looking at Kathleen. Her heart broke at the sadness in

Kathleen's eyes. Instantly she remembered that today Kathleen would return to Pensacola and she felt the emptiness return.

"Will you stay for breakfast?" Cassie asked, trying to keep the catch out of her voice.

"Sure," Kathleen answered softly before getting up and disappearing into the bathroom.

Cassie climbed out of bed and struggled into her clothes. The enjoyment she had felt earlier this morning was replaced with the heaviness of Kathleen's impending departure.

She brushed her teeth, watching Kathleen's shape through the shower wall. Every curve of her luscious body was imprinted on Cassie's soul. She wanted to beg her not to leave or to demand to know when they would see each other again. None of this was Cassie's style and as little as she knew of Kathleen she doubted such demands would be tolerated. To prevent saying or doing something she would regret, Cassie left the bathroom and took the girls downstairs to be fed. She felt like she was being strangled and she left the house hoping fresh air would help her to breathe again.

* * *

Kathleen forced the tears to stop and tilted her face to let the shower spray wash them away. Watching Cassie leave the bathroom without speaking to her, she was overcome by emotions. Quickly her tears turned to anger at her own behavior. She had never responded to any woman this way. She had worked hard to become an independent woman who depended on no one.

The distance between Pensacola and Riverview was not that great; it was crazy for her to act like they were saying goodbye forever. Two hours would be an easy drive for either of them, if they chose to make it. Now she knew where her real fears were hiding. Would Cassie be willing to make the drive? Did she even want to continue this? Whatever this was?

She turned the water to freezing and let it beat down on her until she couldn't stand it any longer. She dressed quickly, already missing the feel of Cassie's clothes against her skin. She said a silent prayer that Cassie would be willing to talk about their future before she left.

* * *

Cassie fed the horses and then one by one checked them over before turning them loose in the pasture. Zoey stayed close to her, but Pandy had chosen to remain in the house. The girls seldom separated from each other, and Cassie knew they would always come if she insisted. This morning Pandy had hung back when she crossed into the office, and Cassie didn't call her. It gave her a warm feeling inside that Pandy wanted to stay with Kathleen.

When Cassie and Zoey returned to the house, Kathleen was already working on breakfast. She was dressed in the khaki pants and button-down shirt she had arrived in on Friday. Cassie thought about the white lace bra she had seen a glimpse of the day before and closed her eyes, focusing on the smell of bacon frying instead. Kathleen was mixing eggs and milk in a glass bowl.

"Scrambled eggs okay?" she asked without looking up.

"Sounds great." Cassie moved behind her and washed her hands at the sink.

They stepped around each other, careful not to touch, as Cassie made toast and placed plates and silverware on the counter beside them. After several minutes had passed, Cassie stopped and watched Kathleen until she made eye contact with her.

"Are we okay?" Cassie asked, wanting to step close and hold her but afraid of pushing her farther away.

Kathleen ran a hand over her face and took a deep breath, letting it out slowly. "We're okay."

Cassie cautiously moved closer. She was sad to see Kathleen leave, but she hoped that it wasn't a permanent goodbye. She had felt the tension in the room as soon as she returned and she was unsure how to clear it. She took another step closer and gently placed her hand in the small of Kathleen's back. Her heart skipped a beat when Kathleen smiled at her.

"This has been an amazing weekend and I'm not sure where we go from here."

Cassie took the wooden spoon from her hand, laying it on the stove and pulled Kathleen into her arms. Their embrace tightened as the tension left their bodies.

"I'm crashing from the high of the weekend too," Cassie mumbled into her shoulder. "Maybe I could visit you in Pensacola?"

"Of course! I'd love that."

"How about tomorrow? Are you free tomorrow? I can make it tomorrow," Cassie continued to mumble, making Kathleen laugh.

Cassie squeezed her before letting go and picking up the wooden spoon to stir the eggs. "Two hours is not that big of a drive. We'll work something out."

"I needed to hear you say that."

Cassie dished scrambled eggs with cheese onto both of their plates, and Kathleen added the bacon. They each took a warm piece of buttery toast from the toaster oven and carried their plates to the table. Kathleen grabbed two glasses from the cabinet and Cassie filled them from the pitcher of water.

They sat close together silently pushing their food around the plate. Cassie took a bite of toast, and it tasted like cardboard in her mouth. The eggs were soft and filled with cheese, but each bite weighed heavily on her stomach. Finally, Kathleen pushed her plate away and sighed.

"I think I should go. Staying any longer will just make things harder."

"Like pulling off a Band-Aid." Cassie smiled, hoping she sounded more cheerful than she felt.

Kathleen started to pick up the dishes.

"I'll get them later," Cassie said, placing her hand on Kathleen's arm. "Would you like a cup of coffee to go?"

Kathleen nodded and followed Cassie toward the office. Cassie watched her pick up her briefcase beside the door and slip into her dress shoes. She stood close, their bodies touching as Kathleen selected her coffee and put a paper cup in the holder. While it brewed, Cassie pulled her into her arms. They clung tightly to each other until the coffee was ready. Cassie pulled a lid from the bottom shelf and snapped it onto the cup.

She took Kathleen's keys from her hand and picked up her briefcase. She unlocked the car and held the driver's door open for Kathleen. When she was settled, Cassie handed her the briefcase and Kathleen laid it on the seat beside her.

"I need the keys too, Cassie." Kathleen smiled up at her.

"Oh, right." Cassie handed her the keys and Kathleen started the car, rolling down the driver's window.

Cassie pushed the door closed and leaned on the windowsill. "Call me when you get home, okay?"

Kathleen nodded. "Thank you for an amazing weekend."

"Thank you." Cassie stepped back from the car and waved. She stood there until the taillights disappeared from her view, then sank onto the steps between Zoey and Pandy.

CHAPTER EIGHTEEN

After passing through Riverview, Kathleen turned her car south toward Pensacola. She could have taken the faster, more-traveled route, but she chose the little two-lane scenic route instead. Time and space was what she needed right now. She felt like she had just awakened from a dream. A wonderful dream where she had been free to act any way she wanted without consequences. She had been wrong though. There were consequences. The biggest was the emptiness she felt inside. Okay, so maybe time and space was not what she needed. She began to play over every second of the weekend in her head. The anxious feeling when she arrived and the feeling of giving in to her desire. Playing each scene and then backing it up and playing it again.

* * *

Cassie watched Pete approach tentatively.

"Hey, Cassie." He sat down beside Pandy on the porch steps. "We're thinking about grilling some shish kebabs for lunch. You want to join us?"

Cassie ran her fingers through Zoey's fur and looked at Pete. "I don't think so, but thanks for asking."

"So, uh, Kathleen headed back to the city?"

"Yeah."

"When are you going to see her again?"

"I don't…uh…I don't know." She looked from Pete to her empty coffee cup. She didn't remember getting a cup of coffee. Getting to her feet, she could feel the fog lifting and her mind begin to feel clearer. "We didn't really talk about details."

"Well, when you talk to her tell her we said it was nice to meet her. Maybe we'll see her again before we leave." Pete got to his feet too. "If you change your mind, come join us. We have plenty of food."

Cassie took her coffee cup back inside and checked the time. Kathleen had been gone for almost an hour. She cleared the breakfast dishes and was surprised by how little either of them had eaten. She downed a glass of water and headed out to the barn. Grabbing the bucket of grooming supplies, she went into the pasture. She haltered Cheyenne and tied her to the hitching post, brushing her from head to tail. Applying conditioner to her mane and tail, she brushed out all of the tangles. She sprayed her down with fly repellent and walked her into the middle of the pasture before turning her loose. She repeated this procedure on two more horses before her cell phone rang. She released Dakota and pulled her phone from her pocket, sitting down on a hay bale inside the barn.

"Hello," Cassie answered tentatively.

"Hey, Cassie. I'm home."

"That's good. I hope it wasn't a bad drive."

"Not too bad. I took the long way to avoid traffic." Kathleen sighed deeply. "I'm sorry for running out on you."

Cassie longed to say how she felt. To just throw it out there and see what happened, but she knew they both needed time to process their own emotions.

She wondered if she had spoken her thoughts out loud when Kathleen's words echoed her thoughts. "I've never felt like this before. I'm a little crazy about you, and I'm having a hard time getting my head on straight. I feel like I've walked out of a dream."

"I was pretty foggy after you left too. I'd like to see you again soon though." Cassie held her breath, waiting for Kathleen's response.

"I'd like that too. Let's talk later in the week. Maybe I can come up on Friday."

"That would be great. I'll call you." Cassie wanted to say tomorrow, but Kathleen had said later in the week. "Wednesday?"

"That's fine. We'll talk on Wednesday. Thanks again for a wonderful weekend. I have a lot to think about this week."

"Yeah, me too."

After they said their goodbyes and hung up, Cassie returned to the pasture and selected the next horse for grooming. She noticed Ana sitting on the grass outside of the fence.

"Hey, Ana."

"Hello, Ms. Cassie."

"You can come in and help me if your parents give you permission."

Ana didn't respond but took off at a sprint, returning a short time later with Anita in tow.

"Hi, Anita." Cassie walked over to the fence. "I'm sorry if I caused any problems. I thought she might like to help me."

Anita smiled. "No problem. We were sitting at the picnic table talking to Pete and Rory. In fact, I think everyone is headed this way now."

Cassie laughed. "The more the merrier. Is it okay if Ana comes in here with me? I'll keep a close eye on her."

Anita looked at Ana dancing from foot to foot. "Yes, go ahead. But," she said, putting a hand on Ana's shoulder. "Pay attention and do what you're told. Okay?"

"Okay, Mom." Ana unlatched the gate and carefully locked it behind her.

Cassie dumped everything out of her bucket and, flipping it upside down, motioned for Ana to take a seat. As she worked, she explained everything she was doing to the horse. Then she allowed Ana to stand and pet the horse's neck. When they finished with Juliet, Cassie walked her away from Ana and released her. She and Ana joined her parents and Pete and Rory at the fence. Ana climbed onto the fence rail, making herself taller and began explaining what Cassie had been doing to the horses. While she was talking, Cassie noticed one of the goats moving closer to inspect the situation. Tate was friendly and curious.

Cassie moved away from everyone and sat down on the grass. Ana talked for a few more minutes and then stopped to watch Cassie. Cassie held her hand out and Tate approached cautiously. When she was close enough, Cassie grabbed her around the waist and pulled her into her lap. At first, Tate resisted, but after a few useless attempts to stand she resigned herself to being held and petted.

"You can come over now, Ana," Cassie called to Ana who was once again dancing from foot to foot.

"Walk slowly," Anita reminded her.

Ana approached and sat down on the ground beside Cassie. "This is Tate." Cassie held Tate's head close to her chest. The goats didn't really bite, but they did nibble and she didn't want to scare Ana.

"She's really cute. I like her," Ana gushed.

Cassie held Tate for several minutes and then explained to Ana that they needed to release her. She had Ana move back over to the fence, and she pushed Tate off her lap. Everyone laughed as Tate kicked up her heels as she ran out into the pasture to join the other goats. It felt good to laugh and Cassie enjoyed the simple pleasure.

* * *

Cassie ate leftovers for dinner as she sat in front of the television. When she finally made it to her bedroom, she found the clothes Kathleen had borrowed folded neatly on the bed.

Cassie tossed them in the closet with her own dirty clothes and prepared for bed. She debated changing the sheets but decided it could wait until tomorrow. She crawled under the covers and settled on her back. The bed felt big and empty. After several attempts to find a comfortable position, she shifted onto her side and slid her arm under the pillow. Her fingers touched cloth and she looped the fabric, pulling it from under the pillow. She sat up and flipped on the lamp. Her hands held Kathleen's silky white bra. Cassie smiled. Not only because of what she held in her hands but knowing Kathleen had gone without.

She pulled her phone off the nightstand and sent a text to Kathleen. *Very soft. Thank you.*

Seconds later she received a response. *You're welcome.*

Cassie put the bra back under her pillow and laced her fingers through it. Sleep came slowly as her mind whirled with thoughts of Kathleen.

CHAPTER NINETEEN

Monday morning arrived fast and Cassie felt like she had barely fallen asleep. She trudged through feeding herself and the dogs, leaving the outside animals to Dillon. She wasn't trying to avoid Dillon or Shelley, for that matter, but she wasn't really ready to talk about the weekend.

Shelley located her on the back deck not long after she and Dillon had arrived. She set two cups on the table between them and flopped into the other chair. "Spill it."

"Nothing to spill. We had a wonderful weekend and she went home yesterday."

"And yet you look like someone beat you."

Cassie shrugged.

Shelley sat silently, sipping her coffee. Cassie had experienced Shelley's tactics before. She had the patience of a saint, and Cassie knew the sooner she gave in the sooner the talk would be over. "We didn't really talk about where things would go from here."

"And that bothers you?"

"Yes, because I don't know how to act or even when I'll see her again."

"Did you ask her?"

"Yes, but she was vague. She might come up this weekend." Cassie loved her farm and the cabins, but at times like this it was frustrating. Two hours was not that long a drive, but she had responsibilities. She couldn't simply walk away for an afternoon.

"So take a day and go see her." Shelley stated it like it was an obvious solution. "Dillon and I can handle things here. You can take her to lunch or something." She smiled evilly. "I know that's not ideal, but at least you have some control of the situation too. Instead of just sitting and waiting for her to make up her mind."

She appreciated Shelley's offer. She was right. She needed to take some control of the situation. "Maybe I will."

Shelley wandered back to the office after a while, claiming she needed to study. Cassie saw her returning from the barn with Dillon for lunch. Cassie chose to eat in the house and did not join them. She knew her silence was killing Dillon, but he would have plenty of time to quiz her tomorrow when Shelley was not around to protect her. She spent the afternoon cleaning Cabin Four and preparing it for the next guests.

She was returning to the office when her cell phone rang. She checked the screen, hoping for Kathleen, but instead she saw Greg's name. He was as sad as she was when he left last summer and was glad that he called often. The last time they had spoken he had tracked down his real father and was thinking about contacting him. She regretted that she hadn't called to check on him.

"Hey, Greg. How are you?"

"I'm good, Ms. Cassie. How are you?"

"I'm good too. Things are crazy here as usual. I'm glad you called. What's going on with your dad?"

"I made contact with him, but he's not a very nice man. I guess I kinda already knew that." He fell silent.

"I was hoping he had changed too, Greg. It's been a lot of years since he walked out on you and sometimes people do change. I'm sorry he hasn't though."

"Yeah, it was disappointing." Greg hesitated. "Are you taking in any kids this year?"

"Believe it or not, I've agreed to four girls." Cassie laughed.

"Wow. Sounds like you'll have a house full."

Greg grew silent again and Cassie tried to draw him back into the conversation. "You know you can visit anytime, Greg."

"Right. I might do that," Greg said, clearly anxious to get off the phone now. "I better go. I need to be at work in an hour."

After they hung up, Cassie struggled with Greg's quick change in moods. She made a mental note to call and check on him later in the week.

CHAPTER TWENTY

Cassie was waiting in the office the next morning when Dillon came in to make his coffee. She had brought the horses in and fed them but had not let them out yet. She wanted to give them baths and thought it would be something she and Dillon could do together.

"Morning, Cass," Dillon mumbled as he selected his coffee and watched it brew.

Cassie waited for him to take a seat beside her before answering him. "Morning."

He looked at her over the rim of his coffee cup while taking a sip. "You look better today."

"I feel better today. I'm sorry I was distant yesterday. The weekend was a bit of an emotional roller coaster and I needed a little time to process."

"I know. Shelley told me to leave you alone today." He shrugged. "I'm not very good at doing what I'm told."

They both laughed and he bumped her shoulder. "I've never seen you as happy as you looked on Friday. If I was you, I'd try to hold on to that."

Sometimes Dillon brought things back to simple. Yes, she would hold on to that. She smiled at him. "Thanks."

Dillon stood. "I'll let the horses out."

"Enjoy your coffee. I thought we'd give them all baths today. They've been rolling a lot with the rain."

"Sounds good."

He drank his coffee silently while she finished answering emails and then they walked together to the barn. The day passed quickly, and Cassie was tired when she fell into bed. Her fingers rubbed the silk under her pillow, and she longed to hear Kathleen's voice. She had checked her texts often, hoping Kathleen would reach out to her. Kathleen had said she was trying to get her head on straight and Cassie wanted to allow her the space to do that. She took a small amount of comfort in knowing tomorrow was Wednesday and they had a plan to talk.

* * *

The beds for the girls arrived around ten on Wednesday, and Shelley helped her arrange both rooms. She put temporary sheets and a comforter on each bed. She wanted the room to look inviting on first glance, but as soon as the kids arrived she would take them shopping to decorate their own living space. In the afternoon, she saddled Cheyenne and took her for a ride. Dillon met her on Dakota, and they rode the fence line in silence. She appreciated his company and his silence. When they returned, Ana watched them from the playground beside the lake. Cassie knew she wanted to ride, but her parents had not signed her up yet and Cassie wasn't sure they would.

She tied Cheyenne to the hitching post outside the office and located Anita and Roz. They were sitting on a swing in the shade watching Ana play. Cassie walked over and joined them.

"She has a lot of energy," Cassie said, taking a seat on the ground beside the swing.

"Yes, most days she wears us out." Roz laughed.

Anita bumped her. "What do you mean most days? Every day."

"I wanted to talk with you without her overhearing. I know you're concerned about the animals, but I was wondering if I could take her for a ride on Cheyenne with me. We've been out for a while, so it would have to be a short one. I need to get the saddle off and let her cool down soon."

Anita and Roz looked at each other.

Cassie continued encouragingly. "We have helmets, and she's small enough to ride in front of me in the saddle."

"I think that would be okay. Roz?"

"It might get her to stop harassing us about riding."

"Or it might make her harass us more." Anita laughed.

"I don't mind taking her for a ride every day if you guys are okay with it. She's eager to learn and she listens very well. I enjoy working with kids like that."

"Okay." Anita looked at Roz again and she nodded her agreement.

"Great." Cassie stood and walked back toward the barn, waving for Ana to join her.

She took Ana into the barn and helped her select a riding helmet. Dillon guided Ana up the concrete steps to the mounting platform. Cassie swung into the saddle, noticing as she did so that Anita and Roz had moved to a bench facing the barn where they could watch from a distance. Ana slid easily into the saddle in front of Cassie.

"Hold on to the saddle horn." Dillon wrapped both of her hands around the horn.

"Are you ready?" Cassie asked. Ana nodded. Cassie felt her little body tense as they started to move, so she held the reins in one hand and put her other arm around Ana's stomach, holding her tight.

"Cheyenne is my horse and she's very gentle." Cassie continued to talk softly, telling Ana about Cheyenne and where she came from. After a few minutes Ana began to relax and ask questions. They circled the small pasture several times, and Cassie nodded at Dillon to open the gate.

"Want to go visit your moms?" Cassie asked.

"Yes!"

They slowly crossed the road and approached Anita and Roz.

"Look at me!" Ana called to them. "I'm riding a horse."

"Yes, you are," Anita said. "I'm going to get the camera." She hurried off toward the cabin.

"You can pet her, Me-momm," Ana said to Roz. "She's very gentle." Ana began to echo the words Cassie had told her earlier.

Anita returned with the camera and snapped several shots.

"Make sure you get a picture of Cheyenne, Mom. I want to show all my friends."

They returned to the barn with Anita and Roz close behind. Dillon waited at the steps and helped Ana get down. She immediately ran to her parents and began telling everything again.

Cassie dismounted and Dillon took her saddle into the barn. She washed the sweat off Cheyenne and then stripped the water off with a squeegee before releasing her back into the pasture.

"Thank you, Ms. Cassie. That was so much fun." Ana waited for her at the gate.

"Yes, thank you." Anita smiled. "This has been the highlight of her trip."

"Well, remember what I told you." Cassie smiled at Roz and Anita. "Come by the office or flag me down anytime."

"Thanks again." They walked off with Ana between them still talking.

"I like them." Dillon stepped up beside her.

"Me too. I think I was testing their limits more than Ana's though. We'll see if they let her ride again before they leave."

* * *

Cassie was successful at keeping herself busy all day, but her evening phone call was never far from her mind. Once Dillon and Shelley left for the day, she fed the dogs and made herself a salad. She planted herself in front of the television, determined to wait until at least six before calling Kathleen. At five forty-five her phone rang, making her jump.

"I was making myself wait until six to give you time to get home from work," Cassie said without offering a greeting.

"I didn't go into the office today and I had to make myself wait until your day was over," Kathleen said with a little laugh.

"You didn't have to wait, you know. Anytime you want to call is fine with me." She paused for a second. "I've missed you."

"Me too."

The silence weighed heavy between them. Cassie had rehearsed a billion things she wanted to say but the words wouldn't come out.

"How has your week been?" Kathleen asked.

"Okay. The beds were delivered today, so we arranged the rooms. I wanted to ask if the girls know they're coming here. Are they okay with it?"

"Oh yes. I've talked with them several times since you were here last week, and they're very excited. By the way, I loved the picture you took of Zoey and Pandy. It was a pleasant surprise."

"I hoped it might be." Cassie hesitated. "Do you think you can come up this weekend?"

"I'm so sorry. That was going to be the first thing I told you when we got on the phone and I forgot when I heard your voice. This weekend is the open house and I have to work it Saturday and Sunday."

"That's a bummer," Cassie said, trying not to sound too disappointed.

Kathleen sighed. "It is, but maybe a little space is good too."

When Cassie didn't respond, Kathleen continued. "Not good but necessary. Does that make sense?"

"I guess so." Cassie took a deep breath.

"I just thought we might need a little perspective."

"Okay." As long as perspective doesn't mean not seeing each other, Cassie thought. "I still want to see you again."

"Me too," Kathleen said quickly.

Cassie wanted to ask when, but Kathleen was already saying goodbye. She swallowed her question and tried to sound cheery as they hung up without any specific plans on when they would talk again.

Cassie stared at the television and thought about their conversation. She hated not knowing when she would see her again, but what bothered her more was the perspective she was supposed to be getting. The kids would arrive in a week and a half and then she wouldn't be able to leave during the week. She would talk with Shelley on Friday about taking Monday or Wednesday off next week to go to Pensacola. Her mind seemed to be whirling but after dozing off several times she finally went to bed.

* * *

Kathleen stared at her phone laying on the coffee table. She wished she could explain to Cassie how unreal life at the farm seemed to her now. The farm had been quiet and peaceful and comfortable. All the things she longed for in her life but hadn't been able to find on her own. The way she felt around Cassie was something she had only read in romance novels. The desire to be with her still emerged anytime she wasn't consciously working to force it away.

Cassie's quiet and gentle demeanor had shined a light on her past. A past she had not chosen to share with anyone as an adult. She had learned to deal with her issues of anger and abandonment in the gym. Punching a bag or running on the treadmill until exhaustion released any pent-up feelings that arose, but it did nothing for the loneliness. She was surprised that she didn't feel any regret for opening up to Cassie, and she was hopeful she would be able to share more should the opportunity arise.

She knew at some point, Cassie would ask for details about the brat pack, and Kathleen wanted to be honest. The parallels between her past and theirs made it hard for her to talk freely. She remembered the night Kaitlyn's call woke her and the way her heart beat wildly as she raced to her car. Kaitlyn was hungry and scared and she wanted off the street. Thankfully, Kathleen had given her a card with her cell number on it when they had met briefly weeks before. For a moment, Kathleen had felt the frigid Chicago sidewalk beneath her instead of the leather car seat. Pensacola was a lot warmer than the streets Kathleen had wandered as a teenager, but the things that lurked in the shadows were the same.

Kathleen wanted to believe Cassie would understand the paths she had chosen—the decisions she had made that caused their lives to intersect. She wanted to be fearless and share herself with optimism, but she knew the soft brown eyes filled with compassion that danced in her mind each time she closed her eyes weren't real. They couldn't be. Life wasn't like fairy tales. The proper perspective would help her explore a relationship with Cassie without all the hype. She couldn't hope for more than that.

CHAPTER TWENTY-ONE

Cassie was surprised when Anita came by the office on Thursday and scheduled a horseback ride for Ana on Friday morning. She had talked with Dillon, and they agreed to have three horses saddled in addition to Cheyenne when Ana arrived. On Friday morning, Anita and Roz looked almost panicked as they approached.

"I thought you guys might like to give it a try since you leave tomorrow," Cassie said, giving them a reassuring smile.

"I don't...I don't know." Anita slowed her approach.

"Sure," Roz said, laughing at the shocked faces around her.

Cassie didn't give her a chance to think about it. She showed her the wall of helmets and helped her adjust one on her head. Cassie knew if she could get Roz comfortably settled on a horse that Anita might give in too. Some people simply didn't like horses, but Cassie believed Anita and Roz had likely never been around them before. Dillon walked Bly over to the steps and held the reins as Roz swung her leg over settling into the saddle.

Dillon handed her the reins and walked Bly away from the stairs. Cassie left him to talk Roz through some basic instructions.

Cassie watched Anita pace nervously. She was holding her camera as if it was a life preserver. Ana already had a helmet on and was standing on the steps. "I'm riding my own horse today, right?"

Cassie grabbed the reins on Greta and brought her to the stairs. Dillon left Roz and came over to steady Greta while Cassie climbed the stairs and assisted Ana. Once settled in, Ana eagerly took the reins and walked Greta over to where Roz was waiting.

Cassie looked at Anita again. "Want to give it a try?"

Anita shrugged, looking at her family. Cassie put an arm around her shoulders and walked her over to the helmets. As they selected the right size and fit it to Anita's head, Cassie talked softly to her so the others couldn't hear.

"Dillon and I will help you get in the saddle. Give it a feel. If you don't like it, we'll help you get down immediately. Riding isn't for everyone, but if you've never tried, you don't know if you like it or not." Cassie smiled reassuringly at her.

Anita nodded.

Dillon brought Angel over to the steps and gave Anita the reins as soon as she was comfortable. Cassie watched her face, and though she seemed tense she was smiling. Cassie mounted Cheyenne, and Dillon opened the pasture gate, which they had closed earlier to keep the other horses out until everyone was comfortable. Dillon whistled for Dakota and quickly haltered him before swinging onto his bare back. Cassie saw Anita and Roz watching him.

"He's been riding since he was a baby."

"He makes it look easy," Roz said.

"Where are we going?" Anita asked, still looking tense.

Cassie moved closer to her, stepping in front of Angel and bringing her to a stop. "Take one hand off the reins and wave at me." Cassie held up her hand and wiggled her fingers. "Like this."

Anita followed her instructions. "Now switch hands." Cassie demonstrated again. Anita looked puzzled, but she did it.

Cassie smiled at her. "You can relax the death grip you have on the reins. Angel will follow and stop when we do. She doesn't like to run if she doesn't have to, so she won't take off on you."

Anita laughed.

"Remember this is supposed to be fun."

"Got it."

Cassie moved back into the lead and pointed to the wooden platform. "See the platform. We'll go to it and then come back. Everyone good?"

Making sure she received nods from everyone, Cassie nudged Cheyenne forward. She looked back several times to make sure everyone was okay. Dillon moved back and forth between them, helping out and telling jokes. Soon Cassie could hear chatting among them and she knew they were enjoying the ride. For first-time riders it was important to keep the ride short. Just as when training animals, you always wanted to end on a good note.

Cassie and Dillon helped everyone dismount saving Ana for last as she continued to ride Greta around the paddock.

"That was so much fun!" Ana exclaimed after she had dismounted.

"We're glad you enjoyed it." Cassie gave her a little hug as she unbuckled Greta's saddle and handed it to Dillon.

With the horses secured to hitching posts, Dillon passed around brushes and everyone followed his instruction. One at time, Dillon released the horses into the pasture. Ana and Roz stood at the fence and watched them.

Anita approached Cassie. "Thank you so much."

"You're welcome. I hope you enjoyed it." Cassie smiled. "Just a little bit."

"I did. We all did. It was really great to share that with Ana. Sometimes it seems like we tell her no so much. She's always eager to try new things. I guess Roz and I are stuck in our ways." Anita smiled self-consciously. "I always swore I wouldn't act like my parents when I had my own child."

"I'm sure it's hard not to when you only want them to be safe."

"That's it exactly." Anita seemed relieved that Cassie understood. "It's so easy to act like an adult and forget the thrill of being a child."

"That's what happens when we get older." Cassie laughed. "We always want to make sure our guests have fun, but safety is a priority. So it's double nice for us when we get both things."

Cassie walked her back to the fence where her family waited and then she and Dillon headed back to the office for lunch.

* * *

It was late Friday afternoon before Cassie remembered she wanted to check on Greg. All of her spare moments and thoughts had been spent on Kathleen. She had talked with Shelley about taking Wednesday off and was trying to decide if she wanted to call Kathleen and warn her or simply show up. Both options had an advantage. She dialed Greg's number and he picked up on the first ring.

"Hey, Ms. Cassie."

"Hey, I've been meaning to call you all week. I felt like you had something you wanted to say when you called last time. Is everything okay?"

Greg was silent for a while.

"Greg?"

"Yeah, I'm still here."

"What's wrong, Greg? You can tell me anything." Cassie sat down on the porch steps and alternated between petting Zoey and then Pandy.

"It turns out my dad has another kid. He's nine and in foster care too."

"Oh, Greg. That's terrible. Did you track him down?"

Again Greg hesitated. "Yeah, but things aren't good for him."

"What do you mean?"

"He's the only kid with this foster family, and there's been some trouble."

"What kind of trouble? What's going on?" Cassie asked. She didn't like the way Greg was being vague, and she could tell he was keeping the worst from her.

"Look. I can't really talk right now. I'm at work." She could hear someone calling him in the background. "I'll call you tomorrow when I get off. Okay?"

"Okay. Take care of yourself. We'll talk tomorrow."

Cassie hung up, feeling a lump in her chest. Greg had never been secretive or evasive with her before. Whatever was happening with his half-brother had him very upset. She ran her fingers through Zoey's soft belly fur until Pandy pushed at her hand. Her dogs had such a tough life. Pandy looked up at her with questioning eyes, and Cassie was sure she was asking when Kathleen was coming back. Pandy had moped around more than she had after Kathleen left on Sunday.

"Let's call her," she said to Pandy. The situation with Greg was a good excuse. Maybe Kathleen could look into things and give her an idea of what was going on.

"Fosters, Inc. Tiffany speaking, can I help you?"

"Tiffany. It's Cassie Thomas. Is Kathleen around?"

"Oh hey, Ms. Thomas. Hold on a sec."

She heard soft elevator music for a few seconds and then the warm voice she was missing answered. "Cassie?"

"Hi. I needed to talk with you about something. I hope it's okay that I called you at work."

"Of course. What's up?"

"I just got a call from Greg. Well, actually he called on Monday and seemed weird when we hung up so I called him today. He's tracked down his deadbeat dad and discovered he has a little half-brother."

"Wow, that's a lot for a kid to take in."

"He says there's been some trouble at the foster home where his brother is. I tried to question him further for details, but he became evasive and said he would call me tomorrow. Is that something you could look into for me?"

"I can see what I can find out. Do you know his name?"

"I guess that would have been a good question to ask, but unfortunately I didn't. I do know he's the only kid with this foster family."

"Well, if he's with Fosters that should be easy to find, but if he's with the state I might not be able to locate him."

"Greg is supposed to call me tomorrow so I'll try to get more details from him."

"Okay. I'll search from Greg's end and see what I can find out."

"Thanks, Kathleen."

"You're welcome. I might not be home until seven or eight tomorrow. Can I call you then?"

"Sure."

Cassie leaned back on the stairs and thought about Kathleen in her borrowed jeans crossing to the pasture. It was hard to believe a week had passed since she had shared a burnt marshmallow with her. Tonight's cookout wouldn't be as exciting for her, but she could always hope next week she would have Kathleen's company again.

The brat pack would arrive on Friday too. She couldn't help being excited. She was also a little relieved to know Dillon and Shelley would be around to help out. The girls were too old to need instructions for their daily life and they probably wouldn't appreciate it anyway. Cassie needed to find a middle ground to give them structure and freedom at the same time. Not an easy task in the narrow window she would have to work with, but she was looking forward to the challenge.

CHAPTER TWENTY-TWO

Saturday passed in a blur. Anita, Roz and Ana checked out around ten a.m. and Jon and Sarah followed close behind them. Cassie spent the afternoon cleaning their cabins in preparation for the three families that would check in later in the day. This would be the first week of the summer where all four cabins were filled. Pete and Rory had extended their stay to see the brat pack arrive on Friday so at least one of the cabins would be easy guests.

Two of the families were checked in by six, and Cassie stood on the porch watching several kids chase each other on the beach. Both families had two kids, one with two boys and the other with a boy and a girl. The girl was young enough she still wanted to play so she followed the boys everywhere they went. The last couple to arrive would be checking into Cabin One late that evening.

Cassie wasn't sure what time Greg was supposed to get off work so she gave him until seven to call her. When she still had not heard from him, she called his cell and left a voice mail.

She checked in the new couple and had barely settled into her recliner when Kathleen called.

"How was your day?" Cassie asked.

"Exhausting but successful. How about yours?"

"Not as exhausting as yours, I imagine."

"Any word from Greg?"

"Nope."

"I was hoping you had." Kathleen sighed. "I reached out to Greg's foster family. Luckily he was excited when he found his brother and had shared details with them. Apparently after he met with him, he became quiet and evasive. They didn't know any details, but they knew his name. Unfortunately he's in Alabama. His record shows he's been passed around a lot, but it doesn't appear that he's ever been a problem. It's just the foster system that's crappy. This family has had him for about a month and last week the husband was killed."

"Killed! What the hell happened?"

"I couldn't get all the details, but it sounds like maybe the family was involved in something illegal. Maybe drugs."

"How in the world do people like that end up with foster kids?" Cassie asked, not necessarily expecting an answer.

"They want the money and they're able to look sane when the state visits." Kathleen sighed. "And there are so many kids that need to be placed and not enough workers to supervise them on a regular basis."

"Oh, man. That poor little boy. No wonder Greg is upset."

"They've moved him again and I wasn't able to find out where, but I'll keep looking."

"Thanks, Kathleen."

"No problem. I hate to hang up so quickly, but I'm very tired and I haven't eaten yet."

"And you get to do it all over again tomorrow."

"Yes."

They said their goodbyes, and Cassie tossed her cell phone on the coffee table. She had forgotten to ask Kathleen for Greg's brother's name. She tried Greg again and left another message for him to call her when he could, no matter the time.

* * *

Sunday morning, Cassie went through all of her normal tasks, including taking the golf cart around to check housekeeping tags. Zoey and Pandy rode on the seat beside her with their tongues hanging out. By midmorning, the beach was covered with kids and parents so Cassie retreated to her back porch. She tried Greg again and still got no answer. This time her message told him he needed to call her as soon as possible or she was sending someone to hunt him down.

She ate leftovers for lunch and then wandered down to the beach to chat with her guests. Everyone seemed to be doing well, and she returned to the house for some much-needed quiet. Stretched out on the couch, she dozed all afternoon and only woke up long enough to feed the dogs their dinner. She didn't feel hungry and thought she would eat later, but she fell back asleep. The doorbell woke her and she stumbled to the front door looking at her watch. She was shocked to see it was after eleven. Guests wouldn't come to the house this late without first calling and the gate was closed to other traffic. Zoey and Pandy waited anxiously for her to open the door.

Greg smiled sweetly when she opened the door.

"Greg!" She pulled him into a hug. "What are you doing out so late?"

"I'm real sorry, Ms. Cassie. I didn't know where else to go." He stepped to the side, pulling a small blond-headed boy from behind him. "This is Chase, my brother."

"Oh." Cassie tried not to sound surprised. She held out her hand to Chase. "Hi, Chase. I'm Cassie."

Slowly he raised his arm and took her hand. She gave it a gentle shake and released it quickly, not wanting to scare him any more than he already was. He was small and his too-large clothes made him appear even smaller. Greg placed his arm across his shoulder, pulling him close. He leaned his head against Greg's side, clearly finding comfort in his older brother.

Cassie sent the girls to lay on their beds and stepped back from the door. "Come in and tell me what's going on."

"Well…" Greg started.

"Hold that thought." Cassie interrupted Greg. "Are you guys hungry?"

Chase hid behind Greg so she looked at Greg and he shrugged.

"I'm hungry." Cassie led the way into the kitchen and motioned for them to take a seat at the bar. "I forgot to eat dinner." She began pulling leftovers from the refrigerator. "We have burgers and hot dogs." She pulled the lids off the containers.

"I could eat a hot dog," Chase said, looking at Greg and then at Cassie. "If it's okay."

"It's definitely okay." Cassie pulled two hot dogs from the container and popped them in the microwave. She put a paper plate with two hot dog buns in front of Chase. "Iced tea, lemonade or water?"

"Water," Greg answered first.

"I guess water would be fine," Chase answered softly, "but iced tea would be good too."

"Iced tea it is." Cassie took three glasses from the cabinet and set one each in front of Chase and Greg. She poured water for herself and Greg and then iced tea for Chase.

"What do you want to eat, Greg?"

"A burger would be great, but I'll get it." He walked over and gave Zoey and Pandy a long pet before pulling lettuce and tomato along with condiments from the refrigerator.

Cassie took the hot dogs out of the microwave and replaced it with Greg's burger. She put the hot dogs on Chase's plate and encouraged him to apply whatever condiments he wanted. He ate silently while Greg talked about work and pulled his burger from the microwave. Sliding his plate across the counter, he joined Chase on the other side.

Cassie fixed herself a bowl of salad and leaned against the counter. She wasn't going to ask too many questions tonight. Both Greg and Chase looked tired, but she needed to understand why they were out so late. "So what are you two doing roaming the streets this late at night?" She smiled hoping to make her question sound less intrusive.

"Chase had a rough week, so I asked if they'd let me take him for a couple of days and they approved."

Cassie knew pretending she knew nothing about Chase's situation would be the best, at least for tonight. "That's great. Do you want to stay here tonight?"

She couldn't ignore the relief on Greg's face. "You know you're welcome anytime, Greg."

He smiled shyly. "I know you always say that, but this is different. I'm not alone."

She met his eyes and then looked at Chase. "Chase is welcome anytime too." She smiled at them both and Chase's brow relaxed as he returned her smile. "Now, which room would you guys like for tonight?"

She offered them either of the rooms with two twin beds, but Chase chose the downstairs double bed instead. Greg went out to grab their bags from the car and Cassie gave Chase a tour of the house. When they returned to the living room, she called the dogs and sat with Chase while he petted them. He didn't seem scared of them, but she wanted to make sure he felt comfortable enough to make it to the bathroom or kitchen by himself during the night.

Once the boys were settled into their room, she locked the doors and called the girls to go upstairs. She lay awake wondering what had really brought Greg and Chase to her door tonight. Greg's face had been rigid and tense when they had arrived. Cassie didn't think she had ever seen him like that before. Tomorrow she would convince him to tell her what was going on.

CHAPTER TWENTY-THREE

The boys were not showing any signs of movement when Cassie came downstairs the next morning. She fed the dogs and then went to the barn to feed the horses. She left the rest for Dillon to take care of when he arrived. She was anxious to fill him and Shelley in on Greg's arrival but waited patiently for Dillon to get his coffee before talking.

"He just showed up on your doorstep?" Dillon asked, taking a sip of his coffee.

"Yep, with his half-brother." Cassie nodded. "Very cute kid. He looks small for his age though."

"I can't wait to see Greg again," Shelley added and Dillon nodded.

Cassie wasn't sure whether she should share what Kathleen had told her with Dillon and Shelley. It felt like an invasion of Greg and Chase's privacy. She kept quiet to give Greg time to share with Dillon on his own.

They talked for a while and planned the week. Then Dillon headed for the barn and Cassie went back into the house, leaving

Shelley at the desk. She scrambled some eggs, then made toast and bacon before knocking on the boys' door.

"It's almost ten, boys. Breakfast is ready."

Greg opened the door, mumbled something and stumbled down the hall to the bathroom. Cassie looked into the bedroom. Chase was sitting on the floor in the corner reading a book. She recognized the cover as an old Hardy Boys mystery that she had on her bookshelf in the living room. She smiled to herself that he must have wandered out there and found it himself. She crossed the room and sat down beside him.

"That's a great book." She nodded at the book he now held tight to his chest.

"I found it in the living room. I hope it's okay that I brought it back in here." His voice was soft and he hesitated. "I'm sorry I didn't get your permission before I picked it up."

"It's fine, Chase. You can look at and touch anything in the house. I read that book when I was your age and I really enjoyed it. Do you like to read?"

"Yes. I usually read when I get up in the morning. I'm not supposed to wander the house before Mr. Timothy gets up." He looked away from her and she frowned, wondering if Mr. Timothy was the foster parent who was now deceased.

Greg returned to the room looking refreshed with his hair dripping wet. "I'm awake now." He smiled at her. "Did I hear someone mention breakfast?"

Cassie stood. "You certainly did. Eggs, bacon and toast. Any takers?"

Chase jumped to his feet with a smile. "I love bacon."

Cassie put her arm across his shoulders. "Then we should go and get you some before your brother eats it all." His little shoulders felt bony, and it was all Cassie could do not to pull him into a hug.

They all sat at the table, and Cassie tried to keep them talking while they dished food onto their plates.

"Chase, do you have a pair of shorts with you that you can swim in?" she asked, watching as he shoveled bacon into his mouth. He nodded, his mouth too full to respond.

She looked at Greg. "I thought maybe Chase would like to join the kids on the beach for a while."

Chase was looking back and forth between them, clearly liking the idea but waiting to be told it was okay. Greg didn't keep him waiting. "That sounds like a good plan."

"Yeah!" Chase bounced in his chair.

"Eat your eggs and then go get changed." Cassie looked at Greg. "Maybe you and I could talk."

He nodded but didn't look up.

* * *

They stopped in the office so Shelley could hug on Greg. Even Chase got a squeeze before heading to the beach. It took only minutes for Chase to make friends with the other kids there. Soon they were jumping in the water and splashing each other. Cassie steered Greg to a park bench nearby and they took a seat.

"Start talking." Cassie said as soon as his butt hit the bench. She wanted to tell him what she knew but waited to see what he would tell her first.

He sighed loudly and stretched his legs out in front of him. "I tracked him down two weeks ago and we met briefly with his foster parents' supervision. Last week he snuck out and called me about midnight. Some men had come into the house and killed his foster dad. Chase was hiding in the closet."

"He was in the house when they killed him?" Cassie was stunned at the news, and it took a minute to sink in. "Did he see anything?"

Greg hesitated. "He says he didn't, that he heard nothing but the gunshot. I guess the police believed him, but of course the state keeps moving him. He's been in three different homes this week. No one wants him, because they're afraid the drug dealers will come after him."

"I guess I can understand that." Cassie touched Greg's arm. "Did you really get permission to take him?"

"I did, but I'm supposed to take him back tomorrow before I go to work." Greg put his head in his hands. "How can I take him back to that? I thought maybe you would let us stay here for a while?"

"Greg." Cassie waited until he met her eyes. "You know I'd love to, but he's a ward of the state of Alabama and I'm not sure they would let him cross into Florida."

Greg looked surprised. "Wait. How'd you know that?"

"I have a friend at Fosters and I asked her to look into what was going on. I was worried when you didn't return my calls."

"I'm sorry. I was trying to decide what to do."

"Let me call my friend and see if she can work some magic." Cassie hesitated. "But if she can't, you have to take him back."

Cassie watched Greg walk toward the barn to join Dillon. She was pleased with the amount of information he had given her. She didn't feel like he had held any details back or evaded any question she had asked. She knew keeping Chase here would be problematic not only with the state of Alabama but how Fosters was going to feel about giving her four more kids. She watched Chase run across the beach and splash into the water. She knew she couldn't save them all, but this one had been dropped into her lap and she had to try. She stood up and stretched, then pulling her cell phone from her pocket she dialed Kathleen.

"You're at home today, right?" Cassie asked as soon as Kathleen picked up.

"Yes, but tomorrow and Wednesday I'm back in the office. We'll be doing paperwork for weeks after this weekend."

"It went well then?"

"We have at least three kids going to permanent homes and about five new potential foster families."

"That sounds successful."

"Having the kids get permanent homes is the best news, but new foster families mean fewer kids in group homes. Plus we can even help the state if we have foster families with space available."

"Can I run something past you?" Cassie asked hesitantly.

"Sure. I thought you sounded funny. What's wrong?"

"With Greg's brother being a ward of the state in Alabama, what's the chance they would let him be placed somewhere in Florida?"

"It happens sometimes, but only if there is a foster family that specifically requests that child."

"How would someone go about that and could you help?"

Kathleen was silent for a second. "What did you do, Cassie?"

Cassie chuckled. "Me? I didn't do anything. Greg showed up on my doorstep with Chase last night."

"Oh no. Did he take him without permission?"

"He says he has permission, but I'm not sure they know he planned to cross state lines. He's supposed to return him tomorrow. Do you think we have any chance of keeping him?"

"I can look into it." Kathleen sighed. "How is he?"

"He seems okay. Greg says he was in the house when the guy was killed."

"What?"

"Yeah, Greg says Chase hid in the closet until they left the house. Then he snuck out and called Greg to come get him."

"And he didn't hear or see anything?" Kathleen said in disbelief.

"That's what I'm being told, but I'm not sure Greg even believes that. Clearly the state of Alabama doesn't, because they've moved him three times in four days."

"What a nightmare. Let me make some calls and see what I can do. I'll give you a call as soon as I know something. It might be tomorrow though before I get any information."

"Okay. Thanks for this. I wouldn't even know where to start this process."

"We'll get something worked out."

Cassie watched Chase and thought about how much her life had changed in the last week. Kathleen had set her world in a spin and then Greg and Chase had kept it in motion. She had seen children traumatized by seeing their parents or someone they loved killed either by violence or in an accident. Though this man wasn't a loved one to Chase, he was still a caregiver—someone who in Chase's mind was supposed to keep him safe. She couldn't imagine the fear Chase must have felt as he hid in the closet. Cassie didn't want him to ever feel that again.

She certainly didn't consider herself the maternal type, but she did understand a mother bear protecting her cub now. Her softer side had become more prominent since she'd left the police force; it was pleasant to not instantly think the worst of someone or to be suspicious. She wanted to make some calls and get more details, but she no longer held any position that allowed her to do that. She had to believe if Chase had seen something that night that he was now far enough away to be safe.

She realized too that she and Kathleen had not talked about how this could affect the brat pack coming to stay with her. She had not even mentioned to Kathleen that she was coming to see her on Wednesday. Maybe it was best to keep that secret. For now, anyway.

She needed to talk with Greg about his plans. It was sinking in that she had asked Kathleen to help her get custody of Chase. Her quiet independent life would be changed forever. She had enough room for Greg to stay too, but he wouldn't be eighteen until the fall. She would have to remember to talk with Kathleen about that too. First she needed to find out if Greg wanted to stay with her and Chase, and then they needed to talk with Chase.

* * *

She stopped at the edge of the barn and watched Greg working with Dillon. He was relaxed around the horses and he followed Dillon's lead. She remembered Dillon saying last year that he wished Greg could stay and she smiled, thinking how happy Dillon would be if everything worked out. Greg looked up and saw her. He stopped working and stood.

"Is it bad?" he asked, stepping toward her.

She nodded toward Dillon. "Do you want to walk?"

"No, it's okay. I told Mr. Dillon everything."

Cassie smiled. This was the Greg she knew. He was no longer silent and secretive. "Okay." She took a seat on a nearby hay bale and Greg took a knee beside Dillon, who had stopped working to listen. "I talked to Kathleen."

"Oh, Kathleen." Dillon smiled.

"Who's Kathleen?" Greg asked, looking back and forth between them.

"Kathleen is my friend at Fosters," Cassie continued, ignoring Dillon's grin. "She says it might be possible for me to get custody of Chase."

Greg jumped to his feet. "That would be awesome!"

"Hold on now, Greg. It's not going to be easy or quick. She's going to call me tomorrow with an update. The question is do you want to stay here too?"

"Of course." Greg looked from Cassie to Dillon. "I've always wanted to stay here. Last summer was the highlight of my life. I can get a job in Riverview and help out around here too."

Cassie laughed. "Okay. One thing at a time. Why don't you go get Chase so we can talk with him? It's time for lunch and he needs suntan lotion."

Cassie watched Greg jog toward the lake and then looked at Dillon. "Have I lost my mind?"

"Not at all. I couldn't be happier."

CHAPTER TWENTY-FOUR

"I could really live here?" Chase's eyes were huge as Cassie and Greg explained the situation to him.

"That's what we're trying to do. Would that be okay with you?" Cassie asked, moving from the couch to kneel in front of him.

Chase nodded. "And Greg too?"

"If he wants to."

Chase looked at Greg, his brow creased as he waited for his answer.

"You know I want to, buddy. I told you this place is awesome." Greg pulled Chase close against him.

"I've never had a forever home." Chase's voice was muffled against Greg's body.

"I know, buddy." Greg squeezed him again, looking at Cassie over Chase's head. "When I tracked down his social worker, she let me read his file while she contacted his foster family. It's worse than mine."

Cassie took a seat on the other side of Chase. “Right now, we’re only trying to get the State of Alabama to let you stay here. Then we’ll ask for a more permanent placement.” Cassie hated to get his hopes up and then have him disappointed, but she wanted to be honest with him. After the week he’d had, it seemed like social services would be happy to have him out of their system.

Chase nodded. It broke Cassie’s heart to look at his sad, little face. “Until we hear differently, we’ll assume things are going to go our way. So let’s be happy,” Cassie encouraged.

Greg squeezed Chase until he began to squirm, giggling.

Cassie laughed with them. “Chase, why don’t you go take a shower, and then Greg is going to take you shopping.”

Greg raised his eyebrows as Chase ran out of the room.

Cassie shrugged. “The tiny bags you carried in last night won’t last you more than a day. Besides, I’m sure Chase could use the outing to process everything that’s happened in the last couple of days.”

She crossed the room and pulled two one-hundred-dollar bills from her petty cash drawer. Greg stuffed them in his pocket and shuffled his feet. “We won’t spend that much.”

She waited for him to meet her eyes. “Please get him underwear and socks and not all toys.”

“Oh no, we won’t get any toys. I’d never waste your money.”

Cassie laughed. “I was only joking. Let him a pick a toy too.”

Greg smiled.

“Grab some lunch first and then shop. I expect you to spend it all. So after you pick Chase a couple of outfits, get whatever you need. Once things are settled, you can make a run to Pensacola and get whatever you left at your foster home. Have you called your job yet?”

“Not yet. I don’t want to quit if I’m gonna be back in Pensacola tomorrow.”

“I don’t think that’s going to happen. As soon as Kathleen calls, I’ll let you know. Tell me about Chase’s file before he finishes his shower.”

Greg slid onto a barstool. "Dad left before he was born, of course, and his mother couldn't hold on to a job or a home. There were a couple families over the years that wanted to keep him permanently, but each time his mother would show up and claim she was prepared to make a home for him. Those idiot judges would believe her every time and after a week or two she'd be gone again."

"What's his mother's problem? Drugs? Alcohol?"

"All of the above. The social worker seemed really upset with his situation, and she worked hard to get permission for me to take him."

"You weren't going to take him back, were you?" Cassie looked him in the eye.

Greg didn't answer her question, but his eyes were wet when he looked at her. "He was crying when I picked him up, and he didn't stop until we were almost here."

She pulled Greg into a hug. "We'll make things work, but we have to follow the rules. Okay?"

Greg nodded.

"There's nothing else you need to tell me, right?"

Greg stepped away from her as Chase bounded into the kitchen. "Nothing. I swear." He turned to Chase. "Let's go."

"Be back for dinner," Cassie called to them as they disappeared out the front door. She heard Greg acknowledge her before the door shut.

* * *

Cassie sighed as she collapsed into the squishy chair beside the coffeemaker in her office.

"Where are the boys?" Shelley asked.

"I sent them shopping. Greg carried two duffel bags in last night, but they were so floppy they couldn't have had much in them." Cassie sighed again. "And I don't have anything to make for dinner."

"I was thinking about running to the grocery store after work. Do you want to go now? We can leave Dillon in charge."

"Good idea. What is Big D up to?"

"He bolted as soon as it became clear there was going to be a serious talk. He doesn't like sharing emotions or watching others do it either, for that matter." Shelley laughed. She called Dillon on the radio and asked him to come to the office.

"Have things really been quiet today, or have I just been out of touch?" Cassie asked.

"Fairly quiet."

"No peep from any of the new guests?"

"Everyone seems pretty happy. I don't think the couple in Cabin One have even gotten up yet."

"Thanks for keeping things going. I'll try not to be so distracted in the future."

Shelley laughed again. "With the girls coming this week, I'll be happy if I see you occasionally."

"This summer will be a whirlwind but I'm really looking forward to it."

"Dillon hasn't stopped bouncing since you told him and now with Greg and Chase here, he is almost ecstatic."

Cassie couldn't help but laugh when Dillon walked in. She knew what Shelley meant but the idea of Dillon outwardly showing excitement was humorous. His naturally calm demeanor was a pillar for her. Aside from a little craziness that crept up from time to time, he would express his excitement in nothing but a smile. It would be a very wide smile though.

Dillon readily agreed to hang out in the office while they were gone. He said he would order feed and supplies, but Cassie knew he would be playing computer games.

* * *

Dillon met them as soon as they returned. He transferred Shelley's purchases to her car so she could take them home, and then he helped Cassie carry in the remaining bags. Cassie could see the worry lines on his face as they unpacked the groceries.

"What's wrong, Dillon?"

"I've been so excited about Greg and Chase that I forgot the girls come on Friday. They're still coming, right?"

Cassie rubbed her hands across her face. "I hope so. I was caught up with Chase too and forgot to ask Kathleen if this would change the plans. I didn't even ask her about Greg."

"What about Greg?"

"He's still in foster care too. At least until the fall. I hope Kathleen will be able to transfer him here."

"I forgot. He seems so mature. He says he can handle all the maintenance on our vehicles now and even talked about getting the old tractor to work again."

Cassie laughed. "But you were going to do that."

"And I will." Dillon paused dramatically. "When I get a chance."

* * *

Greg and Chase returned by six and Cassie had dinner almost ready. Chase took the plates from the bar and set the table. Cassie smiled at him when he returned to the kitchen and took a seat on a nearby barstool.

"Show me." Cassie motioned to their shopping bags with her elbow as she pulled lettuce apart for the salad.

Greg piled the bags on the bar and on the stool beside Chase. "You show it and I'll help with dinner."

Greg pulled carrots and a tomato from the refrigerator and began chopping them.

Cassie removed a casserole dish from the oven.

Greg leaned around her to see the dish. "Is that mac and cheese?"

"It is mac and cheese with chunks of ham and bacon. I remembered how much you liked it. How about you, Chase?" Cassie turned to Chase.

He was surrounded by everything from the shopping bags and sat grinning like a Cheshire cat. "I like mac and cheese."

Cassie carried the casserole dish to the table and scooped some onto each plate. "This needs a minute to cool, so show me what you got."

Chase held up each one of his outfits, and when he finished he pulled a small box of Legos from under the stack.

"Oh, that's cool, Chase. What does it make?"

"A dump truck and a bulldozer." Excitedly Chase turned the box from side to side, showing her pictures of the completed projects.

"Let's eat. I'm starving," Greg said, interrupting the show-and-tell.

Cassie filled three glasses with iced tea and Chase helped her carry them to the table.

The boys took turns telling about their shopping adventure during dinner, and they were still laughing long after the plates were empty.

Eventually, Greg got to his feet and began gathering the dishes. "I'll get these."

Chase continued his story. "And then Greg whipped open the door on this old man in his underwear." Chase laughed hysterically.

"How was I supposed to know you had changed rooms while I was getting you a different size?" Greg gently punched Chase on the arm.

"The door wouldn't lock. I had to move."

Greg pulled him from his chair and threw him over his shoulder. "I'll show you how to move." He spun in a circle, and Chase squealed as he hung upside down from Greg's shoulder. After a few turns, Greg walked into the living room and tossed him on the couch.

"Who wants ice cream?" Cassie asked, stopping the horseplay before Chase threw up his dinner.

"Me!" Chase jumped up from the couch and ran into the kitchen as Cassie pulled the box from the freezer.

"Chocolate, vanilla or strawberry?" she asked.

"Can I have all three?" Chase asked, sliding onto the barstool to watch.

"Of course. Greg?"

"All three for me too."

Cassie scooped ice cream into three bowls. "Let's eat outside."

The boys followed Cassie outside with their bowls.

Chase talked about school while they ate, eagerly telling them about every hour of his day at the last school he had attended. When Cassie asked him about his time spent at home, he stopped talking and finished his ice cream in silence. She loaded the dishwasher as the boys got ready for bed. She left them watching a movie on her iPad in the bedroom.

CHAPTER TWENTY-FIVE

Cassie awoke as the first rays of sunlight were moving through the window. The house was quiet and to her surprise neither dog was on her bed. Eager to see where they had gone, she walked softly down the stairs. Chase and Zoey were curled on the couch watching a cartoon television show, and Pandy lay nearby. She stood at the foot of the stairs and watched Chase's hand slowly stroking the soft fur on Zoey's belly. It was amazing how fast Chase had settled into her house, but she knew his comfort level was related to Greg's presence. She was thankful she could provide a safe and maybe permanent home.

She quietly returned upstairs and quickly showered. Chase glanced up as she entered the living room, a flash of panic on his face.

"Greg said I could watch cartoons if I kept it low." His eyes flicked toward the hallway as if hoping Greg would appear and confirm what he had said.

Cassie took a seat in the chair beside him and spoke gently. "If everything works out this will be your home too and I want you to be comfortable here. You can watch television or read a book without asking permission."

He nodded slowly, still unsure of his new found freedom.

"Now," she stood and started toward the kitchen, "I imagine you and the dogs are pretty hungry."

"Yes, ma'am." Chase stood and followed her into the kitchen.

"How about pancakes and bacon?"

Chase's eyes grew wide and he nodded eagerly.

Cassie opened the pantry door and pointed at the bag of dog food. "They each get one scoop, if you would please. It's easiest if you bring their dishes to the bag."

He crossed the room and retrieved the dog dishes from their rack and scooped kibble into both bowls. Once the dogs were munching happily, he crawled onto the barstool and curled his legs under his butt. "Can I help?" he asked.

Cassie pushed the bowl of pancake mix toward him. "Stir slowly and gently." She pulled a bag of mini chocolate chips from the pantry and watched Chase's face light up again. "Shall we add these?"

"Yeah!"

Cassie put the bacon in the microwave and retrieved the electric skillet from the cabinet. While it heated, she and Chase talked about the horses and goats. He was full of questions, and she promised him she would introduce him to all the animals after breakfast. She handed him a measuring cup and showed him how to spread the scoops of batter so they didn't run together. Cassie moved back and forth between the bacon and turning the pancakes until both were finished. She joined Chase at the bar, and they slathered their pancakes with butter and syrup.

"Is that peanut butter?" Chase asked.

"It is. I like it with my pancakes. Would you like to try it?"

Chase nodded and Cassie put a small scoop on the corner of his plate. "It's best if you get a little bit on your fork with each bite instead of trying to spread it on the pancake."

Chase took a bite, and Cassie watched him roll it around in his mouth before he spoke. "That's kinda good."

Cassie laughed.

They both looked up when Greg walked into the room. He was already dressed in jeans and a T-shirt. "What's that wonderful smell?"

"Pancakes and bacon!" Chase danced happily in his chair.

Cassie motioned to the plate she had laid out for him.

"Oh no," Greg said as he sat beside Chase. "Tell me you don't like that crap too." Greg pointed at the peanut butter on Chase's plate.

Chase laughed. "You said 'crap.'"

"I'm allowed to say crap, but you're not," Greg said between mouthfuls.

"How about if we all try not to say it," Cassie chimed in.

"Okay." Greg pointed his fork at her over Chase's head. "But if I remember correctly you'll have the biggest struggle."

Cassie laughed. "Possibly, but I'll work on it, especially before the girls get here this week."

Greg's eyes widened. "Oh, I forgot."

"Girls?" Chase looked back and forth between them waiting for an answer.

"Four girls and a supervisor are supposed to arrive on Friday," Cassie explained. "They'll be staying for the summer."

Chase wrinkled his nose. "Yuck. Girls."

"Yeah, girls." Greg nudged his shoulder.

"They're all a couple years older than you, and they'll have their hands full learning to live on a farm. You'll already be used to everything by then, so maybe you can help us show them how things work here."

"If I'm still here." Chase's eyes dropped to his plate.

Cassie looked at Greg. "Hey, remember what we said yesterday? We move forward like good things are going to happen until we have to deal with something else, right?"

She nudged Chase until he met her eyes.

"Yes, ma'am."

The sadness in his voice reminded Cassie how desperate their situation was. She hated to keep calling Kathleen, but she needed to see if there was any news. The thought of hearing

Kathleen's smooth voice made her almost forget she had any other agenda. She still wanted to go see her tomorrow. She could leave the boys with Dillon and Shelley for a couple of hours. She realized that her thoughts were running away from her; she needed to see what Kathleen said before she could make plans for the future. If Alabama Child Services took Chase back, everything would change.

She stood, putting her happy face back in place. "Go get dressed, Chase, and we'll head out to help Dillon feed the animals."

Chase disappeared down the hall at a sprint.

"If we stay, will the girls still be able to come?" Greg asked softly.

Cassie stopped cleaning the plates and leaned against the counter. "I don't know." She met Greg's eyes. "But it doesn't matter. You and Chase are my priority right now. We'll deal with everything else as it comes."

Greg gave her a quick hug. "Thanks, Ms. Cassie."

"We really need to come up with something for you guys to call me other than Ms. Cassie and ma'am." She smiled at him.

"I'll think of something good." Greg scooted out of the reach of the dish towel as she playfully attempted to swat at him with it.

* * *

Cassie and the boys arrived as Dillon was feeding the last horse. Greg immediately began filling the buckets for the goats, but Chase remained at a distance silently watching. Cassie was confused by his hesitancy since he had been so excited about working with the animals. She was about to call him over when Dillon beat her to it. She watched while Dillon brought out the first horse and slowly explained their process to Chase. As soon as the eagerness returned to Chase's face, Cassie slipped out quietly and returned to the office.

She pretended to work as long as she could before settling into the chair beside the coffeemaker. Dropping in a canister, she waited for it to brew before dialing Kathleen's cell phone.

"Hey, Cass," Kathleen answered softly. "Can I call you back in a few?"

"Sure."

Cassie smiled as they disconnected. Oh, Kathleen. She sighed. The sound of her voice had washed over Cassie, filling her whole body with warmth. She rested her chin on her hands and stared out the window to the lake where little bodies darted back and forth at the water's edge. As she had a million times since last Sunday, her mind replayed details of being with Kathleen. Her muscles clenched as she remembered the feel of Kathleen's hands on her breasts. Cassie jumped when the phone rang.

"Hello." She struggled to regain control of her voice.

"Are you okay, Cassie?" Kathleen asked with concern.

"I'm fine."

"Then what's wrong?"

Cassie sighed. "I was thinking about when you were here."

"Oh."

Several seconds of silence passed.

"Just oh?" Cassie asked.

"Well, let's just say I'm glad I cleared my office before taking your call because now I'm thinking about that too."

"Glad I could share."

Kathleen cleared her throat. "I was going to call you after my meeting."

"Sorry I interrupted."

"No problem. We were wrapping up anyway." Kathleen hesitated. "I might have a little bit of good news."

"Really? I'm listening."

"Alabama Child Services is happy to release Chase to us temporarily, but you're going to have to do a ton of paperwork for them to release him long term."

Cassie exhaled loudly. "Tell me where to start."

"I'm having all the necessary forms emailed to me."

Without thinking, Cassie cut in. "I was thinking about coming to see you tomorrow."

The silence was heavy between them, and Cassie's voice broke when she spoke, "If that's okay?"

"Of course it's okay."

"Are you sure?" Cassie asked. She wanted to say more but was scared of the silence Kathleen had left hanging between them.

"Yes. I'm sorry if I was hesitant. That's the best plan if you can get away. You'll be able to get the paperwork started quicker."

"Right…yes…get started on the paperwork."

"And it'll be good to see you."

Cassie smiled. She was still confused by Kathleen's silence, but hearing her words made her feel a bit more confident. "Maybe I could take you to lunch. Somewhere quiet so we can talk." And touch, she thought.

"I know the perfect place."

Cassie sat staring at the phone in her hand when they hung up. She would see Kathleen around eleven in her office. She realized she had forgotten to mention Greg's situation or the girls. She dialed Kathleen back.

"Cass?"

"I'm sorry to call right back, but I forgot one of the main reasons I called."

Kathleen laughed. "I understand."

"What do we need to do for Greg to be able to stay here too?"

"Sorry. I guess I was distracted too. I took care of that for you. I contacted his foster family and explained the situation. They're fine, but they'd like him to move his stuff out since he probably won't be back. I didn't get the idea that there was a tight bond there."

"No, probably not. Greg was planning to move out as soon as he turned eighteen anyway." Cassie was relieved. "I'll talk with Greg. If he doesn't have much stuff, maybe I can go by tomorrow and pack it up for him."

"Let me know and I'll call them. We could go by after lunch."

"Thank you. I really appreciate all of your help. I can't tell you how much it means to me."

"I'm happy I could help."

"I'll send you a text after I talk with Greg so I don't interrupt your workday again."

"Okay, but you can interrupt me anytime. See you tomorrow."

"Tomorrow."

Cassie stared at the phone in her hand. She couldn't believe she had forgotten to ask about the girls, again. Where was her mind? She would have to make a point of mentioning it tomorrow when she saw Kathleen. They were down to the last couple days before the girls arrived. She had to think if plans had been changed that Kathleen would have told her.

* * *

Cassie was surprise to see Chase brushing Cheyenne alone when she returned to the barn. She took a seat on the stack of hay bales and watched him stretch on the tips of his toes to reach Cheyenne's back. When he finished, he received a nod from Dillon and then he led Cheyenne into the pasture. Holding the rope, he climbed the stairs on the mounting steps and pulled Cheyenne close. He untied her harness and stroked her neck a couple times, then jumped off the stairs with the biggest grin Cassie had ever seen.

He came straight back to the barn and hung the harness on its hook beside Cheyenne's stall. When he received an approving nod from Dillon, he walked slowly over and sat down beside Cassie. She could feel the excitement bubbling out of him.

"That was the most awesomest thing I've ever done."

Cassie pulled him into a light hug. She could tell he wanted to jump up and down, and she wondered if he was going to explode.

Greg walked over to Chase and handed him a narrow blue two-foot-long ribbon. He pointed to the end of the driveway. "See the mailbox, Chase?"

"Yes."

"Run down there and tie this to the post."

Chase took off at a sprint.

"And then run back," Greg called to him.

Greg and Dillon both exploded into laughter. Cassie looked back and forth between them. "What did you guys do?"

Dillon stopped laughing long enough to explain. "I asked him to remain calm around the horses and now I am letting him burn his energy."

Cassie grinned.

"You wouldn't believe how many trips I made to the mailbox last summer," Greg added.

Cassie shook her head. "I had a guest ask me last summer what the different colored ribbons on the mailbox meant and I was distracted before I had a chance to ask." She laughed. "You guys are just too smart."

"The colors are only to add variety. Sometimes you return with a ribbon and sometimes you don't, but at the end of the day it'll be his job to make sure all the ribbons are back in the barn." Dillon smiled. "My dad did the same thing to me and it's amazing how it works."

Chase slowed to a walk as he entered the barn and Greg handed him a bottle of water. Cassie patted the seat beside her and he flopped down on it. She pulled him close and looked up at Greg. "I have good news."

With all eyes on her, she quickly filled them in on her conversation with Kathleen. "So it's only temporary for now." She squeezed Chase. "But I'm going to meet with Kathleen tomorrow to start the paperwork to make it more permanent."

Chase pumped his arm in the air. "This is the best day ever!"

Greg high-fived with Dillon and then with Chase before looking at Cassie. "Did you discuss me?" he asked hesitantly.

"Yep. And you're good to stay here. I don't know how much stuff you have at your place, but I could pick it up tomorrow when I go to Pensacola. If you want?"

"Could you? That'd be great. I only have clothes there. Anything personal I kept in my car 'cause you never knew who might be in your room when you weren't home." Greg turned toward the pasture and then spun back to Cassie, realization spreading across his face. "I don't ever have to go back there then?"

Cassie shook her head. "You don't ever have to go back there, Greg."

"Wow." He turned back to the pasture again. Cassie watched him rub his hands across his face. When he turned again, he was starting to bounce on his feet and excitement had replaced the stress on his face. "I think the mailbox needs a red ribbon."

"Me too!" Chase jumped to his feet as Greg grabbed the ribbon and they ran toward the mailbox.

Dillon dropped onto the hay bale beside Cassie. "This really is going to be a great summer."

Cassie sighed and leaned back against the wall. "Yeah. I'm gonna need a lot of help, you know?"

"I'm ready," Dillon said eagerly.

"But am I?"

CHAPTER TWENTY-SIX

Cassie left Chase and Greg helping Dillon in the barn and returned to the office again. She sent a text to Kathleen to confirm tomorrow's plan to pick up Greg's clothes and then tried to focus on work. She pulled out her ledger to go over any bills that needed to be paid. Her eyes focused on the pages in front of her, but her mind drifted. She had not felt this overwhelmed in years. Experiencing so much change in only a few days had her mind on overdrive. She eventually settled into the flow of work and the spinning in her head slowed to the speed of a carousel.

She was interrupted several hours later by Dillon and the boys as they clamored past her to make lunch. Chase was talking so fast she wasn't sure he would be able to eat. She steered him to the sink to wash his hands and then helped him make a sandwich while she made her own.

Accompanied by Pandy and Zoey, who had not been far from Chase's side all morning, they carried their food to the picnic table outside.

"Chase." Cassie put her hand up to stop his flow into a new story about one of the goats. Chase met her eyes, interpreting her interruption as concern for the goat.

"I didn't really hurt him when I fell. Mr. Dillon said I just scared him. He was moving so fast and I just wanted to pet him. Greg said I had to catch him on my own. Mr. Dillon explained to me the most important rule around the animals is to never hurt them and—"

Cassie reached across the table and touched his arm. When he took a deep breath, she smiled. "I know you're really excited, but you don't have to see and do everything in one day. You're going to be here for a while." She watched the flash of panic cross his eyes and quickly added, "Hopefully a long while."

Chase's entire face erupted into a contagious grin, and Cassie felt her heart melt. He took the first bite of his sandwich, but his eyes were already focused on the kids playing on the beach.

"Why don't you change into your new bathing suit and play for a while. Tomorrow morning you can help with the horses again," Greg suggested.

"Yeah, that's a good idea." Chase stood.

"Not yet." Cassie motioned for him to sit back down. "Eat your sandwich and then you can change. Today we're going to coat you in sunscreen." Cassie ignored Chase's scrunched-up face.

She popped the last bite of her sandwich into her mouth and pulled her vibrating phone from her pocket. She read the text message and then looked at Greg. "Kathleen says she spoke with your foster family, and we're fine to pick up your stuff tomorrow. Do you think I need to take more than one box?"

"No, one box is enough." Greg was silent for a second. "Do you want me to go with you? You shouldn't have to pack my stuff."

Dillon gave Cassie a wink and then shook his head. "Nope, I need you here tomorrow. Besides Cassie has lunch plans that I'm sure don't include a teenage boy."

Cassie dropped her head to return a text to Kathleen and ignored Dillon's teasing.

"Lunch with who?" Greg asked.

"The beautiful woman who is responsible for you guys being able to stay here." Dillon stood and waited for Cassie to meet his eyes. "Are we going to see her again soon?"

"I was planning to ask her to come up this weekend and help get the girls settled. If she can, of course."

"So the girls are still coming?" Dillon asked as they walked toward the trash can.

Cassie sighed. "I haven't asked yet. It seems like every time we talk there are more pressing matters."

"Better make it a priority tomorrow. Friday is barely a couple days away."

"I know. I will."

* * *

After covering Chase's body with sunscreen, she piled into the golf cart with Chase, Zoey and Pandy. Cassie wanted a little more time for his lunch to settle before sending him to play, so they circled the lake. Chase asked a variety of questions about the bike trails and the woods behind the cabins.

"Maybe tomorrow you and Greg can grab a bike and hit the trails."

"That would be fun. Should we go ask him now?"

Cassie smiled. "Sure."

They parked the golf cart to the side of the office and walked to the barn. Dillon and Greg were in the tack room checking supplies.

"Can we ride bikes?" Chase asked eagerly.

Greg smiled. "How about tomorrow? Dillon and I are going to work on the tractor this afternoon."

"Yeah, yeah. That's what I meant. Ride tomorrow."

"He thought we should ask you immediately," Cassie added. Then she remembered the reason she had actually wanted to come see Greg. "Did you call the garage?"

"Yeah, they said they'd mail my final check."

"Were they upset that you didn't give a notice before quitting?" Cassie asked.

"Not really. I explained the situation, and Carl even offered to put in a good word for me with a friend of his in Riverview."

"Which garage?" Dillon asked.

"Joe's I think," he said.

"We know Jo, too. If you need another reference."

Cassie nodded in agreement with Dillon. "You could have one of us go with you when you drop in to ask about a job."

Greg shrugged.

Cassie and Dillon laughed. "Okay, we'll stay out of it." Cassie bumped her shoulder into his arm. "But we're here if you need us."

Greg smiled. "I thought I might drive in this evening after dinner. Carl said Joe is normally the one that closes the shop at night."

"That sounds fine." Cassie smiled at him and started to ask him if he knew that Jo was a woman, but Chase was beginning to dance beside her. "Ready to go play, Chase?"

"Yep."

Greg gave him a look.

"Uh…yes, ma'am."

Cassie groaned and rolled her eyes at Greg. "Okay. Take off. Be careful and behave yourself. I'll be down in a minute."

Chase tore out of the barn and headed for the beach.

Cassie shook her head. "He's full of energy. Thank you, Greg, for reminding him to be polite, but I've had enough of the ma'am crap."

Greg laughed and Dillon nodded. "Yeah, he makes me tired just watching him talk. I don't think I've been sir'd so much in my life."

"What's the solution then?" Greg asked. "I want him to be courteous."

"We're just giving you a hard time." Cassie smiled at him.

Greg shrugged. "Well, as soon as the paperwork goes through he can start calling you Mom."

Cassie groaned again and left the barn to the echo of laughter coming from Dillon and Greg.

* * *

Cassie strolled toward the beach, watching Chase squeal and run away from another kid. The other children's shouts joined Chase's, and a new game of tag was started. Cassie took a seat on a nearby bench. Kids were so loud. She rubbed her face. What had she gotten herself into?

As though Chase could hear her thoughts, he stopped running and scanned the faces until he located her. She gave him a wave, and even from a distance she could see relief flood his face. He waved back and then splashed into the water to join the other kids. Her heart flooded with warmth. Chase had become attached to her in such a short time, and she was surprised to realize she felt the same way.

Greg's words floated back to her and she grimaced. Mom. She had never considered herself mom material. Nett would have made a great parent and she would have loved Chase. Cassie regretted not giving her the opportunity that she was now going to get even though it wasn't her plan. Unforeseen circumstances had placed her in this position. She took a deep breath and for the first time in days, she thought about the consequences of her actions.

She was going to have a son. Maybe two, though Greg was almost an adult. Chase would need parenting every day and he wouldn't be leaving at the end of the summer. She could ask herself if she was ready for this but did her answer really matter? She had taken Chase in without hesitation and she wasn't an impulsive person. Fortunately, she was at a place in her life that she could offer him something, and as weird as it seemed to her, she wanted to. She smiled to herself as her thoughts drifted to Kathleen. The sound of her voice on the phone that morning had been soft and smooth, and she ached to see and touch her again. How would Kathleen feel about dating a single parent? She would add that to her list of questions. Tomorrow couldn't come soon enough.

After a while, Cassie wandered down to the beach and talked with her guests. Everyone seemed to be enjoying themselves, so she returned to her bench and tried to relax. Unable to sit still, she crossed to the storage shed and began cleaning it out. She pulled everything inside out into the sun and swept the floor. She straightened the racks as she brought everything back in. She was pushing the last bicycle inside when Chase joined her, flanked by Zoey and Pandy.

"Ms. Cassie, is it almost time for dinner? I'm hungry."

Closing the door to the shed, Cassie looked at her watch. "Not for another hour or so. Let's go up to the house and we'll fix a snack."

Chase smiled and turned toward the house. Cassie fell in step beside him and put her arm across his little shoulders. "You look like Superman with your towel cape."

"I could be Superman." Chase began to tell her all the reasons he could be Superman.

She hugged his wet body against her side and brushed the strands of hair from his eyes. When he paused to take a breath, she asked. "When's the last time you had a haircut?"

He hesitated. "I can't remember. Usually someone at the house cuts it."

"An adult or one of the other kids?"

He shrugged. "Both."

Cassie cringed. "How about Thursday afternoon you and I will both go get a haircut?"

Chase nodded, but his voice was unsure. "Okay."

Cassie squeezed him reassuringly. "Go out back with the dogs and I'll be out in a minute. Peanut butter sandwich okay?"

Chase nodded.

"With or without jelly?"

"With, please."

Cassie made a peanut butter and jelly sandwich, putting half in the refrigerator for another time. On another plate she sliced two apples and added a glob of peanut butter for dipping. She carried the snack and two bottles of water outside and put them on the table. Chase had climbed into the hot tub and only his little face was sticking out.

"I got cold," he explained.

Cassie held his towel open and he crawled out of the tub. He quickly ate his sandwich and began on the apple slices. He was eating the last bite when Cassie noticed he was shivering again. She stood and pulled him to his feet.

"Face the house." Taking the towel from him, she held it up between them. "Strip those wet shorts off and toss them on the chair, please."

Chase did as she requested, and she wrapped the towel around him. Pushing open the door, she pointed down the hall. He ran, taking little baby steps in the limited space allowed by the towel. She squeezed the water from his bathing suit and hung it to dry. Clearing their plates, she returned to the office. The beach had cleared except for the couple from Cabin One. She imagined they were enjoying the peace and quiet. Chase was out of the shower when she returned to the house.

"Would you like to watch a movie or read a book?"

Chase grinned and pulled a Harry Potter book from the bookshelf. "Could we read this together?"

"Sure." She sat down in the recliner. When Chase hesitated beside the couch, she scooted to one side and patted the space beside her. The recliner was large and Chase was so small that there was plenty of room for both of them.

"Will you read?" he asked.

"Why don't we take turns?"

"Okay, but I'm not very good at reading out loud."

"That's okay." She smiled at him. "I'm not either, so we'll learn together."

They were halfway through Chapter Three when Dillon stuck his head in the door to say goodbye. He ruffled Chase's hair. Cassie poked him in the gut when he reached for her head.

Greg walked in as Dillon was leaving and flopped down on the sofa. "Did you have an idea for dinner?"

"Not really." She closed the book and started to stand.

"No." He put his hand out. "You guys keep reading and I'll make something. Is spaghetti okay?"

Cassie looked at him in surprise and Greg laughed. "I'll use a jar of sauce and I think I can boil water."

Cassie looked at Chase. "You like spaghetti?"

"Yep."

"What?" Greg asked, giving him a hard look.

"Yes, ma'am. Spaghetti is one of my favorites."

Cassie laughed. "Is there anything you don't eat?"

Chase tilted his head in thought. "I'm sure there must be, but I haven't found it yet."

Chase settled back into the chair and Cassie opened the book. Her mind drifted while Chase read aloud. The ringing phone pulled her back. Greg grabbed it before she could stand.

"Lake View Resort."

Cassie smiled at him for using his sweet voice. Last summer she was always giving him a hard time about how he answered the work phone. She wanted him to sound inviting so guests would feel welcome to call for assistance.

"Hmmm...well, there should be one." Greg paused. "We'll be right over...No, that's okay...We'll be right there."

Greg hung up the phone. "Cabin One can't find a corkscrew."

"They probably don't know how to use the one in their drawer. Chase and I will take them a corkscrew."

Cassie grabbed a corkscrew from the office drawer, and she and Chase walked to Cabin One. Cassie searched her memory for the name of the woman standing on the porch. Chris. And her husband was Shawn.

"We're sorry to bother you," Chris said as they approached the porch.

"No problem at all." Cassie motioned Chase to the porch swing. "Can I come in for a second and I'll show you how the fancy gadget works?"

"Sure." Chris pushed the door open and stepped aside to allow Cassie to enter.

Cassie placed the corkscrew she had brought on the counter and opened the kitchen drawer beside the sink. She pulled out the foil cutter and the straddle-style opener. "May I?" she asked, pointing at their bottle of wine. When they nodded, she showed them how to work the opener.

"Interesting," Shawn said, picking up each piece and looking at it.

"I like these because they don't stretch the cork if you need to put it back in and you don't get pieces of the cork in your wine."

"That's neat," Chris added.

"But…" Cassie held up the corkscrew. "Just in case." She laid it back down on the counter and turned to leave. "Enjoy your evening."

Chris laughed. "We will now that we have our wine. Thanks again."

* * *

Cassie and Chase returned as Greg was draining the spaghetti.

Cassie put plates out and Chase set the table. While they ate, Chase and Greg talked about their day and then made plans for their bike ride the next morning. After the table was cleared, Cassie and Chase returned to the recliner and their book. Greg took a shower and changed into a nice shirt and jeans. He bolted out the door with a "see you later" before Cassie had another chance to talk to him. She liked his independence, but she hoped he wouldn't be too surprised to discover Jo was a woman.

* * *

Cassie heard Greg returning as she quietly exited Chase's room. She had read to him until he couldn't hold his eyes open any longer. It was clear he was trying to wait until Greg returned, so she sat with him until he fell asleep. She watched from the doorway while Greg rubbed Chase's head and whispered softly to him. Chase stirred enough to roll over and then settled back to sleep. Greg followed Cassie to the living room where he flopped onto the couch.

He gave her a little glare. "You could have warned me Jo was a woman."

Cassie laughed. "Did you embarrass yourself?"

"Almost. Luckily she was the only one there, so it only took me a minute to realize she was Jo."

"So what did she say?"

"She said, 'Hi, I'm Jo.'"

Cassie laughed. "You're so funny. What did she say about a job?"

"She said I could work a few hours a week on a trial basis. Carl, my boss in Pensacola had just called her, so she was surprised I came by so soon. Right now she's shorthanded and has to cover Saturdays herself. She said if I come by about noon, I can stay for a couple of hours."

"That's great, Greg. Did you tell her you were staying here?"

"No. I want her to hire me for my ability and not because I live with the only other lesbian in town."

She quickly covered her surprise at his words and threw a pillow at him as she stood. "Think you're so smart, don't you? That's fine. Stand on your own two feet then." She rubbed his shoulder as she passed him. "See you in the morning."

CHAPTER TWENTY-SEVEN

Chase was waiting for Cassie at the bottom of the stairs on Wednesday morning ready to read more of their book. They quietly ate cereal and toast before feeding the dogs and settling back into the recliner. When Dillon and Shelley arrived, the boys went with Dillon to the barn and Shelley followed Cassie back upstairs.

"You're not wearing that, are you?" Shelley asked as they entered Cassie's bedroom.

"What's wrong with what I wear every day?"

"That's what you wear every day." Shelley laughed. "Wear a button-down shirt."

"This is a button-down shirt."

"That's a flannel shirt. It does not fall into the button-down shirt category."

Cassie was giving Shelley a hard time; she had planned to wear a different shirt and it was already hanging on the door of her closet. Cassie disappeared inside and discarded the flannel shirt and T-shirt before pulling on the light purple button-down shirt.

Shelley jumped off her bed when she returned. "Much better. Now how do you smell?"

"I took a shower this morning."

"You know that's not what I meant."

"Honestly, Shelley. Do you think I'm incapable of presenting myself appropriately?"

"Look. Dillon and I have decided that we like her, and we don't want you to blow it." She walked into the bathroom and picked up the bottle of cologne.

Cassie darted out of the bedroom before Shelley could spray her more than once. "I don't want to smell like a brothel."

Shelley followed her back downstairs, and Cassie was pleased to see she had left the cologne in the bathroom.

Shelley crossed the room and stuck her nose into Cassie's neck. "Hmmm. Acceptable."

Cassie stepped away from her. "Stop that!"

"You have passed inspection. Now go."

"The boys want to go for a bike ride today. Please make them take a radio."

"Greg knows what he is doing, and Dillon brought shorts so he might go with them. Now go."

"If I'm too close to dinner time, I'll grab something to bring home with me. I'll call first, though, and see if you and Dillon want to stay."

"Fine. Now go."

* * *

Kathleen stared at the early morning sky through her bedroom window, her mind on Cassie. It had been almost two weeks since they had seen each other, and even though they had talked on the phone she still felt the distance between them. Trying to decide how she was supposed to act today was making her anxious and she closed her eyes, concentrating on their last physical connection.

Memories of Cassie's fingertips stroking her body made her stomach muscles tighten and her body arch with desire. She held the feeling for a moment before she collapsed back onto the bed and groaned, rolling onto her stomach. As much as her body craved release, she knew her own touch would not satisfy her needs. Would there be time to get Cassie alone today? Should she even try? Would Cassie want to?

All the times they had spoken on the phone, Cassie had not mentioned a need for Kathleen other than having her assist with Chase and Greg. Maybe she had simply been too worried about them, but what if she thought their weekend was a mistake? Or only a fling? Kathleen was not a stranger to flings, but she couldn't make herself think of Cassie that way.

She got out of bed and dressed in gym clothes, grabbing a breakfast bar on her way out the door. A workout would clear her head and rid her body of excess energy before her meeting with Cassie.

* * *

Tiffany was all smiles when Kathleen entered the suite. "So…she comes to visit today?"

"She's not coming to visit. She's coming to fill out paperwork for Chase."

"Don't forget the forms for Greg too," Joyce added, entering the office balancing a box of doughnuts.

"You've got to stop buying these." Kathleen pulled a glazed doughnut from the box and headed for her office. "You ruined everything I did at the gym this morning."

"Stop eating them then. They're for our visitors anyway," Joyce said as she pulled a doughnut from the box and followed Kathleen into her office. "Have you talked with Ms. Thomas about the girls yet?"

Kathleen sighed, dropping into her chair. Joyce had been harping at her all week to have that conversation, but Kathleen was afraid of Cassie's response. "Cassie's been very busy with Greg and Chase. What if she says she can't take the girls? They're going to be crushed."

"We'll deal with it. Find out today, so we know what we're facing."

Kathleen dropped her face into her hands, pulling her face away instantly at the feel of glazed icing on her cheek. She glared at Joyce as she crossed to the bathroom. She hadn't been able to find a female assistant to stay at Cassie's for the summer. She had a few more calls to make, and then she was out of ideas. She knew Cassie wouldn't even consider the girls without an assistant—especially with Chase and Greg already there.

An hour later, she hung up from her last attempt, and Tiffany plopped into the chair across from her. "No luck?"

"Why has this gotten so difficult? Never in the past did we have this much trouble finding kids willing to help out."

"Have you thought about helping?" Tiffany asked.

"Yes, Tiffany." Kathleen's tone showed her frustration. "I've been thinking about it constantly. Cassie isn't going to be willing to take the girls without an assistant."

"No, I mean *you* could do it. Be the assistant."

"What? No." Kathleen shook her head. "I have to be here."

"Why? Drive in one day a week if you need to, but really, the phone stuff could be done from anywhere."

"I don't think that would be a good idea."

"What would be a good idea?" Joyce asked, entering the office and sitting down beside Tiffany.

"No, it would *not* be a good idea," Kathleen corrected.

"Okay. What would *not* be a good idea?" Joyce countered.

"I suggested Kathleen be the assistant at Cassie's for the summer."

"Well." Joyce leaned forward. "That would work. Wouldn't it?"

"Yep." Tiffany agreed.

They both looked at Kathleen.

"I don't think…It's not…I can't…"

Joyce raised her eyebrows questioningly. "Maybe you should talk with Ms. Thomas about it when she arrives."

Kathleen looked at the clock on the wall. Ten minutes and she would see Cassie again. Would she hug her? Would she kiss her? Could she kiss her and then stop without touching her more? No. She definitely could not. One taste and she would be out of control.

The chime sounded on the office door, sending Tiffany down the hall at a sprint. Kathleen wanted to follow her. Wanted to run down the hall and jump into Cassie's arms. But instead she assured Joyce she would take care of everything. After Tiffany introduced Joyce to Cassie, they both left, leaving Kathleen alone with her.

Kathleen met her eyes as Cassie studied her. "It's really good to see you," Cassie finally said.

"It's good to see you too." Kathleen forced the words out. Seeing Cassie had awakened her body and she wrapped her legs around the chair to keep from rushing into Cassie's arms.

A rush of desire crossed Cassie's face before disappearing behind her stoic expression. She took a seat across from Kathleen. "Déjà vu? I feel like I've been here before." She smiled.

Taking a deep breath, Kathleen pulled a stack of paperwork from her desk drawer. "Let's start with the easy stuff first." She turned a few papers toward Cassie. "This is the foster paperwork for Greg and Chase. Since they're both under our care now, you won't have to fill out the background paperwork again. We have all that already on file."

"That makes things easier."

Kathleen slid the papers into a folder once Cassie had signed them. "This stack is to start the custody paperwork for Chase. I don't think there'll be any problems except his file shows that his birth mother has appeared every nine months or so to keep a claim on him. You won't be able to adopt him since she refuses to relinquish her parental rights, but permanent custody shouldn't be a problem."

Kathleen explained each group of papers and Cassie signed her name. When the stack was completed, Kathleen stood. She had to get the two of them out of her office quickly. Waiting to kiss Cassie was not going to be an option for much longer. She had tried not to stare at Cassie's lips while they worked, but her resistance was fading fast. "I think we need to get out of here."

"Okay."

"We can take my car." Kathleen led the way down the hall and out the main door without pausing. She heard Cassie offer a quick goodbye to Tiffany.

"Can we swing by my car to get the box for Greg's stuff?" Cassie asked.

"I brought a box too so unless you need to go to your car let's just head out."

Kathleen was on a mission; she hurried through the stairway door, not willing to wait for the elevator. Pulling open the driver's door of her black BMW, Kathleen saw Cassie hesitate. "Get in the car, Cassandra."

Cassie laughed and slid onto the leather seat. The doors were barely closed behind them when Kathleen turned in her seat and pulled Cassie to her. Their lips were inches apart, and Kathleen's pulse raced.

"Oh my," Cassie gasped.

Kathleen leaned forward until their lips touched and their tongues met. She hadn't forgotten the sweetness of Cassie's mouth, but the taste made her body burn with desire. Cassie's response was immediate; her fingers quickly found the buttons on Kathleen's shirt.

Kathleen grasped Cassie's hands in hers, stopping their progress. She sat up, putting distance between them. "I wasn't sure I was going to make it out of the office before that happened."

"I'm glad you did as this could have been a little embarrassing." Cassie's gaze drifted to the exposed flesh on Kathleen's chest. Her hand stroked the top of the black satin bra there, dipping under the material.

Kathleen dropped her head to the back of the seat and inhaled deeply. "We can't do this here." Her voice was hoarse and scratchy. "Nor do I want to." She lifted her head and met Cassie's hazy eyes. "Would you like to see my place?"

Cassie dropped her hand to her lap. "Yes, but can you leave those buttons undone for now?"

Kathleen smiled and started backing the car out of the parking space. "For now."

* * *

Cassie watched the traffic crawl past outside the car window and wondered why neither of them had been concerned about trying to cross town during the peak lunch hour. The silence between them was filled with sexual tension, and Cassie's gaze kept straying to Kathleen's open blouse. She wanted to run her fingers across her creamy white skin and feel the softness she had been dreaming about for two weeks, but something nagged at the back of her mind. She wanted more than an afternoon tryst. She wanted to talk about what was happening between them. She wanted to make plans for a future.

Of course, if they did talk Cassie knew there was a chance Kathleen wouldn't say the things she wanted to hear. She wasn't ready for things to end and forcing Kathleen to put words to their actions might drive her away. Maybe it was best to let their bodies do the talking for now. Cassie smiled to herself as they turned into a short drive with identical red brick townhouses lining both sides of the road. Kathleen pulled the car to a stop in front of a small colorful flower bed.

Cassie placed a hand on Kathleen's arm, stopping her from getting out of the car. "I don't…I mean…I'm not sure."

Kathleen touched her hand as she turned to look at her. "It's okay."

Cassie raised one eyebrow. The disappointment in Kathleen's voice was clear. "I want to talk, and if we go inside I don't think we will."

Kathleen sighed. "No, I can assure you we will not be talking."

Cassie wanted to get out of the car and wander through Kathleen's house, exploring her personal space, but she knew if she did she would be exploring every inch of Kathleen instead. A public restaurant would probably a good thing.

"Mexican or Italian?" Kathleen asked, starting the car.

"Somewhere quiet. I can eat anything."

* * *

Kathleen put the car in gear and backed out of the driveway. She felt a twinge of regret as her body roared its disapproval in the change of plans. All the hours Kathleen had spent thinking about Cassie over the last couple of weeks and now she had her here. She couldn't believe she was driving away. Cassie wanted to talk. And so did she. Sort of. She had never been close to considering sharing her life with someone, but from the moment she had seen Cassie she felt a connection unlike any she had ever experienced.

Kathleen slid her hand onto Cassie's thigh, feeling the muscles there tensing under her hand. "Italian it is then."

Smiling, Cassie placed a hand on top of Kathleen's to stop the caress. "Since only food is in the future some touching is not okay."

"Just for now."

"Yes, just for now."

Kathleen squeezed her hand, and neither spoke again until they reached the restaurant. There was nothing uncomfortable about the silence and the physical connection affirmed their emotional bond as well.

They pulled into a large parking lot packed with cars. Kathleen saw Cassie glance at the line of people extending from the tent overhang at the front door. As soon as Cassie had said she was visiting, Kathleen knew where she wanted to take her for lunch or dinner, depending on how their reunion turned out. She had called Antoine without a specific time, and he assured her it would be fine. She knew he would also have understood, as well, if Cassie had chosen Mexican instead.

Kathleen led her toward the rear of the restaurant, dialing a number from memory as she walked. "We're here."

They stepped up to a door marked Deliveries, which opened into a large kitchen buzzing with activity. A tall woman dressed in a black business suit smiled at them.

"Follow me."

As she led them through the kitchen, a short man in a chef's hat looked up from the creation on the plate in front of him and grinned at Kathleen.

"So good of you to join us."

Kathleen leaned toward him as he kissed her cheek. "Thank you, Antoine, for making space for us."

"There is always space. I'll be up to visit later."

Kathleen was not offended by his dismissal. She hated interrupting him in the kitchen, so she pulled Cassie toward the woman who had paused at a staircase. They followed her up two flights before she turned and led them into a small room with floor-to-ceiling windows covering one side. Cassie was pulled toward the view overlooking the city; as she moved along the window she could see the blue of the Gulf of Mexico between the buildings.

The woman held out a chair for Kathleen.

"Thank you, Maureen."

And then she held out Cassie's chair.

"Yes, thank you." Cassie pulled her eyes from the view and took the offered seat.

"Roberto will be up shortly with your menu and drinks. What would you like?"

"Sweet tea," Kathleen said, looking at Cassie.

"Yes, sweet tea would be fine."

Maureen turned and walked swiftly from the room.

Cassie looked around the room again and smiled at Kathleen. "Impressive."

"I'm glad you think so. I've never requested one of these rooms before."

"There are more than one?"

"Yes, there are six single dining rooms on this floor. The middle floor is for groups and then general dining is on the first floor."

"Wow. So, how did we end up with a private dining area?"

"I called yesterday when you told me you were coming."

Cassie raised an eyebrow. "Okay, but that's not really what I meant. Clearly you're well liked here, but yet you've never requested one of these rooms."

Roberto arrived with their drinks and menus. Once he placed them on the table, he stepped discreetly to one side of the room and placed his arms behind his back. Clearly he was content to stand silently until they were ready to order. The menu was small and listed all the usual Italian dishes. Kathleen didn't open her menu, but she watched as Cassie's eyes browsed the selections.

Cassie glanced at Roberto and then at Kathleen. "I'm feeling rushed. I guess you know what you want?"

"I do know what I want, but I am going to settle for the house special."

"Hmmm. What is that?" Cassie asked.

"You."

This time Cassie couldn't ignore her and smiled, glancing at Roberto. "And the house special is?"

"A small plate of spaghetti and a wonderful house salad."

"That sounds great."

"You can get any pasta in place of the spaghetti if you would like," Roberto said, approaching the table at Kathleen's nod.

"Okay." Cassie smiled at him. "How about lasagna?"

"Excellent choice." He collected their menus and strode out of the room.

"Back to my question."

Kathleen took a sip of her iced tea before answering. "Antoine's father and grandfather owned this restaurant before they passed it to him. When I first moved to Pensacola, a friend brought me here for dinner, and I started picking up orders to take home several times a week. The food was awesome, but their business was very slow. One night I stopped without calling ahead and was waiting for my order to go. I started talking to Maureen and she expressed her concerns about the business. So I looked them up online and couldn't find a website." Kathleen paused to take another sip of tea. "I created a one and showed it to them. They loved it."

"So, you helped them get their business back."

"They helped me too. They were my first website design client. Selling this place was easy. Once I found out about the private rooms, I was able to highlight that feature. You'd be surprised how many people want to dine in privacy and are willing to pay for it."

"That's a very cool story, and this place is awesome."

"I think so too. That's why I wanted to bring you here."

Cassie frowned. "But you gave me the choice of Mexican food too."

"You always have a choice, Cassie. I'm not going to make decisions for you." Kathleen smiled, watching Cassie's reaction to her words.

"And what if I choose you."

"I'd be very happy with that choice."

CHAPTER TWENTY-EIGHT

Lunch was enjoyable though later Cassie barely remembered what she had eaten. Kathleen was relaxed, and they had put aside the serious issues, joking and laughing through three courses. Cassie was shocked when they returned to the car and she saw the clock on the dash. Three hours had passed and she felt like they had just arrived. Though they hadn't talked about where their relationship was going, Kathleen had made it clear she was experiencing all the same feelings. Cassie was also pleased to know everything was still a go for the brat pack's arrival on Friday. Though the assistant position still seemed unresolved, Cassie was confident Kathleen would work something out.

Greg's former foster home was just outside the city and with traffic it took them almost thirty minutes to get there. The modest white stucco house was in a cul-de-sac with a small front yard. Brenda Shaw met them at the door and showed them to Greg's room. She was pleasant and seemed happy that Greg had found a home.

"That was easy," Cassie said as they followed the sidewalk back to the car.

Kathleen remained silent until they closed their doors. "What did you expect?"

Cassie could hear the edge in Kathleen's voice. "I didn't mean to be critical. It's only that Greg has lived here for at least six months and she didn't even express an interest in saying goodbye to him."

"Believe it or not, but this is one of our best placement homes. Brenda and Dale take in about twenty kids a year."

"Like I said, I wasn't trying to be critical. I was surprised, that's all."

"If they weren't able to emotionally detach so easily, we wouldn't be able to move so many kids through their home. Brenda told me once that she keeps a folder on each kid. Where they came from and where they went, but she doesn't hold on to them emotionally. It would wear her down and she wouldn't be able to provide support for the next kid coming in."

"They sound like good people."

"Yes, they are, and unfortunately we have to use them a lot," Kathleen said softly as she pulled behind Cassie's car, which was parked on the street across from the coffee shop outside Fosters.

"I think I'll grab a cup of coffee for the drive home." Cassie nodded toward Java Heads.

"I'll walk with you."

The early evening rush was in full swing, and it was impossible to talk over the noise in the small shop. Each time Cassie glanced at Kathleen their eyes met and Cassie felt herself fall a little more. The smile on Kathleen's lips covered her entire face and Cassie couldn't help but return it.

* * *

Kathleen tried to soak up the view of Cassie in her dark jeans and a button-down shirt opened enough to reveal her deep tan. She had known when they left her townhouse earlier that she would take the chaperone position at Cassie's for the summer. How could she not? She longed to spend more time with Cassie, and this would give her the perfect opportunity.

She wanted to tell Cassie, but part of her wanted to see the look of surprise on her face when she arrived. When they had discussed the brat pack during lunch, Kathleen had been evasive concerning who had been selected for the assistant position. Luckily, Cassie trusted her to take care of the situation.

When they finally received their orders, they carried their cups back outside and slowly walked toward the car. Cassie was quiet, and Kathleen felt the distance growing between them again.

"I'll see you on Friday." Kathleen had readily accepted Cassie's offer to spend the weekend and help the brat pack settle in.

Cassie opened her car door and slid in. Before she could close the door, Kathleen leaned in and kissed her. She had planned to keep it quick, but Cassie's lips responded and she found herself quickly wanting more. She forced herself to pull back and stand.

"Really? Right here on the street?" Cassie laughed. Her face flushed.

"What can I say? I'm feeling bold today."

Cassie shook her head. "I'm sorry I'm leaving then."

Kathleen closed the car door and moved back to the sidewalk. She pressed her fingers to her lips and blew Cassie a kiss before heading down the street to Fosters.

* * *

Kathleen returned to her office, having slipped through the lobby while Tiffany was on the phone. She sipped her tea and contemplated her decision. She was unable to come up with a down side to returning to Cassie's farm for the next two months. Her bond with the brat pack made her eager to spend some quality time with them. She was truly looking forward to it.

Joyce stood in her doorway and Kathleen looked up, meeting her smile.

"You made a decision?"

"Yes, I want to go with the girls."

Joyce smiled. "I think that's a great idea. Let's talk every week, and we can decide if you need to come into the office or not."

"At least for the weekly staff meetings, right?"

"Let's say every other week. No need for you to have to run back and forth too much." Joyce turned to exit and then turned back. "But you'll need to keep working. I'll need those month-end reports and the end of quarter by July fifteenth."

"No problem. I'm sure I'll need something to occupy my day," she said sarcastically to Joyce's disappearing back.

Kathleen was thrilled with her decision. She had just agreed to spend the summer with a very intriguing woman. One that she found very attractive and had a strong desire to know better. It was a dream come true. Standing, she considered following Joyce. Should she tell her she had already slept with Cassie? Would it affect Joyce's agreement to allow her to stay with Cassie and the brat pack?

No. She could handle this. Even though all of those things were true about her interest in Cassie, she wasn't going to be hanging all over her all summer. She would be professional, keeping an appropriate distance from Cassie especially when the girls were around. Joyce had never questioned her choices or decisions and there wasn't any reason for Kathleen to think now would be any different. She would do the job she had been assigned and no one had to know how much pleasure it gave her to have Cassie nearby.

* * *

Cassie called Shelley to let her know it would be almost seven when she arrived home. Dillon and the boys were at Mac's picking up hot dogs, and Shelley was making potato salad. Shelley wanted details and Cassie was happy to replay her afternoon.

Shelley sighed. "I cannot believe you turned her down."

"I didn't turn her down. I just didn't want to fall into bed again. Well, okay I did want to, but I really like her and I don't want us to be only about that."

"Wow. I can't believe you said that on your own with no prompting. Dillon said it would be weeks if not months before you admitted how much you really liked her."

Cassie laughed. "Well, Dillon was wrong. I do like her. I love the way she laughs and the way her face screws up when she's thinking."

"So, where did you leave things with her?"

"She's coming up on Friday and hopefully will spend the weekend to help the girls get settled."

"I hear the boys coming back so we'll talk more when you get here. Oh, wait a minute. Someone wants to talk with you."

"We rode bikes today!" Chase gulped a breath. "We went into the forest and Mr. Dillon went with us. It was awesome!"

"That sounds like fun."

"It was. Maybe next time you can go with us. We went through a creek and there were some deer in the field. Greg saw a squirrel, but he moved too fast for me to see him too."

Cassie laughed. "Okay, Chase. I look forward to hearing all about it when I get home."

Cassie could hear him still talking as Shelley took the phone from him.

"Bye, Cass," Shelley said. "We'll see you when you get here."

Cassie touched the disconnect button on her steering wheel and was surprised to see she only had about thirty minutes left on her drive. She laughed as she thought about Chase and how excited he got about everything. He was such a pleasure to be around. It was hard to understand why some kids ended up in foster care. She remembered what Greg had said about Chase's mother returning often enough to screw up anything permanent for Chase. It sounded cruel even to her own ears, but she hoped she wouldn't return again.

Cassie glanced across her property as she approached the gate. She glanced right taking in the pasture and doing a quick count on the horses and goats. To the left the view of the lake and the cabins behind it were glowing in the dusky light. She circled the office and pulled under the carport.

Chase met her at the car with Zoey and Pandy. "The dogs went with us today. They had fun too. They even swam in the creek!"

Cassie pulled him into a quick hug, and his little arms squeezed her waist. "I missed you today. Did you have lots of fun?"

"I had lots of fun!"

Chase led the way back into the house with both dogs at his heels. Dillon, Shelley and Greg sat at the table, and Cassie grabbed a plate before sitting down with them. After a few minutes of Chase dominating all talk with stories of his day, Dillon suggested a game of catch outside. Greg grabbed a couple of balls, mitts and a bat before joining Dillon and Chase in the backyard.

Cassie was focused on watching them throw the ball around and realized Shelley was watching them as well.

"Nice view, right?" Cassie asked.

Shelley put a hand to her heart. "Touching."

They both laughed.

"Dillon is going to be a great dad." Cassie watched the emotions flutter across Shelley's face.

"I'm not ready to have kids yet."

"That's okay, Shelley. Dillon has plenty of kids to play with here now and when you are ready he will be too."

Shelley sighed. "Dillon understands I want a career but I don't want it to be at the cost of a family."

"You and Dillon are young. You have plenty of time to do both. And in the meantime Dillon will be a surrogate father to all of my children." Cassie opened her arms dramatically, making them both laugh again.

They watched Dillon give instructions to Chase on holding the bat. When Chase finally made contact with the ball on his own, she and Shelley cheered so loudly the boys could hear them outside.

Clearing the table, Shelley looked thoughtfully at Cassie. "You know. When the girls get here we would have enough to make our own team."

"Sounds great. Maybe we should get some practice in."

They put the leftovers in the refrigerator before grabbing mitts from the supply closet and joining the game. They played until Chase became distracted with lightning bugs and he convinced Greg to help him catch them. Dillon, Shelley and Cassie sat on the porch and watched them run all over the yard. The dogs chased too for a while and then gave up, finding a spot at Cassie's feet.

"So hot babe comes back on Friday?" Dillon said with a wink at Cassie.

Cassie groaned. "Please don't call her that."

Shelley laughed, swatting him on the shoulder. "We should go home before you find yourself in the doghouse."

"Thanks, guys, for taking care of the boys today. I had a wonderful day and it was nice to not have to rush home."

"It was our pleasure," Shelley said, pushing Dillon through the back door and into the house.

Cassie turned to Chase and Greg. "Chase. Time to shower."

Both boys came running and followed her into the house. Chase yelled his goodbyes to Dillon and Shelley before disappearing down the hall.

With the house quiet, Cassie and Greg sat in the living room and Greg recapped their day. Wasn't much to tell that Chase hadn't already mentioned, but Cassie enjoyed hearing that Greg had enjoyed the outing too. She told him about the restaurant Kathleen had taken her to for lunch.

"I look forward to meeting her on Friday."

"She's looking forward to meeting you and Chase too."

Greg smiled. "Dillon says she is important to you so Chase and I should be on our best behavior."

Cassie rolled her eyes. "That was nice of Dillon."

"He also says she did all the work to keep Chase here too. I really appreciate that."

"I'm sure she would appreciate hearing that from you."

Chase came dancing down the hall with his pajamas stuck to his body. Cassie and Greg roared with laughter.

Cassie stopped him in front of her. "Did you use a towel to dry off?"

"I did."

Cassie turned him around and pulled the wet pajama top away from his skin. She looked at Greg.

"Let's go work that towel again, buddy. Then we will find you some dry clothes to put on."

Cassie called goodnight to them as they disappeared down the hall. She turned off the main lights, leaving a small one on in the kitchen, and then locked all the doors before heading upstairs with the dogs.

As she settled into bed her hand slid under her pillow and wrapped around the soft material of Kathleen's bra. She sighed, sinking into a deep sleep.

CHAPTER TWENTY-NINE

Thursday passed in a blur for Cassie. She got caught up on paperwork in preparation for the brat pack's arrival. Chase was given the task of checking on all the guests and securing any housekeeping requests. He willingly tackled this assignment because it meant he got to drive the golf cart. He assured Cassie when he returned that everyone was very happy and there were no requests.

Cassie left the phone with Dillon and took Chase to lunch before their haircut appointments. They returned in time to take back the phone so Dillon and Greg could take the family from Cabin Four horseback riding. Turning the ringer volume to maximum, Cassie left it securely at the edge of the lake and spent the afternoon teaching Chase how to paddle a canoe. When the dogs swam out to join them, Chase begged her to let them in, and Cassie pulled each one by their scruff into the little canoe. After a few minutes, though, the dogs tired of being in the boat and jumped over the side—tipping Cassie and Chase into the water.

After much spluttering, Cassie managed to pull the canoe back to shore with Chase hanging off one end. She flopped onto her back as she collapsed on the shore. Chase removed his lifejacket and dropped down beside her.

After a few minutes, he rolled toward her. "That was fun."

"Yes, well, boating is meant to be in a boat, not in the water."

"Yeah." He sighed dramatically. "But it was still fun."

She laughed and grabbed him by the waist, pulling him to his feet. "Let's change out of these wet clothes and decide what to have for dinner. Greg will be returning soon."

"Okay."

They sloshed back toward the house.

"Ms. Cassie?"

"Yes, Chase." She looked down at him.

"I'd like to go on a horseback ride too." He hesitated. "Not today but maybe one day."

"I think we can do that. One day, but not tomorrow."

Chase wrinkled his nose. "The girls come tomorrow."

Cassie hugged him. "You're going to like these girls."

"I don't like any girls." Chase's face fell. "No, wait. I like you and Ms. Shelley. But that's it. No other girls."

Cassie smiled at him. "Okay, but you're still going to be a proper gentleman and help the girls get settled tomorrow, right?"

"Absolutely. Greg told me what to do. We carry their bags and hold the door."

Cassie laughed and held the door open for him to enter the house. "Strip in the laundry room and then shower."

Cassie headed up the stairs to her bathroom.

CHAPTER THIRTY

Friday morning, Cassie opened her eyes to find Greg sneaking into her room. Chase was slung over his shoulder, giggling. She groaned and looked at the clock. Six fifteen.

"What are you guys doing?" she asked, covering her head with a pillow.

"We're ready to start the day!" Chase bounced on the bottom of the bed where Greg had tossed him.

"Okay. I'm up. Leave and I'll be down after I shower."

Chase slid off the bed and bolted out the door.

"Hmmm…what's this?"

Cassie pulled the pillow off her head and looked at the bra Greg was daintily holding with a finger. Cassie felt her face turn red as Greg laughed and tossed the bra back onto her bed.

"Out!" Cassie pointed toward the door.

"It sure doesn't look like something you'd wear," Greg said, backing toward the door with a huge grin on his face.

"Out!" Cassie threw a pillow at him. Cassie smiled as Greg's back disappeared down the hallway. She couldn't imagine Greg doing anything like that last summer. He would never have even walked into her bedroom. It made her feel good to know that Greg was comfortable here and with her. She tucked the bra under her pillow and stood. Her family was waiting.

* * *

Thirty minutes later, she joined the boys in the kitchen. Greg was stirring pancake mix in a huge bowl.

"Are we feeding an army?"

"I called Dillon. He and Shelley are going to join us. This is a big day."

Cassie smiled at him. "Bacon or sausage then."

"Bacon!" Chase yelled from his observation seat at the counter.

"Bacon it is." Cassie reached over and tousled his hair.

They were setting everything on the table when Dillon and Shelley arrived.

"Happy morning!" Dillon called as he burst through the door.

Shelley gave Cassie a quick hug. "Are you ready for today?"

"Ready for them to be here. The waiting is killer."

"What is their estimated arrival time?" Dillon asked.

"Kathleen said she'd call when they left Pensacola. She guessed it would be late afternoon."

"And the supervisor?"

Cassie shrugged. "No idea. I guess we'll find out when they get here."

Dillon clapped his hands. "Okay, then. We should have just enough time to get them settled in before we fire up the grill for the cookout."

Greg added the last plate of pancakes to the table. "Let's eat."

"Who else is coming?" Shelley asked, laughing as a knock sounded at the door.

Cassie opened the front door to a smiling Pete and Rory. "Come in, guys."

"No, that's okay." Rory handed her a basket of muffins and croissants. "We made you some fresh baked goodies on your last day of freedom."

"Seriously, come in. We're just sitting down to breakfast and you should meet Chase."

"Hey, Pete, Rory," Dillon called as he stuffed a bite of pancake in his mouth.

"You remember Greg from last summer, right?" Cassie looked at Pete and Rory as they nodded. "This is his brother, Chase. They're both living here now."

Greg stood and shook hands with both men. Chase followed his brother's lead, shaking their hands too.

"Greg made enough for an army, so please join us." Shelley motioned at the empty chairs around the table.

Cassie set the basket of muffins and croissants in the center of the table and quickly withdrew her hand as Dillon and Greg both reached for a blueberry muffin.

Cassie glanced around the table as multiple conversations went on around her. She watched contentedly as Chase imitated Greg's actions while he ate; he was settling in nicely. As excited as everyone was for the brat pack to arrive, Cassie's biggest concern was that everyone feel welcome. She turned her attention back to Shelley, discussing with her the most important rules for Cassie to go over with the girls when they arrived. The specifics of the role the supervisor would have couldn't be decided until everyone arrived. Male or female, their first responsibility, of course, would be monitoring the girls.

Dillon looked at his watch and jumped to his feet. "The horses are going to stampede if we don't feed them."

Chase laughed and followed Dillon and Greg out the door.

"No, don't worry, boys." Shelley laughed as the door slammed shut behind them. "We'll take care of the dishes."

"What's the rush, Shelley? Let's grab a cup of coffee and sit here for a while longer," Cassie suggested.

"I guess we don't really have anything pressing to do. I'll check messages real quick if you make me a cup too."

"Guys, cup of coffee?" Cassie motioned toward the office where the Keurig machine waited.

"Sure," Rory said and Pete nodded too. "Believe it or not, we're packed already except for what we'll need today."

Shelley checked email and voice mail messages but returned quickly. Cassie saw Chase run by with Pandy and Zoey on his heels. She hurried to the door but stepped back inside when Greg waved to her from the barn.

"What's going on?" Shelley asked.

"Chase is checking the cabins for housekeeping tags. Greg is making him do it on foot."

Shelley, Pete and Rory joined her at the window, and they watched Chase make his way around the lake.

"That's a long way for those little legs." Rory shook his head.

"It's Dillon's way of keeping the kids calm around the horses." Cassie smiled at Shelley. "Does he make you run around the house?"

Shelley laughed.

"Oh, I know this game." Pete laughed too. "I saw Greg tying ribbons on the mailbox last year."

"Yep, that would be Dillon's game."

Rory looked back and forth between them all. "I think I'm lost?"

"Let's go sit and we'll explain the ribbon game to you." Shelley laughed, leading the way back into the house.

When the horses were released, Dillon and the boys came back to the house. Dillon and Greg grabbed coffee before joining everyone back at the table. Chase roamed the backyard with the dogs before collapsing onto the couch to watch cartoons.

Cassie left the room when her cell phone rang.

"Hello."

"Hey, Cassie. We're on our way. We have one more stop after lunch, but we should arrive around two thirty."

"Things are ready here. The way Dillon is pacing you would think Shelley was about to give birth."

Kathleen laughed. "Quadruplets. No thanks."

Cassie laughed too. "See you soon."

Everyone looked at her expectantly when she walked back into the room. "Two thirty."

Pete and Rory headed off to the café for their last lunch before they headed home tomorrow. Dillon and Greg mumbled something about horses and goats and took off for the barn. Shelley and Cassie made several sandwiches and Shelley took them out to Dillon and Greg. Chase ate at the counter before he darted off in his bathing suit. His new friends would be checking out tomorrow, and he wanted to play with them before they left. Cassie pulled a chair into the shade of the barn where she could listen to Shelley and the boys while watching Chase play.

She contemplated the possibility of convincing Kathleen to stay in her room tonight instead of one of the empty cabins. Or maybe she could stay with her in the cabin. There would be a chaperone in the house with the kids. No, that probably wouldn't be a good idea, Cassie thought. That wasn't the kind of statement she wanted to make in front of the girls. She closed her eyes and leaned her head back against the barn wall. She jumped when Shelley dropped into the chair beside her.

"Sleeping on the job?"

Cassie laughed. "I think I might have been."

"Or maybe just daydreaming about the bombshell who will be returning today."

Cassie smiled. "I did have some thoughts about that too."

CHAPTER THIRTY-ONE

Cassie and Shelley looked up as Kathleen's car came into sight. A white van followed close behind her.

"Oh." Cassie sighed. "That's them."

"Places, everyone," Shelley called into the barn.

They laughed when Dillon responded with, "da plane, da plane," imitating an '80s television show.

Cassie met Kathleen at her car as soon as the door opened. She pulled her into her arms for a quick hug.

Greg and Dillon moved to the back of the van and began unloading suitcases. Chase stood with them, dripping water everywhere.

"Chase. Shower." Cassie pointed to the house.

"I'm sorry. I didn't know it was time."

"It's okay. Shower quick and then come back out."

Cassie looked up to see an interested face at the van window watching as Chase bolted inside the house. The dark eyes took in her surroundings with no sign of apprehension. Her cheeks were still plump with baby fat, and Cassie was sure she was looking at Dani, the youngest of the group. Cassie smiled at her before joining Kathleen to greet the girls as they exited the van.

Cassie did a quick appraisal of each, trying hard to keep a neutral look on her face. First out of the van was a short, brown-haired girl dressed in clothes three times her size.

"Cassie, this is Kaitlyn," Kathleen said before pulling the young girl into a hug.

Kaitlyn flung her backpack onto her back and pulled her jeans back up to barely below her waist before giving Kathleen a one-armed hug. She was clearly too cool for hugging but not bold enough to say no. She shyly stepped to the side, making room for the next member of the brat pack.

Attitude came next. Judging from her pierced eyebrow and tongue, this had to be Morgan, the oldest of the group at sixteen. Kathleen attempted to hug her too but was given a look before she circled the group to join Kaitlyn.

Kathleen laughed and shook her finger at the girl. "I will hug you later, Morgan. Just accept it."

Morgan rolled her eyes, but Cassie saw a slight smile cross her lips.

The next girl was the tallest of the group. She ducked her shaved head as she exited the van and pulled Kathleen into a death grip.

"This is Shauna." Kathleen rubbed her hand back and forth across Shauna's barely visible hair.

Dani bounded out of the van and rubbed Shauna's head too. "For luck."

Shauna glared at her as she stepped away from Kathleen. In a deep, soft voice that Cassie could barely hear, she said, "It's Shaun. Please don't call me Shauna."

Kathleen smiled at her. "I love the name Shauna."

"Fine." Shaun turned toward Cassie and stuck out her hand. "Shaun."

"It's nice to meet you, Shaun. I'm Cassie." Cassie nodded to each girl and then turned to the group behind her. "This is Dillon and his wife, Shelley. Dillon is here every day through the week and Shelley is here every other day. Feel free to go to either of them with questions or for assistance." She put her arm around Greg. "This is Greg. He lives here with his brother, Chase." As if on cue, Chase bolted from the house, jumping all three stairs and landing beside Cassie. His shirt, stuck to his wet skin, was tucked into navy shorts and his hair was brushed straight back. Cassie had to look away to keep from laughing at him. She placed a hand on his shoulder. "This is Chase."

Dillon and Shelley moved forward and began talking to the girls. The van driver secured the doors and gave a wave before driving off. Cassie glanced around for anyone she may have overlooked and then raised her eyebrows questioningly at Kathleen.

Stepping closer to Cassie, Kathleen said softly, "You're stuck with me."

Cassie grinned.

Kathleen touched her cheek. Cassie was surprised as a look of sadness crossed Kathleen's face before she turned away to say hello to Shelley.

"Wait a minute," Dillon called over the noise of the group. "The van left and there's no assistant."

"Yes, there is." Cassie gave him a huge grin.

Dillon looked from Cassie to Kathleen to Shelley and then over the kids. His eyes grew large as he focused back on Kathleen. "You?"

Kathleen nodded.

"Well, that's great!" He gave Kathleen a hug. "Let's get you all moved in."

Cassie led the group into the living room and stopped, giving everyone a chance to look around. "Living room, kitchen, laundry room and stairs." She pointed to each location. She turned to address the girls, making eye contact with each one. "There are two bedrooms upstairs for the four of you. One of the bedrooms joins the bathroom that you'll all share. Can you decide who gets that room among you or do we need to flip a coin?"

Dani spoke up first. "Morgan."

The other two girls nodded in agreement.

Cassie looked at Morgan. "Who do you want to share your room with you?"

Morgan looked at each girl. "Shaun."

"Is that okay with you, Shaun?" Cassie asked. When Shaun nodded, Cassie continued. "Morgan and Shaun, your room is on the left. Kaitlyn and Dani, you're on the right. The back two bedrooms are mine and Kathleen's. Go check out your rooms and we'll help bring your luggage up."

The girls took off up the stairs, and everyone else went back outside to carry in luggage. When all the luggage was in the hallway upstairs, Cassie left them to do their unpacking, asking them to return to the living room when they had finished.

Dillon and Greg took Chase and went outside to finish whatever they had been working on and to start the preparations for the cookout. Shelley headed to Mac's to pick up the main course. Cassie fell into the recliner, relieved to have the girls finally here. She hoped her anxiety level would return to normal now. She took advantage of the few moments of quiet to assess Kathleen's reaction when they touched outside. She hoped Kathleen would come down soon and they would have a chance to talk in private.

Cassie could hear the girls running back and forth between the rooms with lots of laughter. After listening for several minutes, she decided to join them. She found Kathleen sitting on Morgan's bed, while Dani ran back and forth between the rooms, carrying on conversations in both of them.

"May I?" Cassie asked Shaun as she nodded to her bed.

"Sure." Shaun turned back to the closet to hang her shirts.

Cassie looked across the room at Kathleen. "How's things going up here?"

Kathleen smiled and then looked away. "Morgan would like something vegetarian for dinner. Is it too late to make that request?"

Cassie pulled her cell phone from her pocket and dialed Shelley. "Are there any other requests while I have Shelley on the phone?"

"Dani, Kaitlyn," Kathleen called. "Any special requests for dinner?" she asked as both girls came into the room.

"Steak, burger, hot dogs, chicken or a mushroom?" Cassie added.

"Burger with no bun." Dani danced out of the room.

"Chicken?" Kaitlyn asked. "I don't want to be difficult, though, so I can eat anything."

Cassie looked at Shaun.

"A burger is fine with me too."

"Are you there, Shell?" Cassie asked into the phone.

"I think I heard all that," Shelley said. "Burgers and chicken, right?"

"And a mushroom," Cassie added.

"Chase and Greg said burgers too. What about you and Kathleen?"

Cassie looked at Kathleen and raised her eyebrows.

"I've been craving a steak since I was here last."

"Steak for both of us," Cassie said into the phone.

"That's perfect. I had ordered ten steaks when I called on Wednesday. I hope two pounds of burgers and one of chicken will be enough."

"Go ahead and grab two pounds of chicken. We can grill it all and eat it over the weekend. I have a pack of hot dogs in the fridge if we run out of burgers too." Cassie answered, only half-listening to Shelley's response as the conversation resumed around her.

"When were you here?" Shaun asked, looking at Kathleen.

Kathleen glanced at Cassie, then quickly looked away. "I came up a couple weeks ago to check things out for you guys." She continued before the girls could ask any questions. "I stayed in one of the cabins. You guys are going to love it here."

Morgan grinned. "She didn't ask where you stayed, Ms. K. Did you, Shaun?"

"Nope. Gotta keep those guilty feelings at bay." Shaun laughed and exchanged glances with Morgan.

"Is everyone ready to go?" Kathleen asked, standing. She glanced at Cassie for assistance.

"Hold on. I want to talk with everyone first."

Dani and Kaitlyn sat on Shaun's bed and Kathleen sat back down on Morgan's bed with Morgan. Shaun turned from the closet and Cassie motioned to the bed beside Dani.

Cassie gave a small cough and avoided looking at Kathleen. "We have very few rules here, but I do expect you to respect each other. That means stay out of each other's personal space and rooms without invitation. It also expands to the animals." She looked at each girl directly. "Follow any directions given by one of us four adults or Greg. Never take out your anger or frustration on the animals or hurt them for any reason. Everyone understand?"

After receiving a nod of agreement from each girl, Cassie led the way back downstairs. She stopped at the foot of the stairs and turned toward the girls. "There's one more thing." She saw Morgan roll her eyes at Shaun, and she hesitated. Kathleen had seen the display as well and swatted Morgan in the back of the head. Cassie laughed and continued. "If you leave the house, there's a white board beside the refrigerator where you need to log out. If you want to take a walk or a bike ride, please check out a radio to carry with you. Next week after you get used to things, we'll make a chore list, but for the next couple of days you are free to do whatever you want. We're all busy here, so please don't make me have to track you down. I'll also log my movements and I'll have a radio with me. If I am not in the house or office, my location will be on the board. Cool?"

"Cool," Dani responded. Cassie was really starting to like her enthusiasm.

"Thank you, Dani." She looked at the other girls until each one nodded.

Cassie turned, leading the way into the office. She gave them a quick tour before heading outside where she pointed out the cabins, giving a short detail of each. They circled through the barn and Cassie introduced them to the goats and horses.

* * *

"I'm going back into the house to make the salads for dinner." Cassie looked at all the girls and Kathleen. "Feel free to join me, hang out with Dillon or just do your own thing." Cassie smiled at each of them. When she got to the porch, she stopped to see what the girls were doing. Kathleen and Kaitlyn were following her into the house, and Dani had joined Chase at the fence to watch the goats. Morgan and Shaun were not moving.

"Don't worry about them." Kathleen held the door open for Cassie and Kaitlyn. "They'll take a little longer than the rest to settle in." She put her arm around Kaitlyn. "Unlike this one."

Cassie pulled tomatoes and cucumbers out of the refrigerator and some onions out of the pantry. After dicing them, she put them in a bowl and added a ranch dressing mix. Kathleen washed lettuce and spinach, adding carrots to make a large salad.

Kaitlyn slid onto a barstool and watched Cassie and Kathleen move around the kitchen. "You guys act like you've worked together before."

Cassie glanced at Kathleen and her heart gave a little tug as Kathleen glanced away.

"So what do you think of this place, Kaitlyn?" Kathleen asked, turning her back to Cassie.

"It's really cool so far. What kind of chores are we going to have to do?" She looked at Cassie.

"I've never had this many kids at one time, so there won't be many. On Sunday evening after dinner we'll all sit down with the white board and go over everything that has to be done each day. Everyone can pick at least one task to be responsible for."

"Like what?"

Chase barged into the house with Zoey and Pandy on his heels. He looked at the clock and then at Cassie. "Can I feed them early?"

"I think that's a great idea, Chase." She looked back at Kaitlyn. "Like feeding the animals, gathering trash, pulling housekeeping tags from the cabin doors and cooking."

"I can cook." Kaitlyn smiled.

"I can't." Chase climbed on a barstool beside Kaitlyn after feeding the dogs.

She smiled at him. "I can teach you."

"Okay." He smiled back at her. "I can teach you to drive the golf cart."

As they sealed the deal with a handshake, Cassie and Kathleen exchanged smiles. Then Kathleen looked away again. Cassie's heart sank. Her initial excitement at having Kathleen here was fading fast. Clearly there was something going on, but she'd have to wait until she could get Kathleen alone to find out what it was.

Cassie heard Shelley return so she grabbed one salad and asked Kaitlyn to grab the other one. As they headed out the door, she heard Kathleen talking to Chase about living on the farm. It had taken Chase only a few moments to warm up to her, and Cassie could hear him starting to replay every detail of the last week.

Greg and Dillon were unloading Shelley's car when Cassie reached the picnic table. She unpacked the bags and began pulling meat out of them. The grill was large enough for everything, so she strategically placed items where they would cook faster or slower depending on the meat. Shelley disappeared into the house and returned with seasonings and dressing.

As the guests began to venture down, Shelley asked how they wanted their steak cooked and then introduced them to everyone. Soon all the guests but the couple in Cabin One were present. Cassie sent Chase and Dani to knock on their door.

"Be polite. They don't have to join us if they don't want to." Cassie watched them walk toward Cabin One. They were quite the pair. Chase, still in his dressier clothes, was a couple of inches shorter than Dani, and she had a tomboy strut that made her look tougher. Cassie smiled as Zoey and Pandy padded along behind them.

They put the youngest kids' table close to but not connected to the adults. The four girls claimed the end table to themselves but were quickly joined by Shelley and Pete. After helping the kids get their plates fixed, Kathleen claimed a spot at the end of the adjoining table beside Shelley. Cassie was last to find a spot after all the meat was off the grill. She was pleased to see that a seat had been left for her beside Kathleen.

Cassie took the long way around the kids' table to remind Chase not to feed the dogs any table food, then sat down beside Kathleen. Though Kathleen had seemed distant since she had arrived, she did not move away when their legs touched under the table. Cassie was confused by the mixed signals but pleased to have the contact. They ate silently, listening to the conversations around them.

When Dillon and Greg finished eating, they pulled a volleyball net from the shed and began setting it up. Cassie pulled out lawn chairs for the guests who didn't want to play. Greg picked Cassie for his team. Luckily it wasn't an intense game—all the smaller kids wanted to play too—because her head was fuzzy from being close to Kathleen throughout the meal. It took a couple punches from Dillon under the net for her to get in the game, but eventually she did, even managing to work up a sweat. They played until dark and then Dillon started the bonfire. Shelley took care of marshmallow duties, and Cassie was free to rest. She sat on the ground away from the fire.

Kathleen sat quietly beside her. Today, she was dressed in her own jeans that hugged her hips and Cassie was surprised to see hiking boots on her feet. Taking advantage of the first opportunity they had to speak alone, Cassie glanced at her and smiled. "I've missed you."

Kathleen smiled back. "It's been a long time since Wednesday."

"No," Cassie said softly. "I've missed you being here."

"Oh."

Chase crawled in between them with a burnt marshmallow stuck to his fingers.

"Where are you going with that marshmallow?" Cassie asked him.

"I'm going to eat it." He stuffed the marshmallow into his mouth. After a few minutes, he sighed loudly. "Morgan is a bully."

"Why do you say that?" Kathleen asked, looking at Cassie over his head.

"She said I couldn't have any more marshmallows."

"Do you know why she said that?" Kathleen spoke before Cassie could.

"Well," Chase recanted, "she didn't exactly say that I couldn't have any more. She said I couldn't stick my hand in the bag anymore."

Kathleen looked surprised when Cassie laughed. "Did you lick your fingers, buddy?" She winked at Kathleen.

"Maybe."

"Okay, so tell her you're sorry and ask her to hand you another one."

"Good idea," Chase said, placing his sticky fingers on their legs to stand before sprinting back to the bonfire.

"Want me to get that off?" Cassie looked at the sticky goo Chase's fingers had left on Kathleen's pants.

"No, I…You can't…I should go get a towel." She quickly stood and walked away.

Cassie stared after her, shocked. Something was clearly bothering Kathleen and she needed to find out what it was. The last time Kathleen was here she didn't bolt at Cassie's touch or even the suggestion of a touch. She was lost in thought, remembering their shared marshmallow when Shelley flopped down beside her.

"What's your problem, chief?"

"What do you mean what's my problem?" Cassie responded defensively.

"Well, normally you socialize with our guests rather than hide back here away from everyone." Shelley smiled to make her words less harsh. "I'd have thought you would be happier with Kathleen being here."

"Yeah, me too."

"Okay. What's wrong?"

"I'm not sure. She's been avoiding me since she arrived and I haven't had a chance to talk with her yet."

"I saw her bolt from you a while ago. I thought you had bitten her."

Cassie laughed self-consciously, "I offered to clean off the marshmallow Chase left on her pants leg."

"Something is wrong if that made her run." Shelley thought for a minute. "Maybe it's the kids."

Cassie replayed Kathleen's actions. There had been kids around most of the times Kathleen had moved away from her. "Yeah, maybe it's just the kids."

After a few minutes, Shelley patted her on the leg and joined the group around the fire. Cassie followed her, but she put her chair outside of the ring around the fire. She listened to Kathleen tell one of the guests about Fosters, but she didn't participate in the conversations unless asked directly. She thought about how good it felt to have Kathleen here. She watched Chase and the other kids play with a glow ball. This was going to be a good summer; she was going to make sure of it.

* * *

At nine, Cassie decided to send Chase in for his shower. He said good night to everyone and then went reluctantly into the house. Zoey and Pandy followed him to the house where they lay down on the porch. Cassie and Shelley carried the remaining food inside with help from Greg and Dillon. Kathleen, Morgan and Shaun went for a walk around the lake. Kaitlyn and Dani went upstairs to shower and get ready for bed.

After everything was cleaned up, Dillon and Shelley left with a reminder to Cassie to call if she needed them over the weekend. Chase had returned to the kitchen in search of a snack and Kathleen was helping him pick something healthy.

"Can I shower while the girls are showering upstairs?" Greg asked.

"I've never had this many people in the house at one time." Cassie laughed. "Try it and then we'll know."

"Okay, if I hear someone yelling I'll shut it back off."

Cassie unlocked the liquor cabinet, removing the blue bottle of vodka. She poured a splash into her glass and added cranberry juice. She poured a second glass and passed it to Kathleen.

Cassie secured the vodka back in the cabinet and took her glass to the living room. Chase flopped onto the cushion beside her.

Cassie softly whispered to him. "So what do you think of the girls now?"

He smiled. "Mostly they're okay."

"Just mostly?"

"Well…Morgan scares me."

Cassie laughed. "She scares me too, buddy."

"I like Dani and Kaitlyn though. We're going to ride the golf cart in the morning."

"Okay. Remember to drive slowly and watch for people and cars."

"I will."

Cassie gave him a hug, and he headed down the hall as Greg came out of the bathroom. Greg waved and followed Chase into the bedroom, shutting the door behind them.

Cassie hadn't noticed Kathleen leaving the house, but she looked up when the door opened. Kathleen, Morgan and Shaun came in together. Kathleen pointed up the stairs and the two girls obeyed.

"Are they okay?" Cassie asked.

"They're fine. I think they were only going to see how long they could stay outside before someone made them come in."

Kathleen picked up her glass on her way to the living room and sat down opposite Cassie.

"Testing us already?"

Kathleen raised her eyebrows. "Of course."

"Do we need to post a guard for the night?" Cassie laughed, but she was also serious.

"I don't think so." Kathleen sighed. "I spent the morning with them before the van arrived. We went over rules and what things would get them sent directly back to the group home. Leaving the house during the night is definitely one of those things."

Cassie stared at her. The soft light from the kitchen silhouetted her face and Cassie longed to touch her. Kathleen seemed unable to make eye contact with her and got up, walking into the kitchen. Cassie followed her. When Kathleen stopped and turned to her, she had tears in her eyes. Cassie pulled her into her arms, breathing her scent in deeply before kissing her. Gently running her tongue along soft lips, she enjoyed the heat from inside Kathleen's mouth.

"I have been dying to do that all day," Cassie whispered into her ear as she pulled her back into a full body hug. She felt Kathleen sob and she pulled her head back to look at her.

"Oh, Kathleen." She smoothed her thumbs over her cheeks, wiping away the tears that were starting to roll down her face. "What's wrong?"

Kathleen sobbed again. "I didn't think this plan through very well."

"I couldn't be happier to have you here for the next two months."

"Yeah, that's what I thought too, but then I saw you and realized we can't do this." She motioned between them. "Us. Not with the girls here."

"Okay." Cassie slowly processed what she was saying. "I thought you were out?"

"I am, but I don't want to put this relationship on display in front of the girls. We barely know each other and all I want to do is take you to bed. What kind of role model can I be when I'm stealing a kiss at every corner?"

"Okay. We'll use this time to get to know each other." She softly wiped the tears from Kathleen's face again. "We can make this work. We *will* make this work."

Cassie bent her head and kissed her again gently. She wanted to convince her that they could hold back their passion. Later, she would deal with the fact that Kathleen would be across the hall for the next two months and she wouldn't be able to touch or hold her.

"Ms. Cassie?" Dani called from the stairs.

Cassie crossed the kitchen in two strides to meet Dani before she came into the kitchen. Dani was starting down the stairs, and Cassie leaned on the banister to stop her descent.

She wanted to give Kathleen as much time as she needed to compose herself. "Yes, Dani?"

"We…" Dani looked behind her and the other three girls appeared at the top of the stairs. "We just wanted to thank you for allowing us to stay with you."

The other girls nodded their agreement.

"Yes, thank you," Kathleen said, placing her hand on Cassie's back before stepping past her. She looked back into Cassie's eyes. "For everything." Turning back to the four teenagers, she shooed them up the stairs and into their rooms.

Cassie waited until all the doors shut, including Kathleen's, and then she locked the doors and turned out the lights. She called Zoey and Pandy, who followed her up the stairs. The excitement she had felt earlier when she saw Kathleen get out of the car was gone. As she crawled into bed with her clothes still on she tried to convince herself that this situation was only temporary. The pain in Kathleen's eyes proved she still wanted her, but the good times they had shared all faded into a fitful night of horrible dreams.

CHAPTER THIRTY-TWO

Cassie woke tired and cranky to a very full, but quiet house. She showered and then made her way downstairs. Pandy met her in the hallway coming from Kathleen's room and Cassie tried not to be jealous. Chase was waiting on her to read their book, so they settled into the recliner together. Greg wandered out a little while later.

"I think I'll feed the horses before breakfast, then we won't be rushed."

"I thought I'd make French toast for breakfast. It's easy to heat up since we don't know when everyone will get up."

"And bacon?" Chase asked.

"I don't see why not." She hugged him and then pushed him to his feet so she could stand.

Dani was the first to make an appearance, and she joined Chase on the barstools to watch Cassie make breakfast.

"Kaitlyn is still asleep and we probably won't see Shaun and Morgan before noon, but I think I heard Ms. K moving around."

"That's fine. Weekends are for sleeping in."

"I never sleep in," Chase announced. "I'm always the first one up."

"Can I help?" Kathleen asked as she walked into the kitchen.

"Can you handle bacon?" Cassie asked.

Kathleen's lips moved into a smile that didn't reach her eyes.

As they passed each other moving around the kitchen, Cassie ran her hand gently down her back. Dani and Chase were talking about horses and swimming. "Did you sleep okay?" she asked Kathleen quietly.

"Not really. You?"

Cassie gave her a half smile. "Not really. I think I might have lost a dog last night."

"I think I might have found one."

"Hmmm…a dog thief." Cassie placed the bacon on the counter in front of Kathleen, raising one eyebrow. "You think you're up for this, eh? I have to warn you. Chase is the supervisor of all things bacon and he'll be watching."

Kathleen laughed and pulled a knife from the drawer to open the package.

Cassie put a microwave plate and a roll of paper towels beside her and then stood back to watch.

"Don't you have something you should be making too?" Kathleen glanced at her before turning her attention back to the bacon.

"I'm just making sure you have the bacon under control." Cassie looked at Chase who was now paying attention to the conversation. "Do you think she can handle it, Chase?"

Chase bounced on his chair. "I'm not sure."

Cassie put her arms around Kathleen, pressing her chest tight against Kathleen's back. Kathleen laughed again as Cassie took the knife from her and opened the bacon. She tossed the knife into the sink and handed the bacon package back to Kathleen.

"I'm not going to watch," she said as she buried her face in Kathleen's hair. "You watch her, Chase. Let me know if I need to help."

"Cassie…" Kathleen's voice quivered.

Cassie stepped away, knowing she had pushed their fragile emotions too far. She was only playing and hadn't meant to lose control. With her back to Chase and Dani, she cleared her head and regained her composure. Retrieving eggs, milk and spices she began making the mix for French toast. She pulled the electric griddle from under the counter and placed it in front of Dani and Chase, handing each of them a spatula.

She coated the griddle with spray oil and placed the first couple of pieces on it. "Let them sit for a few minutes. They need to brown before you turn them over."

She pulled a plate from the cabinet to put the finished pieces on. Kathleen turned from the microwave, leaning on the counter with her back to Dani and Chase. "That was a little dangerous there, tiger," she admonished softly.

Cassie blushed. "Yeah, I was trying to mess with you, but I really messed with me."

"You can't do that in front of Shaun or Morgan. They're already giving me a hard time about how sexy you are."

Cassie's blush deepened. "Oh, yeah?"

"Oh, yeah."

"I'll try to keep my distance or at least maintain control from now on."

"Okay, but so you know…" Kathleen looked into her eyes. "I look forward to the day when you won't have to."

Cassie could read the desire in her eyes, and chills went up her arms. "You have to stay away from me, dog thief."

"I'm a dog thief too," Chase said, interrupting their conversation.

"Yes, you are. You and Kathleen are exactly alike."

Chase smiled.

"Turn the bread," Kathleen reminded them.

Greg returned from the barn with Pete and Rory. Cassie tried to get them to stay for breakfast, but they wanted to get on the road. She left to check them out while Kathleen finished putting breakfast on the table. They had barely sat down at the table when Kaitlyn stumbled into the kitchen.

"What's that smell?" Her hair was plastered to one side of her head and her pajama pants hung so low her feet were covered.

"Grab a plate and join us?" Cassie smiled at her, trying not to laugh.

"Next time brush your hair before you come down. You're a little scary," Dani said between bites.

Kaitlyn only grunted and everyone laughed.

"I thought we'd all go swimming today," Kathleen suggested.

The kids agreed, but Cassie's thoughts immediately turned to their last swim, and she quickly left the table.

"Will you go too, Ms. Cassie?" Dani asked.

From the kitchen, Cassie responded. "Not today. I have to turn two of the cabins, and I'll probably go ahead and do all of them so it'll be finished."

"That's a bummer," Chase added.

"How about tomorrow?" Dani asked.

"Tomorrow we can all swim," Cassie agreed. "But only if everyone remembers to wear sunscreen so you aren't fried before tomorrow."

"Do you need help today?" Kathleen asked. "I could watch the kids and help you at the same time."

"Enjoy the weekend. I'll put you all to work next week." Cassie couldn't look at her as her mind replayed visions of Kathleen in a sports bra and shorts. She really did need to work this weekend if she was going to try to keep her distance from Kathleen.

"How many guests are coming in?" Kathleen asked.

"Just two couples and no kids. First one in gets Cabin Three at no extra cost."

"Oh, that's nice of you."

"I thought you might want Cabin One so you don't have to share a bathroom with teenagers."

"Tempting."

"You could share mine." They both looked at each other and shook their heads. Laughing, Cassie said, "No, I guess not."

Greg looked back and forth between them. "You're not sharing a room? But Dillon said—"

Cassie cut him off before he could say anything else. "Didn't I tell you not to believe everything Dillon tells you?"

"Okay," Greg said, sounding confused.

Cassie shook her head, looking pointedly at the backs of Dani's and Kaitlyn's heads. Greg nodded his understanding. "Well, that sucks."

"Greg said 'sucks,'" Chase called to anyone who would listen.

"What do you think his punishment should be, Chase?" Cassie asked, grinning at Greg.

"He should have to swim with us."

Greg wrinkled his nose. "I have horses to tend to."

When Chase whined, Greg hugged him. "Maybe tomorrow, okay?"

"Tomorrow everyone will swim," Chase announced.

After breakfast, Cassie joined Greg to check and release the horses. Then, since Pete and Rory had already checked out, she began preparing Cabin Two for the next guests. As the rest of the guests checked out throughout the morning, Cassie began working on the other cabins. At noon, she brought sandwiches and chips out to the picnic table, and everyone joined her. After lunch she took a few minutes to talk with Greg and make sure he was doing okay. He said he was enjoying his alone time so she left him to it.

While moving between cabins, Cassie watched the kids playing in the water and tried hard not to watch Kathleen's every move. Cassie was surprised to see all of the girls swimming. Though their bathing suits varied from sports bras and shorts worn by Kathleen to a T-shirt and shorts worn by Kaitlyn, everyone seemed to be having a good time. Both new couples were checked in by five p.m., and Cassie had dinner ready shortly thereafter. The water and the sun had worn everyone down, and Cassie sent everyone to bed soon after dinner.

CHAPTER THIRTY-THREE

Sunday morning, Cassie again joined Chase in the recliner to read his book. Kathleen was the first one down and she and Dani made scrambled eggs with sautéed spinach. After breakfast, Cassie sent Chase and Dani to gather housekeeping tags while she helped Greg with the horses and goats. She hated to leave Kathleen with the breakfast dishes but Kaitlyn offered to help.

When chores were finished, Cassie and Greg pulled the sliding board from the boat shed and carried it out to the floating dock. Greg bolted it down and insisted on being the first one down. Shaun won the battle with Morgan to follow him by pushing Morgan into the water. Cassie retreated to the beach to avoid the dunking. She collapsed onto her beach towel beside Kathleen.

"Too violent for you?" Kathleen asked.

"Absolutely."

Together they watched the kids play until Cassie lay back and closed her eyes.

"Still regretting your decision to join us for the next two months?" Cassie asked.

"No regrets."

Cassie opened one eye to glance at her.

Kathleen patted her leg and stood. "No, definitely no regrets. It's beautiful here and I get to be close to you. I'm taking a swim."

Cassie watched Kathleen dive into the water and swim out to the floating dock before dropping her head back on the towel. Kathleen was putting up a strong front, Cassie thought, but she was pretty sure she regretted sleeping across the hall. She certainly had hated it. Her bed had felt huge and very empty since the weekend Kathleen had left. She took the moment of silence to reminisce about their weekend together and dream about the future. She had barely started to relax when she felt Chase dancing around her head.

"Come out in the water and play with us, Ms. Cassie."

"I'm resting, Chase." Cassie opened her eyes an inch to look at him.

Chase reluctantly moved away, but Cassie felt the silence get heavy. She opened her eyes and then quickly closed them as Chase threw a bucketful of water at her head. Cassie jumped to her feet and chased him into the water. Chase swam toward the floating dock, screaming for Dani and Kaitlyn to save him.

"You better run, Chase," Cassie called to him as she climbed onto the floating dock. She gave a loud growl, making Chase scream again. Dani stepped in front of her to protect Chase and Cassie threw her in the water. Kaitlyn gave up and jumped into the water before Cassie got close to her.

"This dock is mine," Cassie yelled as she tossed Chase off the side.

Cassie turned and realized all the kids were gone and only Kathleen remained on the dock with her. She growled again.

"Cassie."

"Is that your adult voice?" Cassie teased, moving closer to her.

"Cassie. Don't do this." Kathleen sat up and shaded her eyes for a closer look. "I'm serious, Cassie. You don't want to do this."

"You already got your hair wet so why not."

"Because paybacks are hell."

Cassie laughed and then roared loudly, making the kids cheer and encourage her to throw Kathleen off. Cassie turned back to Kathleen. "How about this? We go in together."

"No."

"Come on. It'd be bad for my image to let you win."

"No." Kathleen stood up.

Cassie took another step closer to Kathleen and the kids screamed louder. "Just say yes because you're about to go in."

Before Kathleen could move away from her, Cassie picked her up and jumped into the water. Cassie felt Kathleen's foot connect with her chin as they surfaced.

"I am going to kill you." Kathleen turned to look at Cassie. "Oh my." She pulled Cassie to her.

"What's wrong?" Cassie asked, looking at the panic in Kathleen's eyes.

Kathleen began pressing along her jawline. "You're bleeding, but I can't tell where it's coming from."

Cassie stuck her lip out and tried to view it herself. "That's where it hurts."

Kathleen started to laugh. "Let's go get you some ice before your lip gets any fatter."

They swam to shore where the kids waited, subdued and quiet.

"She's okay, guys. It's only a busted lip," Kathleen quickly explained.

"Yeah, it's all fun and games until someone gets punched in the face," Cassie mumbled with her lip still stuck out.

Greg brought her a bag of ice, and she flopped down on her wet beach towel. Greg sat on one side of her and Kathleen on the other. Kathleen sent the kids back into the water to play, but Chase was slow to join them.

"I'm okay, Chase. Go play for a while longer and then we'll get dinner." When Chase turned and joined the other kids swimming for the slide, Cassie looked at Greg and Kathleen. "Let's get pizza for dinner. I don't feel like cooking or eating."

"Pizza sounds great," Greg agreed. "I can go get it."

Cassie retreated to the house and showered before coming back out so Kathleen could go. After much convincing she finally agreed to use Cassie's bathroom.

"So you guys aren't seeing each other now?" Greg asked as Cassie sat down beside him.

"Kathleen doesn't want us to be a bad influence on the kids."

"How can love be a bad influence?" Greg laughed at her lip pushed out from her face. "Seriously."

"It's not the love. It's the other stuff that she doesn't want to be sneaking around doing."

"I guess I understand that, but you should know the kids are smart. They've got you guys figured out already." Greg shrugged. "Even Chase asked me last night if Kathleen was going to continue to live with us after the girls left."

"Well, crap. I wasn't trying to hide anything, but I also was trying to respect the fact that Kathleen wanted to chill things for a while."

"Don't think it's working, chief."

Cassie frowned at him.

"Sorry. I picked that up from Dillon and Shelley."

"It's okay. I still think we have to come up with something other than Ms. Cassie once the girls leave." She smiled. "Let's let Kathleen believe she is fooling everyone for a little bit longer before we break the news to her."

"You got it." Greg jumped up as Kathleen returned. "I'm off to shower so I can make the pizza run."

By the time Greg returned with the pizza, everyone had been herded into the shower and they were watching a movie Chase had selected. As the hero dog did his supersonic bark to bring down the villain, Cassie paused the movie to distribute plates and drinks. Cassie called a family meeting for nine the next morning instead of after the movie. She and Kathleen decided to take the girls shopping after the meeting. They watched the movie, and then everyone headed off to bed.

CHAPTER THIRTY-FOUR

Monday morning after breakfast, everyone met in the dining room for their first group meeting. Surprisingly the girls were dressed and ready for their shopping trip. Cassie went over some basic rules, and then they picked chores for the week.

As the meeting broke up and the girls headed out to the cars, Cassie stopped Chase in the kitchen. "Would you like to go with us?"

Chase looked up as Greg entered the kitchen. "I'm not sure."

Greg had suggested to Cassie the night before that Chase might like to join them and Cassie had an idea. She looked back and forth between them. "I was thinking about getting a single bed to add to your room." She looked at Chase. "Then you could have your own bed."

Chase looked hesitant.

"You could always sleep in my bed if you wanted. I'll still be right there beside you," Greg added.

"Okay. I guess."

"Great," Cassie said, "then you should go with us so you can pick out your comforter."

"Are you sure you have room?" Chase asked, still torn between staying with Greg and going with the girls.

"We have to take two cars anyway, so there is plenty of space for you." Cassie hugged him. "We'll eat lunch out."

Chase smiled. "Okay, I'm in then."

Chase, Dani and Kaitlyn piled into Cassie's SUV, and Morgan and Shaun chose to ride with Kathleen. Cassie had considered driving to the next town over since Riverview only had one store, but Kathleen had vetoed the option. She thought fewer choices might be better.

"You can stay with us or roam on your own," Kathleen advised the girls as they crossed the parking lot. "You have one hour and then we'll meet up front by the registers. Do not leave the store for any reason."

Morgan gave a rare smile. "We can pick anything we want?"

"We're here for sheets and comforters, but each of you have a budget of an additional fifty dollars for anything else you might want to get," Kathleen answered her.

"Shampoos, deodorants and stuff like that doesn't count though," Cassie added. "Those are items are covered by us."

The girls disappeared together, but Chase stayed with Kathleen and Cassie. As they went up and down every aisle, Cassie helped Chase select hygiene items from a list Greg had provided. Chase selected a Lego bedspread and sheets and a new Lego toy. Kathleen and Cassie moved through the grocery store section making selections for the upcoming week.

Cassie had enjoyed the hour but wasn't so happy when the girls returned. Morgan and Shaun had decided on black bedspreads for their room. Cassie let Kathleen handle that discussion while she checked out Dani and Kaitlyn's selections. Kathleen vetoed complete black and sent them to get sheet and pillowcase sets of a different color. Cassie vetoed the skimpy bathing suit-clad supermodel poster that Kaitlyn had selected for her wall.

"That wasn't as bad as I thought it would be." Kathleen smiled at Cassie. "Aren't you glad we came here instead of the mall?"

"Yes, having less to choose from avoided a lot more vetoes."

"I liked the poster Kaitlyn picked." Chase smiled at them both.

Cassie ruffled his hair. "Don't even think about it. It would be vetoed for your wall as well."

When the girls returned, they checked out. Kathleen, Cassie and Dani pushed the three carts loaded down with their purchases. Chase ran ahead to push the store door open and held it for them. After the carts went through, a man pushed his way into the store through the door Chase held open, separating Morgan and Shaun from everyone else.

"That was rude," Shaun said, looking back at the man who stopped and stared openly at Shaun. "What are you looking at?"

Cassie heard Shaun raise her voice behind them and motioned Kaitlyn to take her cart and keep moving. She turned and quickly appraised Shaun's tight fists as she stared at the man. Cassie stepped between them, facing the man. "Shaun, go to the car."

Shaun hesitated for a second and then followed Cassie's directions.

Cassie met the man's eyes. "Everything okay here?"

"I'm fine. Ask him." He motioned toward Shaun's retreating back.

Cassie knew Shaun could still hear their conversation. "I will talk with *her* when we get home." Cassie turned and herded the kids across the parking lot toward the cars.

* * *

Shaun was sullen during lunch, slamming her tray on the table and pushing every door harder than required. Cassie and Kathleen attempted to engage everyone in conversation, but Shaun's behavior was distracting. Cassie's instinct was to air the situation and clear it up immediately, but Kathleen gave her a headshake when she approached the subject.

On the drive back, Cassie was distracted with her thoughts on how to handle Shaun's behavior. Pulling into the driveway, she swerved to avoid hitting a fast-moving black car with tinted windows. Cassie watched her rearview mirror until the vehicle was past Kathleen and had pulled out on the highway.

While the girls unloaded the cars, Cassie tracked down Shelley in the office. "Did you talk with whoever was in the black car?"

Shelley groaned. "Yeah. Did you see him?"

"We passed him on the way in. He was leaving so fast I almost hit him head-on. What did he want?"

"He was inquiring about renting a cabin." Shelley rolled her eyes. "He didn't look like a nature person. His hair was slicked back with way too much gel, and he wore a cheap suit. I offered to show him one of the cabins but he said no. I don't know why he even stopped."

A door slamming in the house reminded Cassie of Shaun and the impending explosion.

Shelley raised her eyebrows.

"We had a bit of a confrontation at the store," Cassie explained.

"Oh?"

Kathleen entered the office before Shelley could ask any questions.

"We need to separate her from the other girls until she calms down," Cassie said, prepared for Kathleen to disagree with her.

"I agree. Do you want to or shall I?"

"I got this," Cassie said, entering the house. Kaitlyn and Dani were standing in the kitchen, and before Cassie could ask where Shaun was she heard another door slam upstairs. She took the stairs two at a time and pushed open Shaun's door without knocking. "Shaun, follow me. Now."

Cassie exited the room, leaving the door open, and went out the front door. She left it open too without even looking behind her to see if Shaun was following. Dillon gave her a questioning look as she entered the barn, but she shook her head and grabbed two halters from the tack room. Cheyenne wandered over as soon as Cassie approached the fence line, and she placed the halter over the horse's head. Handing the reins to Shaun, she haltered Angel, who stood nearby.

"Have you ever ridden before?" Cassie asked her.

"No."

"Are you scared?"

"No."

"Good. Then climb up those stairs right there." Cassie pointed to the riding steps. "And swing your leg over."

Shaun hesitated for a moment and then did as Cassie directed. As soon as she was on, Cassie handed her the reins and swung onto Cheyenne. Cassie radioed Shelley to mark the white board with her and Shaun on a horseback ride. They rode silently for about thirty minutes before Shaun spoke.

"Are you going to yell at me?"

"No, but I don't think I have to tell you that your behavior was wrong." Shaun didn't respond so Cassie continued. "Can I ask you something?"

Shaun didn't look at her, but she nodded her head.

"What do you think people see when they look at you?"

Shaun shrugged.

"Okay. How about a simple question? Why did you shave all the hair off your head?"

Shaun shrugged again.

"I'm not judging you, Shaun. I'm only trying to get you to think about your actions."

After a few more silent minutes Shaun finally answered. "I thought it would be cool."

"And is it?"

"Not when people act like that man did today. Then I just get embarrassed and angry."

Cassie nodded. "It made me angry too."

Shaun looked at her in surprise. Cassie continued, "Not angry at him exactly but angry because he upset you. People do stupid things. You can't control what they do, but you can control how you react."

Shaun remained silent.

"It's okay to be upset, but it's not okay to take it out on the people and things around you. You made a decision to be different in your appearance, so you have to be adult enough to handle close-minded reactions and not lose your temper."

Cassie turned Cheyenne back toward the barn. "We should head back."

They made the return trip in silence. Cassie wanted Shaun to talk but understood that she might not be the person Shaun wanted to talk with or that Shaun might not want to talk at all. She mentally thanked her mother for the "control of your own emotions" lesson. Newly identified but still in the closet teenage Cassie found every excuse to lash out at the world. She didn't have a lot of great mother-daughter memories but that was one that had stuck with her. It was the first time she realized she had control of her life.

Greg met them when they returned to the corral, and Cassie handed him the reins as she jumped down. "Thanks, Greg. I need to help Kathleen with dinner. Can you brush her for me?"

"Sure. Want me to do Angel too?" He looked at Shaun.

Cassie spoke for her. "No, I think Shaun would like to help you. Maybe you can show her."

"No problem."

Cassie turned to Shaun. "If you want to talk, let me know."

Shaun nodded.

Cassie turned and headed out of the barn, stopping at the doors to look back. Greg was telling Shaun how to dismount without using the stairs or help. She turned back toward the house, thinking about what she had said to Shaun. She was upset with Shaun's behavior, but she also wanted Shaun to think about how others perceived her appearance. All three of the older girls had outward appearances that would make conservative minds think poorly of them.

Cassie could give the tolerance lecture in her sleep. She spent years listening to the words being regurgitated out of the mouths of supervisors who then went out on the street and did whatever they wanted. As chief, she had made it personal for her men and women, holding her own lifestyle up for appraisal. She and Nett were well-liked and faced little resistance in their small town. Any of her officers who exhibited signs of discrimination in their work were asked to adjust their behavior and if that didn't work they were fired for failure to comply with departmental policy. Her officers were expected to follow instructions and put away their personal biases—something it took her parents too many years to learn. She would check with Kathleen but maybe they could have a group discussion with all the kids about it. Tolerance was something everyone needed to learn. The girls needed to understand the people who would be judging them as much as they needed to accept they might not always be judged for who they were.

CHAPTER THIRTY-FIVE

Cassie found Kathleen and Shelley still in the office. Kathleen looked up first. "How'd that go?"

"Fine. I guess. I talked, she listened, but she didn't have anything to say."

"That's pretty normal for her. I think she was embarrassed more than anything."

Cassie sighed. "Probably, but she can't act like that."

"Did you tell her that?" Kathleen asked.

"I think so."

Kathleen and Shelley laughed.

"We sent the nontalker to talk with the nontalker. What were we thinking?" Shelley shook her head at Kathleen.

Cassie blushed. "I talked."

"I'm sure you did, honey." Kathleen touched her arm and then quickly pulled away.

Shelley gave Cassie a sympathetic smile. "I think Dillon and I will get out of here. Guests were quiet today. Joe and Lori took out bikes before lunch, but I saw them come back about an hour ago. I didn't see much movement from Cabin Two."

Shelley left the office and Cassie realized for the first time in days she and Kathleen were alone. She resisted the urge to pull her into her arms and headed for the Keurig instead.

"Cup of tea?"

"Sure. Can we go out back?" Kathleen asked. "I'd like to sit in the quiet for a few minutes."

They made their tea and crossed back through the house. Cassie erased her name from the white board before following Kathleen onto the back porch. They sat side by side without touching, and Cassie glanced at her.

"What?" Kathleen asked with a smile.

"I'm happy you're here."

"Me too."

"That said, though…I still want more."

Kathleen smiled again.

"You have no comment?" Cassie asked.

Kathleen winked at her. "What could I say?"

"Oh, I don't know. Maybe you want something more from me too."

"Oh, I want something more all right." Kathleen gently slid her hand down Cassie's arm entwining their fingers. "I'd give anything to take you to bed right now."

Cassie squeezed her hand and, leaning back in the chair, closed her eyes. "I can imagine the house to ourselves and that happening right now."

Kathleen stroked her thumb across Cassie's hand.

Opening her eyes, Cassie looked at her. "I want more than that though."

Kathleen raised her eyebrows.

"When the girls leave, I want to explore this relationship. I'll respect your request for distance as long as we can sneak moments like this occasionally."

"This is fine. You just can't kiss me."

"I know." Cassie sighed. "But I want to."

"The feeling is mutual."

Cassie savored the feel of Kathleen's touch against her skin. "Why is it so quiet?" Cassie asked, opening her eyes.

"The girls are rearranging their rooms and washing bedding. They were very unhappy with me when I said everything needed to be washed before being used. I haven't seen Chase since we unloaded the cars."

Cassie laughed. "I'm glad you thought to tell them that. Chase is probably in his room reading. It was a full afternoon, and I'm sure he needed time away from the girls."

Cassie had barely finished speaking when Greg interrupted them. "Have you guys seen Chase?"

Cassie stood up. "Not since we returned. I thought he was in your room getting away from the girls."

"He's not there," Greg said. "I just checked."

Kathleen stood up too. "Anything on the white board?"

Greg went back into the house with Kathleen and Cassie behind him. Cassie studied the empty spot beside Chase's name.

"He didn't come to the barn when he got back," Greg said, the panic growing in his voice.

Cassie took the stairs two at a time and knocked on the girls' doors as she passed. Doing a quick check in her room and Kathleen's, she met the girls in the hallway.

"Has anyone seen Chase?"

The girls looked at each other. "He helped carry all the bags in but then we came upstairs," Dani said. "What's wrong?" She looked at Kathleen and Greg standing at the foot of the stairs.

"Let's separate and check outside," Cassie said, sending everyone in different directions. As she started to head outside too, Kathleen grabbed her arm. "I haven't seen Zoey and Pandy since we returned either."

"That's good then. It means they're with Chase." Cassie walked from cabin to cabin, checking with guests and entering the empty ones, then she called Dillon and Shelley. They returned immediately and began helping to search.

It took almost thirty minutes for the area around the cabins to be checked and everyone to return to the porch. Cassie forced her panic down and sent the girls into the house.

"I don't see any reason not to call the sheriff's department," Kathleen's voice wavered.

"All the bikes are here." Dillon nodded his agreement.

"Not that he would take one, but all the horses are here too," Greg added.

Cassie pulled her cell phone from her pocket and punched in a number. She stepped off the porch as Deputy Steph Williams answered her call. Cassie quickly explained that a ten-year-old was missing. After a few minutes, she returned to the porch.

"Deputy Williams has issued an Amber Alert and will be here in a few minutes. She thinks we should widen our search area."

Kathleen nodded, taking her hand. "We should update the girls."

Kathleen and Cassie entered the house. The girls stood when they heard the door. Shaun stepped forward, and there was anguish on her face. "Did he run away because of the way I acted?"

Kathleen dropped Cassie's hand and pulled Shaun into a hug.

"He didn't leave because of you, Shaun," Cassie said. "He probably just wandered off and got distracted." She prayed her words were true, but deep down she knew it was something more. Chase wouldn't wander off any more than he would get distracted and forget to check in.

Cassie and Kathleen exchanged a silent glance. Cassie's unspoken fear registered on Kathleen's face, and she withdrew from Shaun, keeping her arm around the girl's waist.

Cassie continued. "As a precaution we've called the sheriff's department and they're going to send some deputies out to help us search."

"We want to help too," Dani demanded.

"I need you guys to stay here in the house." Cassie looked at Kathleen and she nodded her agreement.

* * *

Kathleen watched Cassie sprint up the stairs before she sank into the chair. She wanted to ease the girls' fears, but she didn't like the unease she had seen on Cassie's face. When Cassie returned, she crossed into the office and returned with several radios. She handed one to Kathleen and pulled her into the kitchen out of sight of the girls.

"Please stay in the house and keep the doors locked," Cassie whispered. "I have a bad feeling about this."

Kathleen nodded.

"I have my cell on vibrate, so call it if you need me. Don't use the radio unless it's an emergency."

Kathleen felt numb as Cassie pulled her into her arms. Her hands slid around Cassie's waist, and she gasped when her fingers touched the cold steel under Cassie's shirt.

"Why?"

"I'm afraid Chase didn't leave on his own."

Dillon called through the front door. "Steph's here."

Kathleen held on to Cassie a moment longer and then took the quick kiss she offered before releasing her. Kathleen moved to the door as it closed behind Cassie. Through the side window, she watched her pass Dillon, Greg and Shelley and head straight for the police cruiser and the blond, ponytailed woman standing beside it. Even in jeans and not her uniform she clearly was taking charge of the situation. Kathleen knew at a glance that this was the woman Cassie had mentioned that she dated. She watched the deputy touch Cassie's arm, and she forced herself to remain behind the closed door.

Steph wasn't a threat to Kathleen or her new relationship with Cassie. She was here to find Chase. The reassurances didn't stop her heart from racing as she compared the two women. Cassie's tan face held more maturity than Steph's light features, and though they were the same height, Cassie's shoulders were broader. Kathleen longed to hold on to her right now, but as another cruiser appeared she stepped away from the door and joined the girls in the living room.

* * *

Cassie told Steph everything she could think of concerning Chase, including the possibility he may have witnessed a murder and then stood back while Steph radioed her fellow deputies. When she finished giving instructions, she addressed everyone. "There's a black Chevy Impala with dark windows sitting at the side of the road outside your gate. Nobody in it at the moment."

Shelley gasped. "That's the guy that was here earlier."

Cassie explained about their visitor and then let Shelley give his description. "He asked about kids, but I thought he meant he wanted to bring his kids. He was so sleazy. I should have known!"

Cassie sat on the steps beside her and pulled her into a hug. "It's not your fault, Shelley. I saw him when we came in, and I didn't think about it either."

Several deputies arrived and Steph left the group to brief them. Cassie sent Greg and Shelley into the house to stay with Kathleen.

"Can we use your horses?" Steph asked as Dillon and Cassie approached the group of deputies.

"Of course," Cassie answered immediately.

"We'll need four horses. We have a search and rescue group coming as well, but they'll have their own horses and dogs," Steph explained. "We'd like to go ahead and get out there though."

Cassie and Dillon headed for the barn and began saddling horses while Steph and the deputies went over a map on the hood of her car.

"We're ready," Cassie called to Steph when the horses were saddled.

"You and Dillon are coming with us, right?" Steph asked.

Cassie felt her gaze rest briefly on the bulge of her pistol, and she waited until Steph met her eyes. "Yes," she said firmly.

Steph nodded. "Good. You guys will notice anything out of place faster than we will. We separated your property into three divisions. Once we reach the property line, we'll meet back up to decide how to handle the federal park. By then we should have Search and Rescue here and they can help."

The teams separated; Steph and Cassie took the middle section. They crossed the pasture area, slowly looking for any clues that Chase may have left behind.

At the edge of the woods, Steph checked in with Search and Rescue and directed them to begin on federal land, working their way back toward Cassie's property. Cassie let Steph take the lead as they entered the woods. They traveled quietly and circled left and right to the perimeter of their area. It was almost two hours later when they exited the woods, crossed to the edge of Cassie's property and reunited with the other teams. Cassie pulled the gate latch to allow everyone to cross onto federal property.

CHAPTER THIRTY-SIX

They were losing the last rays of sunlight as the deputies gathered again around the map. Steph used her cell phone to check in with Search and Rescue again before assigning new areas for each team. Cassie texted Kathleen with an update. She wanted to call her, but she knew she didn't have anything to tell her.

Dillon rode up beside her. "Come look at this." He led her to the section of fence they had repaired the previous week. There was a small piece of fabric stuck to one of the wire patches Dillon had made.

Cassie returned to Steph. "We found where Chase crossed the fence." She pointed to where Dillon sat on Dakota. "There's a piece of fabric stuck on the fence. It's the same color of the shirt Chase had on today."

Steph surveyed the scene. "I wonder why he didn't go through the gate."

"Maybe he was in too much of a hurry," Cassie answered anxiously.

Steph nodded. "Let's get going. Check-in texts every thirty minutes with your GPS location," she reminded the deputies.

Everyone mounted, and they began their search again. Cassie knew Chase was hungry and he had to be tired. She thought about Pandy and Zoey and wished again she could call for them. She knew they would respond, but Steph thought, and she agreed, that it would alert the driver of the black car, who they had to assume was searching for Chase too.

As darkness surrounded them, Steph pointed out a broken limb and dismounted, using her flashlight to take a closer look. When Cassie dismounted too, she placed a hand to her lips and motioned for them to tie their horses in place. Quietly they followed the broken limbs through the forest. Cassie heard a voice in the distance, and her eyes grew wide. Steph nodded; she too heard the voice. They advanced close enough to see and hear the owner of the voice.

A short man in a dark suit was pacing as he ranted into his phone. "Don't worry. I'll find the little fucker." A pause. "I'll call you if I need a ride back to my car." Another pause. "Then I'll kill him where I find him."

Motioning Cassie to stay in place, Steph began to move to their left directly behind the man. He slammed the phone shut and jammed it into his pocket. Slapping at nearby tree limbs, he started moving again. Seeing Steph emerging from the tree line, Cassie stomped her feet. It didn't make a lot of sound, but there was enough of a rustle to pull his attention away from Steph, who slammed into his back, driving him to the ground.

His compact body was muscular and he pushed back against Steph like a bucking bronco. Before he had a chance to try to stand, Cassie dropped beside her and placed her knee in his back. Using her body weight, she helped Steph hold him down and together they cuffed him.

Adrenaline pumped through Cassie's body and she almost wished he had put up more of struggle. She didn't think she would be doing this again and had forgotten how much she enjoyed the thrill of an arrest. Then she remembered Chase and why she was out here in the middle of the night.

She held his arm while Steph radioed back to base and sent texts to the other deputies. Cassie helped her get him back to the horses, and they tied a rope around his wrists so he could walk and Steph could ride.

"Call your dogs. I feel confident that he's out here alone," Steph said, stepping away from their captive. "I'll question him as soon as I get him back and let you know if I learn anything different."

"Thanks. I don't think it'll take me long to find him now."

"Good luck and stay alert."

Cassie was relieved to be able to turn her attention to finding Chase. She called Kathleen as she mounted Cheyenne.

"We found the guy, and Steph is headed back with him. You guys are safe." Cassie paused. "I can call for Zoey and Pandy now, so hopefully I'll find him fast."

"That's great," Kathleen gushed. "Hurry and find him."

* * *

Kathleen turned off her phone and faced the room. Greg was standing, so she shook her head at him. "They found the man who was after Chase. The deputy is bringing him in now."

"But not Chase," Shelley said softly.

"Not yet. But Cassie is able to yell for Zoey and Pandy now, and they'll come to her." She touched Greg's arm. "It won't be long now."

"Can I go outside?"

Kathleen appreciated him asking and she couldn't deny him the opportunity to be a little bit closer to Chase. "Yes, but please stay close."

Kathleen sat down at the table and looked at the girls stretched out across the living room. Morgan was the only one still awake, and her eyes met Kathleen's across the room. Kathleen smiled at her and she went back to watching the program on television.

Shelley set a cup of coffee in front of her and then joined her at the table.

"Oh, I don't think I can drink another cup." Kathleen rubbed her face with her hands.

"It's decaf."

Kathleen picked it up and sniffed it. "Maybe I'll just use the smell to wake me up then." She took a sip. "That's good. Thank you."

"It's my favorite. I'm sure we'll switch to tea when Cassie returns. She'll need some downtime before bed too."

"When she returns, I just want to crawl into bed with her and hold her all night."

Shelley laughed.

Kathleen covered her face. "I said that out loud, didn't I?"

"Must be sleep deprivation."

"Or just insanity."

"There is nothing insane about love," Shelley chastised her.

"Who said anything about love?" Kathleen frowned at Shelley, looking to see if Morgan could hear their conversation.

"Everyone knows, Kathleen." Shelley smiled at her. "You can't hide the way you look at her."

Kathleen frowned again and lowered her voice. "I do like her, and after the girls leave this summer we're going to explore a relationship."

"Right. You're just going to ignore each other for the next two months."

"Yes."

"Ignore each other like you've been doing for the last couple days."

"Yes."

Kathleen's frown deepened when Shelley laughed again. "That's what I'm telling you. You aren't hiding anything from those girls. Wouldn't it be better to show them a loving relationship rather than someone trying to ignore the way they feel?"

"I want to enjoy the feeling I had when I was here last, and I can't do that with those eight eyes watching us."

"Why not?" Shelley asked. "Let them see you fall in love. It's a wonderful thing."

Kathleen rubbed her face again. "I'll think about it once Chase is home and it's not the middle of the night."

* * *

Cassie called again and then stopped to listen. In the distance she could hear a bark, so she yelled again. When another bark followed, she kicked Cheyenne into a gallop. They were both tired, but Cassie needed to find Chase. She could hear Search and Rescue teams in the distance, but when they yelled there were no answering barks, so she continued to yell, hoping the teams could follow her voice.

As she entered a clearing, she could see movement on the other side. She gave another yell and Zoey came sprinting across the clearing. She jumped down to pet her and left Cheyenne to follow when Zoey took off into the tree line. Zoey led her straight to Chase, who was fast asleep snuggled against Pandy. Cassie scooped him up and his eyes flew open.

"I thought I was dreaming."

"You're not dreaming." Cassie squeezed him close against her, wishing she had brought a blanket when she felt his little body shiver. She stepped into the clearing and almost immediately they were surrounded by Search and Rescue personnel.

"Let us take him for a minute," a soft-spoken female voice said into Cassie's ear.

Cassie didn't want to, but she allowed a rescue worker to pull Chase from her arms.

Chase began kicking and screaming. "No, Ms. Cassie. There's a bad man here."

She stepped into his line of sight. "Everything's okay, Chase. These people are going to make sure you're okay so we can go home. The bad guy is gone."

Chase didn't look convinced, but at least he stopped kicking and screaming. Cassie knelt down, taking both her dogs into her arms. Unlike their normal behavior, they licked her face and she talked softly to them. They had stayed with Chase even when they heard her calling, and she was so proud of them.

Dillon came at a gallop and jumped down beside her. He was on the phone. "Yes, she's right here." He passed her the phone. "It's Greg."

"He's fine, Greg."

She heard a sigh of relief.

"We'll be on our way back shortly, and I'll let him call you."

"Okay." He paused. "Hang on." She could hear Greg yell in the background. "They found him and he's okay."

Cassie listened as excited voices talked, then a soft, soothing voice said into the phone, "My hero."

"Well, that's an exaggeration."

"It's my opinion and you can't change it. Are you on your way back yet?" Kathleen asked.

"Not yet. Search and Rescue are checking Chase out." When there was no response, she continued. "He seemed fine though when I held him."

"Okay, good. Call us when you start back." Kathleen paused and then said softly. "I'll be waiting for you."

Cassie released her breath. "I love you." In the few seconds of silence that followed Cassie couldn't make herself regret the slip.

"I love you too, Cassie."

Cassie smiled and she handed the phone back to Dillon. "Let's get our kid and go home."

Dillon smiled back at her. "Yeah."

Cassie looked at Chase's little body sitting on the ground surrounded by people. She pushed her way through the crowd and found the woman who had talked her into giving Chase up. "Can we take him now? His brother needs to see that he's okay."

"Yes, he seems fine. You can follow up with your regular doctor tomorrow if you feel like you need to."

"Thank you for coming so quickly." She wanted to say more, but she needed to get Chase home more than they needed praise. There would be time to show her appreciation later.

She scooped Chase up and handed him to Dillon while she mounted Cheyenne. Dillon passed him up into her arms and helped make him comfortable in the front of the saddle. One of the rescue workers passed up a blanket for Chase and a jacket. Cassie quickly pushed her arms into the sleeves one at a time while holding tight to Chase. It was the first time she realized she was cold. It was probably still sixty degrees, but without the sun and with the lack of sleep the jacket felt good on her bare arms.

As they traveled back across federal land, walking slowly to avoid injury to the horses, two of the deputies joined them. The trip seemed to take forever. When they crossed back onto Cassie's property, she dialed Greg and handed the phone to Chase, holding him tightly against her chest.

"Greg! Where are you?" Chase exclaimed when he heard his brother's voice, and then he began to talk quickly, explaining to Greg that he had been on his way to see him after the shopping trip when the guy that killed his foster parent had appeared. He was between Chase and the house, so Chase's only choice had been to run away from the house. He made it across the pasture to the tree line before the guy realized it and began to pursue him. By then it was too late to yell for help, so he continued to run.

By the time Chase finished his story, they could see the lights from the house. Greg met them halfway across the pasture, and Cassie handed Chase down to him. Greg pulled Chase into his arms. "Don't ever do that again," he said sternly.

Chase looked up at Cassie as she dismounted and his surprise at Greg's words showed on his face. "He was scared, Chase. We all were." She patted Chase's head and then Greg's back. "There'll be time later when you can talk about what he should do, God forbid, this ever happens again. But not right now."

Greg looked at her with tears in his eyes and nodded. He hugged Chase hard and then stood, taking Chase by the hand they walked toward the house. Kathleen and the girls were waiting at the fence, and they all hugged Chase as he left the pasture.

Cassie hugged Kathleen before turning back to unsaddle Cheyenne. "Where's Shelley?"

"She's making breakfast." Kathleen looked at the deputies. "And she says there'll be enough for everyone." They nodded their agreement.

With help from the deputies and Greg, Cassie and Dillon unsaddled and brushed all the horses before leading them into their stalls. They would release them with the other horses after they were fed and rested.

Cassie followed the crowd toward the house. Steph waited at the door of her cruiser, a tired smile plastered on her face.

Cassie squeezed Kathleen's hand. "I won't be long."

Kathleen smiled and, with a quick glance at Steph, left her.

"Looks like we need to talk," Steph said as Cassie approached.

"Yeah, a few things have changed." Cassie smiled. "Thanks for everything."

"Happy to help. Our scumbag is on the way to the station and a few deputies are waiting for the man he was talking to on the phone to arrive." She gave Cassie an evil smile. "We made him call his partner and tell him to come give him a ride back to his car."

Cassie laughed. She watched the pink sky swirl with light as the sun fought to break through the morning clouds. Though she was relieved to have her family safe inside the house, she wished she had been more suspicious of the stranger when he showed up. She needed to convince Chase to spill every detail from the night of the murder.

Interrupting her thoughts, Steph spoke them. "Someone needs to see what that boy really knows. Someone he trusts."

"My first task when things calm down."

Steph slid into her cruiser. "Call me and I'll put his official statement on record. We can do it here if that makes him more comfortable."

"I appreciate that."

Kathleen emerged from the house and handed Steph a wrapped sandwich. "Thanks for all your help."

Steph nodded. "Thank you." She held up the sandwich.

"It didn't appear you were staying."

"Nope, paperwork is calling. And then sleep."

Cassie slid her arm around Kathleen's waist as they climbed the steps. "That was nice of you."

"You didn't think I could be nice to your former lover?" Kathleen joked.

"Not lover."

"I didn't ask."

"I think you did."

* * *

After everyone had eaten, she walked the deputies out and thanked them for their help. When she returned Kathleen was waiting for her in the doorway. The breakfast dishes were washed and loaded into the dishwasher. The kitchen was spotless.

Kathleen took her hand. "Let's go to bed."

"Where is everyone?"

"I sent the kids to their rooms, and Dillon and Shelley are in my room."

Cassie smiled. "And where do you plan on sleeping?"

Kathleen pulled her up the stairs without answering.

Cassie took the bullets out of her pistol and secured it in the closet before climbing onto the bed with her clothes on.

"At least take off your boots," Kathleen commanded with a laugh.

Cassie unlaced her boots and kicked them off before pulling the comforter over both of them. She was asleep before Kathleen had a chance to snuggle in.

CHAPTER THIRTY-SEVEN

Cassie awoke to find Kathleen and Chase sitting at the bottom of the bed, their voices soft as they whispered.

"What's going on?" Cassie growled at them.

Kathleen turned to look at her and smiled. "Aren't you a fright when you wake up?" Kathleen looked at Chase. "I think we woke up the bear."

Cassie glared at them when they both laughed.

"Mr. D says we should have a party," Chase said excitedly.

"Okay, but only if you give me a hug and then leave the room quickly."

Chase jumped onto the bed beside Cassie, and she sat up, pulling him into a hug. "Now go quickly and wake everyone else."

Chase bolted out of the room and began knocking on the girls' doors.

"Oh, that was mean," Kathleen said with a smile.

"If I must be awake then so must everyone else," Cassie growled.

Kathleen leaned over and kissed her on the lips. "Take a shower and then you'll feel better."

Cassie took in her fresh clothes and the refreshing smell of body wash. Her hair was styled back, but it fell forward around her face when she leaned in to kiss Cassie again. This time Cassie captured her and pulled her against her body, inhaling the smell of her shampoo.

"No more kissing."

Kathleen frowned at her in response.

"I need to brush my teeth and besides kissing is not allowed." Cassie narrowed her eyes. "Remember?"

"I remember, but I think we should talk."

"Hmm. I like the sound of that." Cassie climbed out of bed and headed for the shower.

"Later," Kathleen said over her shoulder as she left the room.

* * *

Kathleen helped Chase wake the girls and sent them off to the shower. She talked with Dillon and Shelley, who headed out to get food for the party. Then she went into the office and checked the voice mail messages. She called both of the cabins with guests and spoke with them, giving them a brief recap of the previous night and inviting them to the party.

Deciding she had delayed making her call as long as she could, with a deep breath she dialed Fosters, Inc. She spent a few minutes catching up with Tiffany and then asked for Joyce. Joyce had already heard some of the details because the Amber Alert had reached her office.

"I'm so sorry I didn't call you sooner," Kathleen apologized when Joyce said she had tried to reach her earlier.

"I wasn't too worried once I heard Chase had been found. I figured you guys were probably sleeping after being up all night."

"Yes, we just got up, and we're planning a party. Would you like to come?"

"Tempting, but probably not the best use of my time."

"You could come up on Friday for the cookout. Cabin One is empty so you could stay."

"Now that's a good idea. Dave and I could come up after work."

"That would be great." Kathleen liked Joyce's husband Dave.

"Okay, thanks for the details. Send me a written report when you get a chance, and I'll get the police report from the deputies. Talk to you later."

Joyce hesitated when Kathleen didn't respond. "What else?" Joyce asked.

Kathleen took a deep breath. "I want to date Cassie."

"Okay." Joyce paused. "Are you asking for my permission?"

"Yes, I mean no. I guess I'm resigning."

"Why are you resigning?" Joyce asked, puzzled.

"I can't chaperone the girls if I'm dating Cassie."

"Kathleen, I have worked with you for years and I trust your judgment. You're a professional and I trust you will be discreet with your sex life. I'm confident it will be fine."

"Thank you, Joyce."

"This woman has really gotten to you?"

Morgan stepped into the office and leaned against the doorframe. Kathleen made eye contact with her before answering Joyce. "Yes, I really like her."

"Well, I look forward to meeting her on Friday. Let me know if there is any problem with us renting the cabin."

"Okay. Talk to you later." Kathleen pressed the off button and pocketed her phone before looking at Morgan.

"You should know by now that we're too smart for you to hide something like this from us." Morgan snickered at her.

Kathleen smiled back at her. "I should have known."

"We like her too and Chase needs a family."

"Let's not jump the gun, Morgan. We're only dating."

"Yeah. Okay. Whatever." Morgan crossed to the outside door. "Greg took the kids to the beach so you guys do…" she waved her hand around. "Whatever."

Kathleen laughed as Morgan closed the door behind her. She ran back through the house and up the stairs to Cassie's bedroom. As she entered the room she ran into Cassie on her way out. She threw her arms around Cassie's neck, pushing her back into the bedroom and kicking the door closed behind her.

"What?" Cassie asked in surprise.

"Greg is watching the kids at the beach, Dillon and Shelley are getting food, and I've checked in with all the guests." She continued to push Cassie toward the bed, unbuttoning her shirt as they walked.

"What about our no-kissing rule?"

Kathleen pressed her lips to Cassie's before pulling away again. "There are no rules now." She kissed her again. "I've changed my mind and I need you in so many ways." She slid Cassie's open shirt down her shoulders, past an eye-catching blue sports bra, and pushed her onto the bed before climbing on top of her.

Cassie pulled Kathleen's shirt over her head and ran her hands down her chest, lifting one eyebrow. "No rules, huh?"

"No rules," Kathleen said as she leaned in for another kiss.

Bella Books, Inc.

Women. Books. Even Better Together.

P.O. Box 10543
Tallahassee, FL 32302

Phone: 800-729-4992
www.bellabooks.com